Books by January Bain

Brass Ring Sorority

Winning Casey

I0542079

Winning Casey

ISBN # 978-1-78686-196-2

©Copyright January Bain 2017

Cover Art by Posh Gosh ©Copyright 2017

Interior text design by Claire Siemaszkiewicz

Totally Bound Publishing

Published in 2017 by Totally Bound Publishing, Think Tank, Ruston Way, Lincoln, LN6 7FL, United Kingdom.

Brass Ring Sorority

WINNING CASEY

JANUARY BAIN

Dedication

Dear Reader: This book you hold in your hands is a special book for me, more special than I can truly say. The journey to this point has been incredible for I got the privilege to spend time with some awesome men and women during its unfolding, and I know how blessed that makes me. Some of these people are within the pages of this novel, some are in my real life, because for me, it often blends, in a good way.

This is for all the kickass heroines of the world! Some of whom I wish to thank personally, Noa Xireau, Cara Lake, Bella Brooke, Sierra Brave, Tara Nina, Wendi Zwaduk, Aurora Russell, Amy Gonzales, Tabitha Cockburn, Zoe Mullins, Ute Carbone, Judy Griffith Gill, Jude Johnson, Cathy Colburn, and Patrick Khayler, honorary goddess. To Karen Emilson and to the town of Ashern, thanks for all the wonderful support over the years. A special thank-you to my brilliant editor, Rebecca Baker Fairfax, who was immensely helpful in the creation of this series, and who even inspired one of the characters. I could not have made this journey without you. You made it happen!

And to Don, my inspiration for all the heroes in my books. And in memory of my dad who told me he thought I was really onto something this time. My dear beloved brothers who left us far too soon, Donald, Robert, and Garrel, meet you on the other side...

And of course, to all the wonderful people at Totally Bound Publishing who have made this journey possible. Thank you for your faith in my work and the huge welcome I've so generously received to the family. (Thanks, Desiree Holt, for sharing that!) It does a heart good. And to Emmy Ellis for her beautiful cover, a big bouquet of fresh flowers.

Chapter One

"Yet it isn't the gold that I'm wanting; So much as just finding the gold." *Robert Service*

Casey glared at the stuffed moose head and it stared right back at her, its one broken antler leering.

"What are you looking at? You think this is easy? Who piles this many friggin' rocks over their treasure, anyway? Yeah, yeah, I know — someone trying to hide it."

She took a deep breath, adjusted her white and blue striped canvas work gloves and inserted the heavy red-tipped crowbar under the final stone slab. Air hissed out of her mouth and nose as she exerted her back and thigh muscles to the task, straining to pry it loose.

"Ach-choo!"

She sniffed loudly, her nose dripping. The damn soot-covered rocks had been in use as a fire pit. *Give it to Hefty, though — clever ruse.*

Ignoring the black soot, she leaned against the huge pile of stones and wiped her nose on her hoodie sleeve before shining her flashlight onto Hefty McGee's journal. She thumbed through the tattered pages, still confident that the university wouldn't miss the dusty old thing for one weekend.

"Hmm, says here Hefty won a moose head from a saloon keeper in a card game right here in Dawson City. Furthermore, that you lost that antler in the ensuring fistfight when it turned out that the gambler was a poor loser. Know anything about that?"

She tucked the journal back into her hoodie then reinserted

the crowbar.

"Okay, here goes!" She attacked the slab with all her might. A loud squeal of protest as rock ground against rock. *Ah, it moved. Just another few inches.* Grunting, she pushed harder until the heavy cover slid off enough that she could shine her flashlight inside the hole pickaxed into the cave floor.

The sight of a large rotted pile of leather securely wrapped and tied with a cord quickened her breath. On top, weighing the package down, was a small smooth rock, and underneath it a torn piece of brown butcher paper. She pulled it out and shone the light on it.

She read the faded handwritten words aloud, figuring the moose had a right to know, as well. "'Abandon hope all ye who steals Soapy's Gold. It be cursed. Gave me the pox. Hefty McGee.'" Casey chuckled, despite the discomfort of the past few hours of digging in the tight, damp quarters, and gave the moose head a glance. "Just proves, old man, I'm in the right place!"

She thrust her arm inside the large hole in the cave floor and tugged on the heavy parcel. *Damn, not enough room to lift it out.* The blasted stone needed to be moved farther over. She glanced back at the doorway of the cave. Only a short while and the spring waters of the rising Yukon River would flood the low-lying cave.

"Be nice if you could lend a hand, buster." She directed her comments at the moose head. It was beginning to creep her out, staring down at her with glassy, lifeless eyes. Okay, so perhaps coming alone had not been so smart, but she needed to know if all her research was going to pay off. And, just maybe, it was about to. *Big-time.*

The pry bar slipped as the rock jerked under the extreme pressure. It swung in an upward arc toward the moose head, pitching her forward as it did so. It also hit the beast a solid blow on its huge bulbous nose, knocking it loose from its perch on the rock wall and right down onto her head.

The last thought as pain drilled into her brain was that

the old miner who had gone to the trouble to hide his stolen gold in the wilds of Northern Canada might have gotten it right. The curse was effective — if one was a klutz.

Casey woke with a start, shivering uncontrollably. Her head pounded from a possible concussion and her clothes were soaking wet. She blinked hard, gingerly touching the top of her skull, and felt a lump as large as a goose egg under her platinum braid of hair. *Damn.* If she had a mirror she could tell her if her eyes were dilated. But at least there was no blood. She rummaged in her pocket for her cell phone and checked the time. Double damn. She'd been out for more than an hour!

As her vision cleared, she focused on the cave's entrance. Waves slapping around the opening made her heart race. Swallowing hard against the shock and the pain, she struggled to pull herself to a sitting position. Her brain swam with the effort and she punched the downed moose right in its over-sized moth-eaten nose.

"It's all your fault! If you weren't already dead..." Casey threatened. She managed to get to her feet by holding on to the clammy moss-covered stone wall. Trickles of moisture created darkened trails down the ancient walls, dampening her palms.

A flash of something sliding by the doorway drew her attention. Her boat! Left tied to a tree on shore, with the rising waters it'd somehow managed to work itself free. Headache forgotten, she splashed through the frigid water, lunging to snatch hold of it before it drifted away in the current. Swaying dizzily, she managed to tug it inside the cave's broad mouth. Thank goodness the cave floor sloped down toward the river, otherwise her transport might have floated away while she was knocked out.

She held hard to the canoe's frayed rope, maneuvering the sixteen-foot boat closer to the treasure. Once she tied it securely to an outcropping of rock, she hauled the offending moose head off to the side, grateful the one good antler hadn't pierced her skull. She relaunched her efforts to retrieve the booty. Thank God her flashlight was still intact and working.

"No fucking way I'm leaving here without my gold!" she muttered. "God damn it—move, won't you!" she exclaimed in frustration, pushing as hard as she could manage. It was now or never. At least the weight training was paying off. She put everything behind the effort, every muscle in her body struggling and screaming at her to give it up already.

With an ominous creak like a banshee screaming in the wind, she inched the stone lid off bit by bit, the pit reluctant to give up its treasure. Finally, against the clock, Casey jolted the stone lid far enough off to allow her full access to what lay beneath. With a tug at the rotted string that bound the package, she thrust it out of the way and pushed her hand inside to pull apart the decayed leather.

She froze and took a deep breath, heart hammering. Was this the moment? Would all her intensive research now pay off? Or was it an elaborate hoax set up by an ornery old conman with a wicked sense of humor?

She touched it reverently, a laying-on-of-hands. Took a deep breath.

This was it. The moment of truth.

And yet, she hesitated, her hands trembling. So much rode on this. Finding the treasure would fund another adventure, her life's blood. Give her the freedom she needed. Craved.

Open it already!

Okay. Stop shouting at me.

The war within quieted as she slowly peeled back the edges of the musty old covering. Was that a choir of angels singing? No, just her imagination working overtime. Whispers from the past upping the roaring clamor in her head as the color revealed itself.

Shiny yellow nuggets. Gold! Soapy's stolen hoard!

The nuggets gleamed brightly under the flashlight's beam. Nestled between the lumps of gold, someone had packed old leather pouches filled with gold dust. She'd found it! She swallowed hard. Glanced back at the cave's entrance.

Crap. The water was rising. Faster.

Hurriedly, she scooped up the heavy nuggets and packets, flinging them into her backpack and glancing back at the cave's entrance every few seconds to make sure she could still free herself. Running out of room in the pack, she pulled another black carryall from the canoe's bottom and loaded it. At the last possible second, she threw in the moose head, knowing she was being loopy. The damn thing must weigh twenty-five pounds, broken antler or not, but he'd helped point the way.

After wading through the rising flood waters that lapped and sucked at her jean-clad knees, she leaped into the boat as she got near the entrance, grabbing one of the paddles to maneuver the canoe through the doorway. Head throbbing and eyes aching, she ducked under the rough edge of the opening and worked the canoe onto the open water of the Yukon River. The river was narrower at Dawson City, a half mile down the river from the cave, making the expanse that much more difficult to cross. She needed to find a safer place to be on this side of the river soon as possible.

The waves were rough. Far rougher than before. Dismay filled her. Heart racing as adrenaline pumped through her depleted system, she focused on keeping the front of the canoe centered with the tailwind at her back, her muscles aching brutally from the strain. She wasn't scot-free yet, but she was going to do her damnedest to make it happen.

Of course, as she fought the current of the swollen river, the heavens opened up, releasing their bounty, a driving rain that stung her eyes and blurred her vision. The buckets of cold water drenching her head made her teeth chatter nosily. *Really. You had to send rain...*

"It's all your damn fault!" she exclaimed, ranting at the moose to keep her mounting fears at bay. He rested in the bow, his one antler pointing jauntily skyward, completely oblivious to the freezing rain, covered snugly by his thick brown hide. The sound of the rain endlessly pelting the water, her oar splashing rhythmically into the river, all combined into a marching drone pushing her onward.

Spying a low-lying area, she awkwardly steered the rented craft toward it, fighting the river's intense current, which was magnified tenfold by the rising water. She needed to build a fire to dry out her drenched clothing. The comforting vision of a roaring blaze kept her going and she gave it all she had left. The high, angry waves fought her every step of the way, battering the canoe bow, threatening to overturn the craft, her depleted muscles screaming for relief and leaving only her fighting spirit to push her body onward. A lifetime passed until she felt the canoe touch bottom.

Shaking with relief, knees turned to jelly, she climbed out and pulled the boat the rest of the way onto the shoreline. Behind the small alcove, seventy-foot fir and birch trees thickly carpeted the high hillside, marching right out of sight. How far to bring the boat up? How high would the water rise? Shivering with bone-chilling exhaustion, she dragged it an extra few meters for good measure. Rummaged around in her bag for supplies. Her frozen hands were almost useless and wouldn't follow a simple direction, making it seem an eternity until she found her life-pack of emergency supplies. Life and death lurked menacingly in the shadows. Her mind shutting down, her bruised brain screaming for relief, she wanted nothing more than to lie down and sleep.

No. Focus. Even now hypothermia's lethargy crept into her veins, leaving no room for error.

Just. Keep. Moving.

Finding a drier spot under a thick canopy of trees, she used her hands to scoop out a depression in the soil, adding a few dry twigs and moss from her pack. Brown Owl, her Girl Guide troop leader from days long past, had harped on being prepared. Maybe she hadn't been referring to rustling someone's gold, but still. Casey gave a snort of hysterical laughter at the very idea of rustling gold in modern times. The sound echoed eerily in the dense forest, which seemed devoid of human life. Tall trees stood guard, frowning their disapproval.

Her hands shook uncontrollably as she struggled with her lighter to kindle a flame in the uncooperative moss. Wearily, she gathered sticks of wood strewn about, pinpoints of white light in her vision making her sway drunkenly. Hours, not minutes, passed until the life-giving heat blazing into the sullen gray sky mimicked her vision in the boat of building a fire to warm her. Life-giving warmth.

"Ah, that's better, eh," she remarked to the moose head she'd propped against the trunk of a tree. She rubbed her hands together as near to the dancing flames as she could without sustaining burns. Rummaging around in her pack again produced a protein bar, a large bottle of water and a small one of aspirin. Between bites of the bar, she drank water and chewed on aspirin. Other than the thumping headache, she was better.

She wrinkled her nose against the sharp stench of polyethylene as she shook out a blue plastic tarp stiff with newness and hung it between four trees as shelter. Once a second tarp was unfolded and spread on the ground, she laid rocks at the corners to flatten and secure it. The familiar fragrance of smoke burning off the damp wood filled her nostrils. Pine needles added to the potpourri, giving off their own sharp scent as she lurched about, crunching them under her boots and releasing their fragrance. Casey sneezed three times in a row, shivering in her wet clothes.

After pulling off her wet hiking boots and turning them upside down, she impaled them on sticks, setting them close to the fire to dry. She added her socks, pants and jacket. Quickly donning her one change of dry clothing, she wrapped the distinctive red and black Hudson Bay blanket around her freezing body, the scratchy wool tucked up around her chin.

She sat on the tarp and smiled at the moose head. "Let that be a lesson to you. You can never be too prepared."

A twig snapped.

She turned her head toward the sound. Another twig. A longer crackling noise. She held her breath, her mind spinning.

Man or beast?

She rummaged blindly at her side, reaching for her bear spray, while she scanned the bush line. Her fingers closed around the black plastic trigger of the colorful metal canister with the brown bear's photo in proud display, sharp incisors and all. Not a comforting sight — for a human intruder.

She braced it in both hands, moving stealthily toward the forest. Working her way across the ground, careful to step softly, all senses alert. A slight movement on the perimeter drew her attention. *Wait for it…*

Sighting a bit of yellow fabric attached to a leg from behind a tree, she stopped in her tracks. *Human.*

"Stop or I'll shoot," she shouted the warning.

"Don't shoot!" a voice called out.

"Show yourself then."

The full figure emerged from behind the thick tree trunk. An unkempt man wearing a dirty yellow rainslicker locked gazes with her. He stopped ten feet away.

"What are you doing here?" she demanded keeping the bear spray pointed at him.

"Whatcha doing with Hefty's moose?" he asked, ignoring her question. He pointed at the offending object lazing against the tree trunk, demanding answers with his belligerent stance, hands braced on hips.

"What's it to you?" she shot right back.

"You been messing around in his cave?"

"It's on public land — no law against it." She lowered the bear spray to her side but kept her finger on the trigger.

"Ain't right to disturb a man's things when he ain't here to defend them," he muttered.

"Just took a liking to this guy." She gestured at the moose with her free hand. "He fell on my head and knocked me clear out."

His slate-blue eyes narrowed suspiciously. "You look okay now."

"Throbbing headache, but it'll pass. Anything else I can do for you, Mr...?"

He hesitated for a moment. *Alzheimer's setting in?*

"Duncan MacLean." He pursed his lips, scratching at his thick beard intertwined with threads of gray and red. A dirty cap that might have been red at one time was pulled down over his ears, grizzled hair sticking out the sides like that of a mad professor.

"I'm Casey." She didn't offer her hand. Her finger tightened on the trigger of the can, alert for any sudden movements.

"You know the legend of Soapy's Stolen Gold, lass?"

Casey shook her head. No point in telling him she knew all about it—it would only bring more suspicion her way that she might have gone after the treasure. Best he thought it was just the moose she had taken a shine to.

"Fer the price of a hot coffee and a wee nip of the spirits, I'd share it with ya. Hell of a tale."

She shook her head. "Sorry, I have neither. Just water and protein bars."

He screwed up his wrinkled face, grimacing. "Wouldn't give ye two cents for that shite."

"Sorry, all I've got." She kept her tone neutral, wishing he'd leave. "I'm not feeling up to company, anyway. Been a long day."

"Ah, sorry to bother ye, lass. Another time."

"Maybe."

"Ye staying in Dawson City?"

She nodded, wondering where this was going.

"Water's too rough to cross tonight. Best watch yer back. And keep that bear spray handy. It's the four-legged creatures ye need to watch out fer most, lassie."

"Thanks for the advice."

"Yer welcome." He turned on his heel and strode back to

the bush line, vanishing into the forest.

She let out a sigh of relief, hoping she'd seen and smelt the last of him. Even though she was ten feet away, a strong, stomach-turning odor rose from his unwashed clothing. Meeting a virile mountain man in the bush appeared vastly overrated. Or at least that particular one. Now, having one of the studs from her friend Rebecca's hot and steamy books drop into her lap... That would be awesome.

Sleep would be awesome, as well, but she needed to stay on guard. *Going to be a long friggin' night.* She threw off the blanket, glancing into the bottom of the canoe as she went by it, selecting more firewood from the ground to add to the growing pile. Though the treasure was well concealed, she knew her visitor had most likely headed off to check the cave she'd abandoned, if he wasn't still watching her. Her one consolation? He wouldn't be able to enter to see the destruction of McGee's fire pit until the water receded. *When would that be? Sometime tonight?* She scanned the river. *Choppy waters.* Effective barrier to keep him out for a while. And her pinned down. *Some impasse.*

A screech owl hooted as it flew silently overhead, joined by a few wolves sounding the ancient call a few minutes later, making the nerves in her neck tingle. She checked her phone for bars. *Thank God.* She called the hotel to let them know to keep her room. They were obliging, then it was back to waiting. Endlessly waiting. At least the rain had stopped.

She sucked back more bottled water, wiping her mouth with her hand. Wait. Were the waves lessening? She got up, scooped a large red plastic bucket from the canoe and hurried to the shore. Dipping the edge of the pail in the river, she let the cold water rush in. Lugged the heavy pail back to camp and set it by the crackling flames. All set.

The minutes ticked by.

She let out a deep breath, blowing it through her teeth. *Bed. Tonight. Please let that be part of my memory of Dawson. Sweet, the gods must be listening.* The sun glimmered enticingly, slipping out from behind the cloud bank. She doused the fire and stripped the campsite, throwing everything into the canoe.

Once she'd shoved the boat into the water, she took up the wooden paddle and headed the bow straight across the river. A sudden thought. Wouldn't it be great to have her rowing team from the university help out at this precise moment? Of course, she wasn't willing to share the booty quite that far, so solo it was going to have to stay. Besides, they'd shared enough glory winning a ton of meets together. She laughed out loud, the exuberance of the moment overcoming her.

Muscles straining, she paddled like she had never paddled before, racing an internal clock. The wind further tousled her disheveled hair, sending strands flying into her face and making her wish she'd dealt with it in camp. She swiped the perspiration from her forehead with the back of her hand, her sweatshirt clinging to her skin. Scanning the horizon, she grimaced at the renewed throbbing in her head. Leaning into the wind, she doubled her efforts, quickly rewarded with the tantalizing view of the shoreline inching closer.

The canoe struck bottom suddenly, squealing in protest. Arms deadened, she stumbled out, tripping over her own feet. Landed on her ass. She got up, rubbing at her posterior, and pulled the boat the final few feet to safety before sinking back down onto the ground. Took a few deep breaths. The air tasted sweet, tinged with the fragrance of freedom.

Hide the gold. The mantra kept her moving. She followed the pre-existing plan to the letter. Bore the heavy weight of the treasure one full backpack at a time to the hole she'd dug last night inside an old hollowed-out tree trunk. Covered it over with soil and leaves. Pulled the phone from her jacket pocket to mark the spot with a photo.

Somehow, she made it the quarter mile back in the canoe. She docked the boat in its rental spot ready for its next adventure, doubting the craft would ever again see what it had just gotten her through. Hefting her backpack, she picked up the moose head and wearily trudged back to the hotel. Slipped through the side entrance. Each stair felt a mile high as she forced her feet to move. Inside the room, door closed, she fell face-first on the bed. She just needed five minutes…

Her cell phone chirped. She groaned. Rolled over. Checked the number. Aha. She should have known. This would take more than mere *talking*.

Casey crawled over to the side of the bed and grabbed her laptop, quickly opening it. She leaned back against a nest of pillows, exhaustion forgotten for the moment. With a few quick clicks of her mouse, she set it up.

A few seconds later and the video conference screen dinged and opened, a montage of happy female faces filling the twelve-inch screen. She savored the moment, quashing down her secret, which was bursting to escape.

"So, did you find it?" Rebecca asked, her honey-blonde waves of hair swaying around her animated face.

"Find what?" Casey teased.

"You know! We've got heavy action on this. 'Fess up!" Lacey demanded, her red curls sparking with megawatt voltage, an all-too-true indication of her wild-child character. Her green eyes shone. Her identical twin's face crowded in from one side, nearly interchangeable with Lacey's, and Miranda, the sweetest pixie in the whole world, huddled too, her short dark hair gleaming under the overhead light. Casey could barely see Ava's thick golden-brown bangs perched above black-framed glasses in the background, next to uber-blonde Elin who towered above her. Oh, and there was the top of Tessa's curly head. All the Ringers accounted for.

"Okay. Oh, yeah, we're in business!" She couldn't hold out as long as she would have liked, enjoying the immediate whoops of satisfaction from her friends more than relishing the secret another second.

"So, what time did you find it?" Lily asked, biting her

bottom lip in concentration.

"About four o'clock this afternoon. Who wins?"

"Damn. I had this morning between ten and eleven-thirty," Lacey grumbled.

"I had three to four-thirty," Ava said, pushing in between Miranda and Lacey to look right at Casey. "Right smack-dab in the middle. I win!" Her usual solemn lawyerly expression had gone, replaced by full-on exuberance.

"All yours, Ava. You get the forfeits. Sweet, now we get to watch Lacey do a pole dance for Will and won't he be surprised," Rebecca confirmed, grinning. William James Thornton III, the twin's BFF, could use the distraction, having recently returned from his tour of duty in Afghanistan.

"Not much of a stretch," Lily deadpanned, rolling her eyes. The forfeitures were chosen by others in the group — not the one who had to pay it. Kind of unfair, but a whole lot more fun. Some good-natured grumbling filled the airwaves.

"How did it go? Any problems?" Rebecca asked, pushing in closer.

"Nothing I couldn't handle," Casey said, dismissing their concerns.

"Tell me. I can sense something popped up."

"Pretty uneventful, really." She shrugged. "Just one visitor. No biggie. Name of Duncan MacLean."

"You can't be too careful. I'll check him out."

Casey yawned, exhaustion crowding in. "Okay, up to you. I gotta get some sleep, guys. Congrats, Ava. See you all soon."

She closed her laptop lid. Lay in the dark, grinning ear-to-ear. She'd done it…

* * * *

Casey woke with a lurch, disorientated, muscles stiff and aching. She checked her phone. Five o'clock. Just enough time for a hot shower. Humming under the hot flow of water, she soaped and scrubbed the night away.

"So, what shall I call you?" she asked the cocky moose, drying her hair briskly with the fluffy white hotel towel. "Howard. Fits you to a tee, I think. You know, you've got a lot more going for you than that last guy I went to dinner with. He didn't see the point of my adventures. Would have seriously objected to this trip. And, hell, thought the safest place for a woman was staying in one spot and most likely catering to just his needs. *Sooo* not going to happen! Well, since you're not objecting, I'll take that as a yes."

Chapter Two

"Of all the gin joints in all the towns in all the world, she walks into mine." *Casablanca*

Just as Casey began driving the small black rental across the short causeway toward Oak Island, her cell phone chirped. Ignoring it, she turned right at the end of the bridge connecting the island to Nova Scotia and pulled into the small visitor parking lot. She snatched up the phone. Hit Redial.

"Hey, girlfriend."

"Thought you'd be home by now," Rebecca said.

"Just wanted to take the opportunity to reconnoiter the famous Money Pit. Not going to waste my final day of vacation. Not with what's coming up this week. Plus, I could use photos for that new course I've talked the admin into letting me teach—Mysteries and Lost Treasures of the World. Just got approval last week."

A foghorn blared in the distance.

"Finally! That should be fun. Surprised admin went for it."

"Had to get approval before our new department stooge arrives—who knows what will happen then?" Casey let out a deep sigh. Just how bad was the new suit going to be? *He can't possibly be as useless as the last diabolical department head, right?*

Rebecca chuckled. "Well, be careful. Remember the legend says just one more person needs to die on Oak Island for the treasure to be revealed."

"And all the red oaks to die. Well, can't say that part

hasn't happened. Don't worry. Not planning on being the seventh sacrifice. Booked another plane for tonight, by the way. I should be in around ten."

"I only called because I learned a bit about the guy you ran into, then I'll leave you alone. He's a local legend. Considered a real troublemaker by some. Thought you should know," Rebecca said.

"Okay, good to know." Casey ended the call. She frowned, thinking about the intruder. Was he going to be trouble? Hmm. She'd need to keep more of an eye out. She picked up her backpack, scrambling out of the car. Only one other vehicle on the lot. Probably belonged to the guide. She'd been lucky enough to book a private tour.

Hoisting the pack onto her back, she pushed the button on the key fob for the rental, locking the doors.

The sun broke through the clouds at that moment. Eyes closed, she tilted her face upward. Then got a move on toward the information center. Deserted.

"Hello. Anyone here?" *Good stuff.* Time to recon the area.

Song birds filled the air with their sweetness as she strolled along the well-trodden path. After yesterday's hard labor, today's treat beckoned, waving her in to home plate with open arms. Occasional arrows pointed the way and she pressed on. She continually scanned the area for signs of human and animal life with her cell phone in hand, snapping photos and wishing black ants hadn't killed off the lofty red oaks.

Suddenly, the ground rumbled ominously beneath her feet. She froze. Listened. What the hell was going on? Earthquake? Something crashed-landed? Which direction? Unfreezing and spinning around on the spot, she looked intently for a clue as to what was happening. Did someone need help? Her heart beating wildly, she had no choice but to wait, unsure of which direction the sound had come from.

A loud shout. *There.*

She took off running, shoving the phone into her pocket,

adrenaline coursing through her veins, feet pounding down the path.

She raced around a curve in the trail to find a sinkhole opening a meter away, the ground still tumbling.

"Holy shit!" she exclaimed, stopping dead in her tracks. Should she move any closer? Would she destabilize it even more? She backed off a couple of steps.

As the dust settled, a man emerged, standing upright in the pit. Not just any man, but a truly pissed-off one. She could only see him from the shoulders up until she moved in closer for a better view. He appeared unharmed.

"If you wouldn't mind lending a hand, darlin'," he said, his tone suggesting she was not being very helpful just standing there gawking. "Just in case this thing decides to settle even more."

"Oh, yes, of course." She extended her arm. The poor guy was covered in dust and debris. He grasped her hand, she gave a mighty pull and he scrambled up the side of the hole. He slipped at the last possible second on the unstable edge and tumbled forward, landing right smack on top of her.

Fuck. She went down with a thud, the breath whooshing from her lungs in a wild rush, his sudden closeness to her person a hell of a shook. The scent of cologne or aftershave, mingled with a natural underlying musk, washed over her as he lay prone on her body, his head cradled by her breasts. She stared into the bluest eyes ever as his startled glance locked with hers. A complete stranger, embracing her. Albeit a very handsome and hot one who gave off a tantalizing fragrance, if that made it any better.

The man had the grace to look even more horrified than her. When he seemed to realize his hands were on her person, and more specifically, squeezing one very sensitive breast, the nipple pebbling from the intimate contact, he extracted himself, got to his feet then bent to give her a hand up.

"My God, I'm so sorry. Are you okay?" he apologized.

"I'm fine," she croaked, swallowing hard. Her backpack

had absorbed most of the fall.

He took a moment to shake and pound the soil off. Her hands trembled as she retrieved a water bottle. She drank deeply, offering a second bottle to him as she did so. He took it with a nod of thanks and downed half in one quick go.

"Wow," she finally ventured. "That really was something."

"Yeah, that was something all right," he agreed. She got a better look at him as he emerged from his dust cocoon. Topping six feet two at least, he towered well above her, wide shoulders encased in a blue work shirt, sleeves rolled up to the elbows, jeans hanging on narrow hips. His blue eyes blazed and his square jaw was tight. He reminded Casey of a young Robert Redford from the movie *Butch Cassidy and the Sundance Kid. Golden Boy. Sweet Jesus.*

"Oh, goodness, I'm so sorry! What happened? Are you okay?" A voice intruded as a young man dressed in a beige uniform, clipboard in hand, expression aghast, rushed up. *Oak Island Tours* printed in white on his red baseball cap signified his occupation.

"What happened is a blasted pit opened up under my feet. And I nearly hurt this young lady by landing on top of her."

"I'm so sorry…" The man looked down at his clipboard. "Professor Harrison. I didn't get the chance to warn you. I was running late, oh, my goodness—you're not going to sue the company or anything? I could lose my job."

"Weren't you off the marked path?" Casey interrupted, glancing over at a black backpack lying at the base of a pine tree at least ten feet off the trail.

"What? Uh, yes, okay. I did go over to look—"

"Well, then, you'd better not sue the tour company for your own negligence."

"What in the world are you talking about? Who said anything about suing anybody?"

"Well, it was obviously your own fault." A devil made her

say it. Blame it on the last few confusing moments. Things needed to get back under control. Her control.

"My fault!"

"Yes, you strayed from the path, didn't wait for the tour guide to give his safety speech." She crossed her arms over her breasts, pursing her lips.

His blue eyes flashed and narrowed. "And you did? Why are you here, anyway?"

"I booked a private tour. A perfectly acceptable reason for being here, I believe."

"I see you didn't wait for the tour guide, either. Isn't that a breach of the rules?" he noted, his jaw tightening.

The tour guide piped up, "Oh, I'm sorry about that. Apparently, I'm double-booked for a private tour today."

"You sure are sorry about a lot of things today," the guy muttered, not letting up on his scowl.

"Mr. Harrison," she began.

"Truman," he said.

"Truman Harrison," she parroted. *Wait.* That name sounded familiar.

"Precisely, darlin'. And you are?"

"Uh, Casey Madison." She appreciated his pronounced southern drawl. It sounded vastly more charming than her stark Canadian prairie flatlander accent. Even when pissed. Make that royally pissed.

The tour guide spoke up, glanced her way. "Casey Madison from the U of M. Right?"

"University of Manitoba?" Truman asked, furrowing his brow. He leaned forward, pulling something from her hair. He held out a dry bit of twig. She took a step back, chewing on her bottom lip.

"Yeah, so?" She smoothed the braid curving its way down her breast. She regretted having tied a bright red ribbon around the blonde ends that morning. She glanced at his hair, shining bright gold in the sunlight. *Oh, yeah. A real pretty boy. And being a bit of a jackass.*

"Department of Archeology?"

"Yeah?" Casey repeated.

"Don't you think it only right and proper to welcome your new department head?"

Just. Fuckin'. Great.

Casey pressed her lips together into a grim line. Of all the people to run into here, in Nova Scotia, he would have been the seventh billion in plausible possibilities on her list. Was this payback for stealing Soapy's Gold? Her fingers twitched to squeeze the life out of the stress-ball printed with the chancellor's image, thoughtfully presented to her by a fellow Brass Ringer last Christmastime.

So, this pretty treat for the eyes is a professor at the University of Manitoba. Where does she get off, suggesting I'm in the wrong? No warning signs around the area. No suggestions about its instability. Okay, he had ventured from the path, and without a proper escort. He needed to accept some responsibility.

But Casey Madison had just done the same, which spoke volumes. He smothered a chuckle. Poker was a favorite game in the deep south. Something told him she was also a master of the game.

"Ah..." Casey began.

He hid a smile, watching her struggle for words. This was proving to be fun.

"I imagine you would prefer to cancel your tour?" the earnest young guide interrupted, his Adam's apple bobbing obsessively in his skinny throat as he ping-ponged his glance between them.

The look of gratitude she gave the guide was beyond priceless. *Maybe you're not as good at poker as you think, Miss Madison.*

"Nonsense. I'm here now. I would prefer to continue. This may be my last chance for some time to visit your fine province of Nova Scotia," Truman assured the guide.

Casey upped the ante. "I want to continue, too. I need the experience and documentation for one of my courses. It's important. Very important to me."

"I-I need to report this to my boss. Get permission to continue. I don't know if he will allow it, but I can ask."

"Good. In the meantime, I would like to take more photos," Casey added.

"Uh, sure, go ahead. I'll be right with you." The young man pulled out his cell phone and punched in some numbers. He turned his back and began speaking to someone, explaining what had just occurred, absurdly waving his hands to point out what the guy on the other end of the call could not possibly see.

Truman skirted the raw edges of the hole and retrieved his backpack, strapping it on. Hmm. With the island riddled with so many manmade shafts and pits, what had happened was not surprising. Hindsight being twenty-twenty, of course.

"Ready, darlin'?" he asked Casey, enjoying watching her eyebrows rise at his use of the word *darlin'*. Totally inappropriate, of course, but he couldn't help himself. Her lovely animated face with those gorgeous blue eyes was so expressive he could read her conflicted thoughts. He was her new boss. She wasn't sure what she should do. She was pissed off about it yet intrigued and she wanted to continue the tour. Pretty much in that order.

He waited. *One, two, three…*

"Okay, let's go." She gave him a determined look and strode off, digging her cell phone from her jeans' pocket. The action drew attention to her body and a quick memory of her being pressed against him, his hand on a luscious breast. Warm and curvy and smelling so damned fine. Like magnolia blossoms after a spring rain.

He strode down the path, enjoying the view. His mind focused, he nearly banged into her again as she stopped dead, clicking photos of bore holes and the landscape. She turned around and said, "I'm taking the right fork."

He looked ahead to see two different paths. *Hmm.* "A road diverging in a wood, eh? What does that remind me of?"

The smile she gave in acknowledgment made him bet that she knew the famous poem and that she'd always been drawn to the uncharted route. She made a little curtsy for fun. "Gotta follow your instincts. You take the other and see who arrives first," she ordered and took off at a fast clip.

Damn. Now he didn't get to follow that fine ass.

He rounded a corner and found himself face to face with the legendary Money Pit. A death trap, pure and simple—if he hadn't already known its secrets. Though its history demonstrated it certainly was not pure in the taking of six lives, just as its underground schematics showed it to be anything but simple in its mesh of underground labyrinth and booby-traps.

The approximately twelve-foot diameter opening was surrounded by chain link fencing. Tall grass dominated the inside of the fence line. *Not much to see.* An abandoned hole covered over with some wooden ties. What was here was more alive in the human imagination as visitors envisioned a treasure hoard hidden in the dark depths of the island hundreds of years ago. *If they only knew the real story.*

Truman glanced at the large sign nearby, depicting what lay beneath—the nine layers of oak platforms, the single one of flat stones not indigenous to the area but to Gold Island carted in from a few miles away, the layers of fill including some of charcoal, blue clay, spruce, metal pieces the auger had been unable to bring to the surface and very old carbon-dated coconut fiber from centuries past. It continued down to the ninety-eight-foot depth where it had famously flooded for the Onslow Company one dark night in 1804.

Salt water now filled the pit to the thirty-two-foot tidal mark, no matter how much bailing went on or how powerful the pump. Modern excavations had dug deeper to the nearly two-hundred-foot level, still without the pit giving up its secrets. And now all this legal wrangling. He shook his head in dismay.

He continued reading the posted literature. *Nice, the*

planners did a good job of sharing what they knew of its history for tourists. The illustrations of the famous heart-shaped stone, a fragment of parchment with strange lettering from the days of Shakespeare and Sir Francis Bacon and the oddest find of all—a large rock discovered upside down somewhere between eighty to ninety feet with glyphs cut on it. Glyphs commonly decoded as meaning Forty Feet Below Two Million Pounds Are Buried.

All laid out quite well. Though I could add volumes to the short history included alongside the diagram on the black and white sign.

"It was booby-trapped to flood before the treasure could be found. Quite the engineering marvel," a female voice threw in and Casey came up to stand beside him.

"Do you think there was a way to avoid that tragic outcome earlier on?" he asked though he knew the answer, turning to look at her. Her small body vibrated with excitement, stirring his…imagination.

"Possibly, if you were the ones who built it," she said. "Do you think it was a tar pit for the British navy, as has been recently suggested?"

"Not likely—too many layers involved. No tar kiln in the world has ever been dug to such a depth. And why rig it to flood with ocean water? And go to all the trouble to build an artificial beach to keep the flood tunnel operational? And those five box drains found set up with eelgrass and smooth stones made to last centuries? More likely to hide something. Stolen treasure or possibly a burial site."

"So, is your money on the Egyptians, Vikings, Mayans, Aztec, British Admiralty, King George, Marie Antonietta, Sir Francis Drake, Shakespeare or Bacon, the always suspect Vatican and Templar Knights or as the locals figure a pirate like Captain Kidd or Blackbeard? The list of possible suspects seems to grow with each new theory."

She shook her head in mock-dismay as a slight smile played around her lips. Truman throbbed with the sudden, deep urge to kiss her. *What the hell?* He gave his head a slight shake. Chalked it up to the way they'd met. A dangerous liaison always kick-started the libido. He didn't appreciate being part of the scientific proof. Put him off his footing.

"My money's on all the treasure being long gone. A lot of people have gone over the island with a fine-tooth comb for two hundred years. I really am here just for the research value. Coming up to work in Canada, the opportunity just fell in my lap."

"Really?" Casey asked, looking disappointed.

"Yes, and even finding out more of the history is going to be difficult. All the original stones and artifacts have been tampered with." He was quick to lower her expectations.

"Where do you think one should look for the best chance to learn more?" She would share his thirst for knowledge. She was an archeologist, after all.

He grinned. "Now for that choice bit of information, darlin', you'll just have to wait and find out when my book's published."

"I got a friend taking care of that for me. Uses all my exploits in her plots," she teased, her eyes filling with glee. "Of course, I really just want the information for my classes, that authentic touch of having been there to add a proper sense of reality for my students. Every little bit helps, Professor."

Not so easy to impress. Hmm.

"Say, how about after the tour — ?"

The tour guide came scurrying up at that moment, regard for timing not being his strong suit.

"I'm sorry, but you'll have to leave — "

"But I'm not finished yet! What about the cave-in pit and the manmade beach? The giant cross or where the stone triangle lay before it was destroyed? How can I explain them to my class without proper photos?" Hands on her hips, Casey confronted the interloper, her expression equal parts belligerent and horrified.

"Casey — " he began.

She glared at him, her eyes glinting dangerously. "In the

last twenty-four hours, I have been pushed to the limit. Pelted by rain, hit over the head by a confounded moose with only one antler and knocked unconscious and waylaid by an old miser. No way am I leaving here today without what I need and have paid for, damn it!"

"Okay, no need for profanity, darlin'. Surely we can work something out with this good man. Your name, sir?" Truman asked, holding up the palms of his hands in a gesture of reconciliation toward the tour guide.

"Uh, Mason. Mason McGinnis."

"Well, Mr. McGinnis, I would be most pleased if you would accept my humble apologies and an offer of a monetary reward to assist this young lady here in obtaining what she so vitally requires. You know the old expression — you can't stop a woman when she's out of control? No?"

Mason shook his head, his expression bewildered, shuttling his gaze back and forth between the pair of them.

"Well, it states the obvious, I'm sorry to say. I think it's in best our interest if we both see to what the young lady wants. Surely, that would be the best course for the two of us to follow?"

"Uh, yeah, well, the owner's going to be delayed for a bit —" Mason began, lifting off his hat to scratch at his sweat-flattened hair before plunking the hat back on his head.

"Well, there you go, then. We'll be out of your way in a jiffy if you would kindly consent to just giving us a few more minutes more of your precious time." He was laying it on a bit thick, but it would serve his purposes. He needed to see one spot in particular. For comparison.

"Okay, sure. But we have to hurry."

"Of course. Please lead the way, Mr. McGinnis."

Casey's expression and mood turned on a dime.

"Don't ever refer to me as a 'young lady'. And stop calling me 'darlin'' while you're at it. I'm nobody's darling!" she whispered out of the side of her mouth as they dutifully followed the now fleet-footed tour guide to the next landmark.

"If you insist, but I find it hard to believe. You being so sweet-natured and all."

She squinted her baby blues at him, sparks glinting through the narrowed openings. He pursed his lips.

"I'll zip it for now," he said with a wry smile. "Take your pictures. I'll reimburse our Mr. McGinnis."

"Like hell you will! I pay my own way."

"The department will reimburse me." They wouldn't, of course—he'd never ask—but he wanted to see her expression as he reminded her who he was.

She clamped her lips together.

"Tell me about this moose that bonked you on the head," he said.

"You'll have to read Rebecca's book to find out."

Touché.

The tour guide was here, there and everywhere, rushing through his rehearsed speech, including the legendary superstition of a Devil Dog with the glowing red eyes appearing on the island in days long past, and soon they were back in the office. Truman handed Mason fifty dollars on the sly while Casey made use of the ladies' room.

She emerged, her face scrubbed clean and fair hair tidied. He liked her natural good looks with no need for artifice, so unlike most southern belles he was acquainted with.

"How did you get hit on the head with a moose?" He had to ask again. "I don't have time to wait for the novel to be written."

Mason stopped fiddling with some papers on the counter and looked up.

"Long story," Casey sighed. "Suffice to say, it was more my fault that his. He fell off a wall and clunked me on the head." She didn't meet his glance but studied a brochure she'd pulled from a display, unfolding it to peer at it carefully.

A man burst through the door at that second, his expression grim, his John Wayne swagger a good match for his big hat and scuffed boots.

"What happened here? Mason?"

"Mr. Byrne, I'm sorry, but I was running late 'cause my car broke down—"

"What do I pay you for? To be on time. No excuses. Why didn't you call me?"

The short, stout middle-aged man with the handlebar mustache wore a pair of jeans and a faded work shirt emblazoned with the company logo. His armpits were ringed with sweat, his raspy breathing loud.

"I accept the entire responsibility for causing the ruckus. I walked off the pathway."

"And you are?" The man turned his attention to him almost before Truman finished his apology.

"Professor Truman Harrison."

"Well, Professor, much as I appreciate your defense of Mason—"

"No harm's been done—not really. You now have an interesting new location to explore and show on tour." Truman said.

"Truman Harrison. Say, wait a darn minute! I know that name." The portly man squinted, his brow furrowing and reaching skyward to meet up with his sweat-rimmed Stetson. "You're the guy trying to get a diggin' lease here."

"Is that true? Have you applied for a digging lease?" Casey demanded.

"Yes, I have applied for a lease, but it's not for digging. That's incorrect. It's because I want to spend more time here and learn more about this legendary island for prosperity's sake. Oak Island is listed as one of the top ten mysteries of the world. How could I not come to Canada and use this opportunity to observe the area more closely?"

She eyed him, eyes narrowed, hands on hips. "Why didn't you tell me?"

"Why, you didn't ask, darlin', and we just met," he pointed out. "I'm going to use the research for a book. Just like you do with your friend Rebecca."

"Enough of the books already! You see the last one? That dang blasted author had the gull to suggest there's nothing here! Made out we're a goddamned tar pit, for Christ's sake!"

"Now, Mr. Byrne, it was just a theory, meant to start a discussion, like all good theories."

"No discussion! I want you gone. Now!"

"Of course. Please accept my apologies if I have offended you in any way. And don't worry. I have no intention of suing you for any suffering on my part for falling into the pit."

"I'll be more than offended if you don't get the hell out of here!"

The crunch of the gravel path was the only sound as they left the office. That and Casey's heavy breathing directly behind him as she hurried to keep up with his longer strides.

"That went rather well."

Truman grunted. Gave her a quick look. She grinned at him and he returned it. He appreciated her moxie. Here he was expecting theatrics and instead he got substance.

"Yes, perfectly, just like I'd planned."

"So, tell me more," she purred, her eyes alight with expectations.

"Nothing much more to tell, really. I'm writing a book and just wanted the opportunity to learn more. You know, talk to the community, neighbors, set up a small operation as home base to work from."

"That's the only reason you're here?"

"Yes. Sites like this fascinate me."

"I understand the fascination." She still sounded skeptical, though her expression softened. "My grandpa loved tales of high adventure. Seafaring and the like. I was hooked on *Treasure Island* almost before I could walk. He read and told stories most nights at bedtime—he came to live with us when I was three. My mom always said I was spoiled smart. And it bothered her that she didn't get her dreams to come true. She wanted to travel the world, meet all kinds of people, but she found my dad, fell in love, and the rest is history. Taught me not to give up my dreams—for anyone. I'm committed to living life to the fullest."

"'Two roads diverged in a wood, and I...I took the one less traveled by, And that has made all the difference'," he quoted with a smile.

"That about sums it up."

He enjoyed the brief moment of harmony. Wanted to extend it.

"How about we adjourn to a local eatery and share a repast?"

She turned from tossing her backpack into the rental's trunk, her lips pursed. "Okay. But I warn you, I want to know all you know about Oak Island."

"Just like you shared your moose story," he teased, hitting the button on the black key fob to unlock the vehicle's door.

"I would have shared if there was more to tell. I love to tell a tale as much as the next person. But it would have to be a tall tale in this case. Just a simple accident—nothing more." She was lying through her teeth.

Nobody goes to that much trouble to explain nothing. "Hmm. Well, how about we eat at Captain Kidd's Café?" It seemed all the tourist spots in the area were named in honor of the pirate the locals thought to be the treasure's most likely depositor.

"If you're buying," she said with a half-smile. Of course, it was the opposite of what he expected her to say. She intrigued him. He was going to have to be careful. Once burned, twice shy about fit him to a T. Plus, she was one of his employees.

"Sure. I'll let you keep all the treasure you've been finding. I'm sure you have better uses for it."

She ignored his probing. "Actually, I'm far more interested in discussing your theories about what's gone on historically. I've read engineering reports. A cavern with a sturdy oak ceiling lurks deep in the bedrock." She looked him right in the eyes. "But I don't think that's the only place treasure was found in the past," she counter-punched.

"No?" he inquired, enjoying watching her eyes light up with mischief. She jabbed at his upper arm with her forefinger. He pretended to be in pain, holding his injured arm.

"No!" Another grin. "Now, I'm starved. Meet you at the café." She ducked into her rental, gunned it and sped off in a cloud of dust.

* * * *

"I was told to call if I had anything." Byrne, thinking about the pair of professors who had just left *his* island, held the business card between his fingers and absently rubbed his thumb over the raised lettering. It gave only a phone number. The enticement was in the reward offered by the businessman when he'd given him the card, seeking any information about recent activity on the island. An expensive drill had broken down again and funds were running low. A quick buck would certainly help.

"Yes, Mr. Byrne. How good of you to call."

"The guy said there was a reward for information?" he pressed.

"Of course. That goes without saying. I'll have my man deliver the promised amount later today." The soothing voice calmed his fears.

"Well, a Professor Truman Harrison applied for a license to dig on the island."

"I see. Have you met the professor?"

"Yeah, he was just here," Tom muttered, bile rising in his chest. He reached into his pocket and automatically pulled out a roll of antacid tablets, using one finger to pop one off and into his mouth. He sucked on it and continued, "Booked a private tour. Like butter wouldn't melt in his mouth. Guy works at the University of Manitoba. Another girl that works there was here, too. Casey Madison, but it's not important. Just coincidence — some kind of trouble with a double booking. Anyway, then this Harrison fellow has the audacity to think his snooping around is warranted. He had an encounter with a new sinkhole—"

"Is that right?" the man spoke up, interrupting him. "Where?"

"Not far from the Money Pit. Just a shallow hole. I've checked it out. Not that interesting. Oh, and the guy says he's just here to get information for a book he's writing on the island. Though it might be legit. He *is* a professor."

"Okay, good. Keep an eye on things. Let me know if he comes back. There'll be more money in it for you."

"No problem. Don't want his kind here, anyway. Damn guy will just get in the way. You know what those ivory tower assholes are like. Always thinking they know it all and not wanting you to touch anything so it can be saved forever."

"Thank you, Mr. Byrne. Please call again when you have more news. Especially if they start to dig or drill."

"Yeah, sure," he muttered. "Just make sure the money is sent. Today. I need a new drill. ASAFP."

"Excuse me?" The voice sounded surprised.

"As soon as fuckin' possible," Tom spelled out.

Silence for a brief moment.

"You have my word." The phone went dead.

Chapter Three

"There are no accidents; we're all teachers." *Marla Gibbs*

"The clam chowder sounds good."

"Make it two bowls," Truman said. He handed the plastic menu back to the waitress. He turned to give Casey his undivided attention as if she were the only woman in the small family owned café — or so the outside signage proudly announced — his intense blue eyes locking with hers for a brief second. The connection made her uncomfortable and she turned to stare out of the window at the street.

"I think you and I have one thing in common, at least," Truman commented, drumming his fingers on the tabletop.

"And what would that be?" She had nothing in common with a suit, even if he was more tan than most. *Blame it on the longer daylight hours in the States.* She racked her brain for a safe topic, not wanting to insult the new department head. Problems would arise soon enough. Just look at her track record.

"Our interest in archeology, of course," he said sweeping a hand through his golden hair in a futile effort to keep it off his forehead. A boyish lock came tumbling right back down. Something stirred inside Casey.

"Yeah." *And that's the only thing we have in common.*

"What do you do in your spare time, when you're not off chasing adventure?"

"I'm part of a group of friends that came together during university. The Brass Ringers. We're a sorority of sorts — not officially recognized or anything like that, but our main goal's always been supporting one another. You know, helping to reach for the proverbial brass ring. Getting one wish to come true for each member." She rubbed absently at the spot on her upper shoulder where the loonie-sized tattoo had been inked a few years back. All the Ringers had one. Eight interlocking rings with a stylized running *R* inside.

"I like it. But that's got to be expensive — granting wishes," he mused. "So, tell me, darlin', how do you raise the funds?"

The plump waitress with the pencil pushed into the thick bun of brown hair tied to the top of her head plunked down their bowls of steaming clam chowder just then, saving her from answering right away.

"Hmm, this is good!" She grinned at him after tasting the fragrant soup and sharing a look of bliss.

"Yes, it is. But you didn't answer my question," he persisted, raising his eyebrows.

"Well, there's lots of time to get to all the wishes on the list."

"You have a list? What's yours?"

"World peace."

He chuckled.

"Not sharing too much, *eh*?" he queried, stressing the ubiquitous Canadian-ism.

"Far too soon for the sharing of secrets. Besides, you still haven't shared your best theories."

"I'm more interested in *who* buried the money there in the first place. Who would you place your money on?"

Now, this intrigued her, with her having spent many weeks sifting through the evidence and postulating theories with her adopted sisters. Though she wanted to hold her tongue and hide some facts, enthusiasm got the better of her. "Well, it's a fact that the pit had to have been completed prior to 1750 when settlement would have made construction impossible to keep secret and yet not before the carbon dating going back to — best guess — early 1300s. That rules out the Mayans or Micmacs. Vikings, too, because they had neither the means nor the motive. And it's ludicrous to think that ship repairers would choose the site when so many better ones existed at the time for careening boats. Farther north in Halifax, for example." Casey stopped to take a sip of water.

Truman leaned forward and took up the thread. "What was buried there had to be of considerable value to make it worth the time and effort that went into constructing the pit, flood towels, false beach, drains and land markers. A year or more is my best estimate. And, more importantly, that the creators had to have been very knowledgeable about hydraulics. Not your average pirate, that's for damn sure. Excuse my French."

"Don't worry, I speak French — very well," she reassured him. "Yeah, pirates were known for burying quickly and in shallow pits. And never getting back to claim it. Nothing like this marvel of engineering. Had to have been a more advanced civilization."

Casey made a point of scraping her bowl clean. "Good soup." She licked her lips and added in a more serious tone, "You know, a lot of historians wonder if the Scottish earl Henry Sinclair, whose family was enlisted to be the hereditary guardians of the religious and monetary treasure of the Templar Knights, isn't the best bet."

She bit at her thumbnail as she collected her facts. "It's been theorized that Sinclair came to Nova Scotia in 1398 with the Venetian, Antonio Zeno, younger brother of the man who saved Venice. And the carbon dating for the coconut and oak fibers found suggests a timeline early as that entirely possible. This could be a treasure with a thousand-year provenance. Imagine such treasure, the likes of which the world has never seen. Everything else would pale by comparison. Makes you wonder where it is now." She lowered her voice to a whisper. "Maybe even proof of a historic bloodline conspiracy like Dan Brown wrote about in *The Da Vinci Code*."

"Are you leaning toward that school of thought?" he asked, shifting forward in the booth. The bergamot and cedar notes combined with a slight bit of lemon in his cologne tickled her nostrils, making them flare.

Seductive – must cost a fortune to smell that good. Most suits did not smell or look quite so good. She pulled back and dabbled her lips with a paper napkin.

"Then there is that small bit of parchment brought up by a drill bit? The one with the stylized 'V' on it, that's led some historians to think it might be the original work of Francis Bacon, posing as Shakespeare? It's theorized that Bacon didn't really didn't want to be known as the author of books that lambasted his queen or exposed him. Gave credit to an illiterate man in some historian's opinion, not mine of course – it seems hardly credible – to avoid any possibility of prosecution. But those must have been some turbulent days to live in. If only we could time travel – that wormholes really existed for our use."

"Your students are fortunate to have such an inspiring, obviously very dedicated and knowledgeable teacher who is unafraid of controversy," he said. "You appear to have a genius for making complicated things simple. That's a hallmark of a good teacher, as my father used to always say. And if you can tell good stories that relate these facts in a fascinating way, why, there could be no stopping you. They'd swarm to your classes, even the ones the university makes you give, you being a junior and all. And, with more official recognition, you'd get to teach more what you wanted to teach, become the best professor you could be. Have far more input. Your students would greatly benefit from having you choose the direction and courses you present."

"Why, Professor, you do know how to sweet talk a girl," she said, embarrassed. *God, if I have to teach Intro to Standard Practices and Statistics one more time...* She wished it was just a popularity contest, as his words had suggested. In the churning cauldron of political intrigue that was the university's academic community, she was occasionally broadsided with doubts in her struggle to become a tenured professor. *Maybe that's why I donate so many finds to the university archives? Trying to make up for my other failings?*

She needed to make her mark, forge her own way and write important papers if she was to have any chance of getting *that* brass ring. 'Dog eat dog' was a cliché invented just for the suits, in the Ringers' sympathetic opinion. That helped. Problem was, she loathed writing the necessary, always boring, research papers expected of her. And she liked being a part-timer. Gave her more time for running off on adventure when it called, and it always called. A definite conundrum.

"But if you must know, my courses are usually filled up early on," she said with a small, self-depreciating smile.

"I know. I asked for the stats on all the profs, even part-timers," he said. He sat back on the leather seat, draping one arm along the top edge. It squeaked slightly in protest, making her want to giggle – if only the stakes weren't so high.

"Then you know I'm still on probation." She met his stare.

"Yes, you've had your issues. But where it matters – delivering in your classes – you're in your element. I'd like to see you offering more."

She smiled at his compliment. Teaching was important to her. When she turned a mind to the wonders of archeology, she felt immense satisfaction, as though she was sharing the very essence of what it meant to be human.

"But, and this is very important to your achieving tenure, you still need to focus on delivering on your research. You're lagging behind in this vital area."

Casey's stomach knotted into one giant fist. He'd hit a raw nerve dead center and it didn't help that his assessment was correct. Same old ivory tower shit. He wasn't any different from the other suits – just better disguised. *What a fucking loss.*

"It's my job to help you in any way I can to assist you in performing better in that arena – "

"Well, I do appreciate you pointing out the obvious,

Professor Harrison. I must decline any offer of assistance. It's my job to do it myself." Her lips were so stiff the words were hard to say. She knew she was being an ass but nothing could stop her. Not even the reality that she was trampling on any chance of her ever acting on the attraction she felt for this man. She resented feeling it as much as she hated that she couldn't stop herself. *Fucking Catch-22*.

"Okay. I can see you're upset, Casey," he said, giving a charming smile, obviously meant to diffuse the situation.

Good luck.

"Please, let me help you. My expertise lies in—"

"I'm fine. Thank you for your suggestions, but I really have to be going. Plane to catch—you understand." She got up, congratulating herself on being polite, and snatched her carryall bag from the red leather seat. *Exit stage right.*

Chapter Four

"To be prepared for war is one of the most effective means to guarantee peace." *George Washington*

"I see you brought Howard home," Rebecca said, nodding toward the spot where Casey had recently fastened the moose head proudly above the inlaid pink marble mantel of the fireplace. "I think he fits right in beside the squirrel Miranda lugged home last year because she couldn't stand the thought that her mother was about to throw it out. What's wrong with burying dead animals is all I ask?"

The stuffed squirrel named Sammy was perched on the mantel, its tail less than bushy after a brush with a fire gotten out of control during the winter. A little puff of fur on the end of his rat-like tail looked as ready as a dandelion about to be scattered to the wind. Howard did indeed look right at home. Anybody visiting would quietly wonder if they were practicing discount taxidermy.

Casey had inherited the rambling house in River Heights on legendary Wellington Crescent with its spectacular view of the Assiniboine River from her eccentric Aunt Milly. She'd died childless during Casey's last year of high school. The Victorian-style mansion had soon become a home base for the Brass Ringers. Aunt Milly would have been happy to know of all the chatter, excitement and sharing it barely contained.

Casey's favorite part of the house was the den, with its main focus the round table she'd splurged on, hand-crafted by a local artisan. The well-oiled teak featured an embedded map of the Earth. Around the circumference of the three-foot globe were the Latin words they'd once considered for their tattoos, plus the extra motto that held just as much meaning for all the Ringers — *Forget your fears, fight for the future.* The spacious table had been dubbed Eden with a flute of champagne, like the Round Table of the Knights of Camelot. The sorority members came together as equals around it, setting down any squabbles at the door. At least, in theory.

Sometimes she imagined her beloved aunt watching the Ringers' follies from her favorite armchair, a white lace antimacassar laid out precisely behind her head, and drinking from her bottomless cup of Earl Grey tea, the only brand she deemed worthy of brewing. From her command center while reading the latest romantic thriller, Aunt Milly would view the wide and lazy river meandering by the property behind the boathouse. Casey loved to sit there. Right now, it was the center of an explosion of books laid out on the floor and end table studded with little yellow stickers and handwritten notes. What had her friend found out?

Rebecca drew closer to the moose and rubbed his big brown nose. She sneezed as dust motes drifted off, landing lazily on the hardwood floor. "To think he once hung above a saloon in Dawson City. Just imagine the tales he could tell us."

"He told me all I needed to know," Casey said with a half-smile, not looking up from rummaging in her carryall.

"How'd it go on Oak Island?"

"Don't get me started," she warned before she spied what she was searching for. "Ahh, look at this!" She unfolded the shoe-polishing cloth she'd swiped from the hotel room and held out her palm toward her friend with the booty nestled inside. A handful of gold nuggets. They glittered like the beckoning of an ancient blood lust under the soft glow of the living room lamps.

Rebecca approached, her eyes wide.

"May I?" she asked before plucking a gold nugget from

Casey's palm. "Heavier than I expected." She hefted it as if to gauge its weight. "While you were gone, I did some digging on my own—excuse the pun—on a possible connection between Solomon's Temple, Rosslyn Chapel and Oak Island you might be interested in," she said, a teasing tone lowering her sexy, throaty voice even further. She never looked or sounded more like Kathleen Turner than when she was hiding a secret. Casey secretly envied Rebecca her thick waves of honey-blonde hair that framed her gorgeous features to perfection. Her own strands represented a clash of wills—too silky to hold a curl or do anything else she wanted when a special occasion presented itself. Good thing that hardly ever happened.

"Spill," Casey demanded.

"I need a glass of wine first. You?"

"Sure."

Rebecca filled two wine glasses from a jug of red wine already laid out on the sideboard.

"To Soapy's Gold," she toasted and took a swallow, making a sour face. "Maybe we can afford better wine now."

"Yup. Not to mention fund another wish or two for the Ringers. Won't know how far we can stretch it until we weigh the gold. I'll have to head back up there this weekend and lug the rest of it home. Only way I could keep suspicion away. As it was, the baggage handler gave me a funny look at the weight of my luggage. Asked if I liked hauling rocks? Okay, no more stalling. What's up?"

Rebecca's green eyes glowed as she pointed at the pile of tomes dragged home from the university's archives, which reminded Casey she must get her own borrowed book back ASAP. "I've followed the thread from Jerusalem and Solomon's treasure to the Sinclairs of the Orkneys and Rosslyn Chapel to Nova Scotia and the Money Pit, all soundly researched. I made Coles Notes-style entries for you."

She paused to tuck her hair behind her ears, reverting to

her most serious. An endearing quality which meant she was about to launch into something that truly interested her. "Now, the historical connection between the three locations is the trail of Templar artifacts and treasure, as long suspected. No surprises there. The physical connection, I think, is the well. This sounds crazy, but one has to be lowered down to get into a tunnel that leads to the vast vaults under all three locations. Find the well—find the treasure." She finished with a smug smile and took another swallow of wine.

"The tunnel entrance has to be above the ninety-foot level to avoid the constant flooding from the first tunnel," Casey said, worrying about the serious depth though she'd long been aware of what it was going to entail. The stark reality hit home, making her shudder. "I hate confined spaces and that's a long way down into the earth."

"I know. But just imagine what might be down there. What's a few minutes of discomfort to find priceless artifacts? Maybe even the Lost Ark or the Holy Grail! You've done it lots of times before. Your career would be made and I get to document it all. We'd both be famous in one stroke of genius."

Rebecca's brass ring wish was to become a famous novelist.

"Yeah, and do you have any idea just how many others are chomping at the bit on that island? When could I possibly find the privacy to spend the time searching for a well?" Even as she spoke, an idea popped into her head. But...*and isn't there always a damn 'but'?* It would mean cozying up to the new nemesis. *No damn way.* Besides, he'd never get a permit. She'd been trying forever.

"Yes, you'd need to get permission or exercise a plan of stealth," Rebecca admitted. "But, if we knew going in exactly where it was located, think of the time saved."

Casey shook her head. "I don't know. I think the chances are slim. And you know what happened the last time I got too obsessed with a case."

"When has that ever stopped you before? Something you're not telling me?" Rebecca was polite enough to ignore her reference to the Mexican debacle. *Lucky to get out alive when the cave ceiling collapsed.* At least she'd managed to rescue that Aztec fertility statue before the Federals chased her out of the country. And it was now safely hidden in the archives of the university, a peace offering for the problems she sometimes caused. Never of her own making, of course. A girl just had to do what a girl had to do.

A golden man with intense blue eyes popped into her head. *Damn, what a shame he turned out to be just another suit.* Well, maybe it was for the best. Freed her to do what she wanted. She didn't need some guy dictating the terms of their mission.

"Spill. I can see you're hiding something."

"There was this guy I met on the tour."

"I thought you had a private tour scheduled?"

"Some kind of mix-up—doesn't matter. Anyway, I heard this loud rumbling and ran to help, only to find this really pissed-off guy up to his waist in a newly discovered sinkhole." She grinned at the memory and took a swallow of wine. "You'll never guess in a million years who he was."

Rebecca shook her head, watching her.

"Professor Truman Harrison, the new department head!" Casey cried.

"You're kidding, right?"

"I kid you not! He has an interest in the treasure—I mean, who doesn't? It's such an alluring mystery, two hundred plus years trying to discover how to get at it."

"What's he like, this professor? Lame guy or real hunk?"

Casey shrugged. "I guess you'd call him a hunk. But a suit is a suit." She carefully repacked the gold into her case. She'd weigh it later.

"And you wouldn't? I can tell. You're interested!" Rebecca crowed, her smile widening to a full grin. "Maybe he won't wear a suit and tie all the time, or do something else to piss you off on the first date. Hey, remember Alex Wood and his preference for eating his corn one kernel at a time instead of scooping them? You've got really lame reasons for giving up on a guy. Have you ever made it past the third date?"

"I've got *good* reasons for ending it quickly. Besides, I don't know if I'll ever want to settle down. So not me," Casey said with a snort. The last thing she wanted was any guy thinking he could control her. "Fuck, I just remembered — " Guilt made her edgy and she stood. The Hefty McGee journal needed returning.

The kitchen door slammed a split second before Lacey and Lily Cameron, affectionately known as the twin tornadoes, burst into the room. Two beyond gorgeous identical female P.I.s with their bright auburn hair, big green eyes and sexy curves. They always got their man or whatever else they wanted. They'd both taken education at the U of M and lasted exactly one morning in the classroom of a rural high school before breaking their white board pointers in half and throwing their keys down on the desk, immediately resigning. They'd never looked back and had begun their own private investigators business. Their specialty of uncovering insurance scams was just getting noticed by the industry and paying the bills of their growing company.

"Will's away gone again!" Lily complained. William James Thornton III to be exact. The twins shared the fun-loving multi-millionaire's affections. Insisted it was platonic. Maybe it was.

"Really? He's been away a lot lately. Maybe he's found someone? Some exotic mysterious female on the other side of the world," Rebecca said, obviously looking to get a rise out of the twins. *Not too hard to do.*

"Seriously?" Lacey, the most headstrong of the pair, gave her a look. In point of fact, she was the most headstrong woman Casey had met. Ever. She seriously doubted any man would ever turn Lacey's head. "I mean, don't get me wrong, he's a great guy to hang out with, but he's no man of mystery. But, hey, it's going to work out just fine. I got the pilot's details and permission from Will to use his plane, so it's all good."

It was a boon to their private investigative business that Will was so generous. Casey silently agreed with Lacey on her stance on not giving up anything for a man. Look what it had done to her own mother, tossing back anti-anxiety pills like candy after ditching her dream of going to L.A. to become an actress. And she had been so good, in that one movie role she'd gotten in that made-in-Manitoba movie before throwing it aside to marry Casey's dad and having to be content with local productions put on by Celebrations Dinner Theatre. Casey wouldn't let herself think of the many times she'd found her mom asleep on the coach, too depressed to make food for her young family.

"Casey's got something to share that will take your mind off Will," Rebecca said.

"Yeah? Did you bring some home?" Lacey's emerald-green eyes lit up, turning as round as saucers. Casey opened the carryall and plucked out the 'borrowed' cloth housing the treasure. She'd left a generous tip to allay her guilt at the theft.

The twins whistled in unison, Will's defection all but forgotten.

"Where's the rest?" Lily asked.

"Hidden just outside Dawson City. We can all fly up there on the long weekend and retrieve it. What do you think?"

"Sure. Love a road trip with the Ringers and we have the transport. Yes—it's still a road trip if we fly. Don't start. Though I wish we could take the RV and pack everyone in like we did last summer. Give those Dawson City cowboys something to really stare at when the eight of us disembark," Lacey said with a wide grin.

"And you know what else this means?" Casey asked triumphantly.

"What?" Lily asked, picking up a gold nugget and inspecting it in the palm of her well-manicured hand.

"We could maybe buy or lease a boat—go after a treasure sea hunt like you've been pining for. Wednesday, we'll vote." All of the sisterhood always tried to make their monthly poker game. She missed having the other Ringers live with her full-time like they'd done all through university having been friends since grade school, but she understood. Things change. The only thing one could truly count on in life.

Another low whistle came. "Maybe our turn. Sweet!" Lily clapped her hands together.

"Hey, Sammy has a new friend!" Lacey spotted Howard.

She approached him and angled her head to the side, lips pursed. "I think he needs a decoration." She reached up under her short dress and pulled down her red lace thong, proving yet again she was a natural redhead. Stepping out of the tiny scrap of material, she dangled the panties from a fingertip. "What do you think, kids, wouldn't this make his antler festive?"

"Go for it!" Lily egged her on.

And Howard attained his badge of honor. Rescued from a cold, damp cave in Dawson to live in a warm, cozy home in Winnipeg, Howard wouldn't be complaining anytime soon. In fact, she imagined a grin.

Chapter Five

"When you have eliminated all which is impossible, then whatever remains, however improbable, must be the truth." *Sir Arthur Conan Doyle*

"Ladies and gentlemen, I would like all of you to give a warm U of M welcome to our new Department Head of Archeology, Professor Truman Harrison."

Casey barely heard the introduction, busy scanning the agenda for the staff meeting for the second time, finding it challenging through her sunglasses. Hmm, she'd skip the luncheon and head back to her office, lower the possibility for any one-on-one time. The last time, ending in such complete disaster, still rankled.

The department administrator droned on, his speech identical to last year's.

"And finally, I want to remind everyone that you need to get a permit from admissions for the staff parking lot before the end of the day. We need exact numbers, folks. And remember to keep it placed prominently on the upper left-hand corner of your windshield. Last year —"

Casey took a swallow of coffee, her head throbbing. An impromptu celebration to heap honors on Soapy's Gold. *Best kind.*

"Ms. Madison, I would like to see you in my office." Truman loomed over her. She kicked herself for not paying better attention. Others were leaving and she should have made her getaway. Quick like a bunny.

"Uh, sure, now?" she asked, praying he meant later. "I've got to get my parking pass." She failed to keep a straight face.

"I think it would be for the best."

Oh, shit. Was he about to fire her? The stark memory hovered of that important benefactor's dinner held at the late department head's house, and her showing up late in her field clothes, thinking it would be quite enough to present him with the latest find, the awesome Jeweled Dagger of Salome. What? So it had taken a *wee bit* more time to find than originally anticipated and left her classes uncovered for two extra days. Huh. Turned out it hadn't been *nearly* enough to tame the head or his feelings about her absence.

"O — kay." She chewed on a fingernail as she walked side by side with him down the long, long hallway to his corner office. *Brazen it out.*

He waved her in ahead. She took an appreciative look around.

"Very nice. You must have rated high on the popularity meter," she said with forced cheerfulness. A great view of the campus and the football stadium that housed the new digs for the Blue Bombers, Winnipeg's football team. Other than the prerequisite skyscrapers, Winnipeg was a flatland city built on clay that turned to boot-sucking gumbo when it rained. A city that housed more than half of the citizens of the province of Manitoba — one million, three hundred thousand strong in the latest census.

"It'll do. Sit. Can I get you anything?"

"I'm fine, thanks." She held up her travel mug of coffee as proof. He leaned over her and slipped off her sunglasses, his tantalizing scent invading her personal space. She blinked rapidly, too stunned to protest.

"You left so suddenly the other day we didn't get to finish our conversation," he began, sitting behind his impressive desk that commanded attention. He leaned forward and tented his fingers, giving her an unfathomable look. She had absolutely no interest whatsoever in finishing that conversation.

"So, why I called you in here is to discuss Oak Island. I know you have an interest in enriching your classes" — he punctuated his point by toying with a string of the Mardi Gras beads she'd picked up while taking her class on an ill-advised field trip to research local culture, chiefly voodoo practices, among the Haitian community — "so I'm prepared to offer you the opportunity to learn more when I go back to do research for my book."

Had he gotten access? *Damn.* She'd been trying to get a license to snoop on the island for years. She'd wanted it since she'd been a child and read an old 1965 copy of the *Reader's Digest* story on Nova Scotia's Money Pit in a dentist's office. The 1909 photograph of Franklin Delano Roosevelt, future president of the United States, had been a call to action. *And a suit gets one — just like that. So fucking unfair.* She clamped her lips together.

"It can only help your position here at the university. As you know, historical site visits are encouraged, especially when they lead to published results that add luster to the university. I've set up a conference call with the chancellor to explain our position and get approval for this joint venture."

"Right now?" She swallowed hard. *Fuck. Fuck. Fuck.* He was boxing her in.

"Yes, of course, right now. I want to set my schedule for this coming year. You will be one of my projects. My way of encouraging an untenured teacher under my direct tutelage to get the help she requires to publish research papers."

Gritting her teeth so hard they ached in protest, she struggled to remember the words of wisdom shared by Rebecca the previous night. *Stay calm. Don't fly off the handle. Sounded a whole lot easier to do last night after a few drinks.*

"Ready?" he asked, fiddling with the phone system on his desk.

She nodded, her body so tense she was afraid to speak. Who knew what would fly out of her mouth?

"Chancellor Adams, yes, I have Casey Madison in my office and we're discussing that proposal I submitted to you yesterday about the Oak Island venture?"

"Yes, yes, of course. I have it right here." The sound of papers rustling. The chancellor's voice scraped her nerves raw. Pompous suit who thought he was a benevolent god. *Worst kind of fucking –* The grating voice interrupted her internal tirade.

"I am delighted to hear Miss Madison is prepared to accept your help in writing research papers. Her performance review is due soon and your proposing to help her could not be more timely. She now stands a chance of achieving a better outcome – with your help, of course, Professor. Good of you to take such an interest."

Casey rolled her eyes, biting off the tip of her thumb nail and spitting it out onto the floor. *And I thought bringing back that medicine man guest lecturer from the Amazon would carry weight, but no, not nearly good enough for the likes of him.*

Truman's eyes widened.

Calm down. Stay quiet. This will soon be over. Please make it so.

"Miss Madison, do you agree to Professor Harrison's proposal? Are you willing to put in the time expected? May I hope to see results of his efforts soon?"

She cleared her throat, swearing under her breath. "I haven't actually agreed to it yet. We were just discussing the idea."

"Oh, it was my understanding this was in the works already? You are aware of how badly you need this opportunity that your department head has so graciously offered you?"

"Fuck!" The word exploded from her shaking body. Try as she might, she could not contain it.

"Excuse me!" The chancellor's tone had dropped its pompousness. An ominous chilly edge replaced it. Her hands tightened around her coffee.

"So sorry, but Miss Madison just dropped her cup on the

floor and spilled coffee all over my new carpet. She's very sorry," Truman gave her a look of warning she ignored, staring out of the window, chewing on her bottom lip.

So much for following good advice. *You can lead a horse to water, but you can't make him drink, jackass.*

"That is unfortunate, but there's no need for profanity, is there?" The chancellor tsked-tsked. She imagined his fat jowls moving like a bowlful of jelly as her fingers desperately longed to squeeze her stress ball. Every interview with him set her on edge. "Very well, I'll leave you two to work out the details."

Professor Harrison cleared his throat as the call ended, waiting as if he expected her to speak first.

What does he want from me? To tell him he's such an annoyance factor to my normally untroubled life? That he smells too good to be true and I'm far more attracted to him than I care to admit? Sure, she wanted to go to the island. But alone. With no distractions. Sleuth the area thoroughly, check out her theory. Not with this guy and with all these fucking strings attached. Maybe it was time to quit swearing. *Nah, that's going too far.*

"Well, that went well. Are you always your own worst enemy?"

She bit her tongue so hard she drew blood. A metal taste filled her mouth. Where to begin? If only her head wasn't aching so much, her nerves would be steadier. Blame it on the tequila shots. "I can't go this weekend. I promised the Ringers a road trip." *Stalling, perfect start.* For her.

"That's unfortunate. It's a long weekend, as well."

"You got your license to investigate the island, then?"

"I did," he said, his tone suggesting complete satisfaction with the outcome.

"How did you manage that so soon?" *So unfair.* She deserved it more than him.

"I appealed to their special interest in the Money Pit making history with my book. Debunk the 'tar pit' theory that I'm fairly certain is not to their liking. Then, when that didn't work, I bribed the guy with green bucks."

Casey couldn't hold back a snort, caught off-guard. "That usually works." A trick she'd often employed in the past, as well. She recalled the Mexican heist, the Federal's surprise at finding her in his territory one fine morning and her willingness to part with a substantial sum to cross his land unimpeded. *And that's Business 101 for treasure hunters. Money buys cooperation.* She chastised herself for not thinking of it sooner, though she hadn't expected Canadian officials to be open to such dealings. *Turns out the world is more alike than different.*

"Well, we're agreed then. We start working together to further both our careers. Win-win," Truman said, his wide smile blinding.

She hated the expression 'win-win' almost as much as she hated stodgy department heads. She got up from her chair, stubbing her toe against the leg of his desk in her haste.

"Ow!" she winced, holding back more colorful language with great difficulty.

Truman got up and came around the desk. "I'm so sorry. It's too large. I'm having the damn thing replaced next week. I don't want to intimidate the staff. Something lighter and more modern would work far better."

"Good idea," she muttered while cautiously bending her numb toes in an effort to convince herself they weren't broken. "I have to be going." She limped as quickly as possible out of his office. So much for dignity on the battlefield. *Exit stage left.*

Chapter Six

"Millions of spiritual creatures walk the Earth.
Unseen, both when we wake, and when we sleep."
John Milton, Paradise Lost, Book IV

"I don't need much right now. I have newish digital equipment to capture the Electronic Voice Phenomena just fine and my EMF detector's picking up electromagnetic fields as good as ever." Miranda paused in her thoughtful perusal of what her paranormal investigator team could use some of Soapy's Gold for.

Everyone huddled around the Eden table, making pitches. Casey tapped her toes underneath. This meeting had already taken a few days to arrange.

"By the way, you guys should think about coming. I'm bunked into the Fort Garry Hotel, Room 202, specifically. The famous haunted room. Maybe I'll even find that elusive inter-dimensional doorway or portal that so many insist exists between the world of the living and the land of the dead," Miranda said with a grin, her pretty elfin face as skeptical as ever about the field she so determinedly investigated. The recent change of her thick black hair into a pixie cut suited her. Made her violet eyes pop even more. "But if you have funds to spare, I could use more travel money and a better digital camera, if you're offering. I want to head into the Interlake and investigate the Medicine Wheels then over to Spirit Sands — the Devil's Punchbowl."

"Yeah, count me in. But I've always thought that portal existed in my shower. Every time I take one seems a new idea pops into my head, making me hop around naked scrounging for pencil and paper," Rebecca said, grinning.

"Seeing that appealing sight would attract the otherworldly creatures, not dissuade them!" Miranda laughed.

"What about you, Elin? Need any funds?" Casey asked of the beauty sitting back quietly while the others made their cases. The tall drink of Scandinavian water that she so wished she could emulate, with mile-long legs to die for and a gift for consuming chocolate in vast quantities and not gaining an ounce, was their resident expert on ufology.

"I'm good, thanks," she said with a wink from one of her periwinkle blue eyes as she tucked her fair hair behind her ears.

"Okay, I think we know enough now to vote," Casey said with authority. The one who called the meeting chaired it. She raised the gavel and gave the directive. "All those in favor of using the funds for deep-sea treasure hunting, say aye."

A chorus of ayes filled the room, warming her heart.

"Good." She brought the gavel down with a satisfyingly resounding crunch on the wooden sound block. "It's settled then. We're all onboard—no pun intended."

The eight women got to their feet in unison.

"I can hardly wait for next summer," Lacey said, her eyes beaming her excitement.

"Going to be a *fine* time. Hope some of you can go with?" Lily said, prompting a few noncommittal shrugs.

"Well, I, for one, will be there with bells on," Casey said with aplomb.

"Group hug!" Lacey said. Casey threw her arms around her as they crowded together.

She reluctantly pulled away, smoothing down her sky-blue robe with its pattern of stars swirling and twinkling about the shining rich silk. The robe was identical to all the others', chosen to represent the sky and the unlimited potential of reaching for the heavens.

She picked up her wine goblet and took a sip.

"Hey, Casey, when do you want to get away tomorrow?

Will says the plane is available anytime we like," Lacey said, coming up beside her and linking arms.

"The earlier the better," Casey said. She turned to warn the Ringers as they all filed into the conservatory where the hot tub stood waiting. The room also featured a glass globe arched roof, exposing the full glory of the night sky. "Go light on the booze tonight, pretty please. We need to arrive in Dawson with some of our wits about us." A chorus of groans.

A rustling of silken fabric and everyone climbed into the warm water in their colorful bikinis, holding fresh drinks. Casey closed her eyes and allowed herself to relax, really relax for the first time since she'd gotten home. Heavenly.

"Did you see that?" Miranda's voice intruded on Casey's calmness and she reluctantly opened one eye. Miranda was focusing intently on the woods that led down to the riverbank through the conservatory windows. Casey swung her head around but could see nothing. The property was gated and no one lived *that* close by.

"I saw something move," Miranda insisted, peering into the darkness.

"You want me to pull the shades?" Casey asked.

Miranda didn't answer, but Lacey spoke up, "If we have a perv, we should give them a real show!" She leaned over and gave Casey's breast a light squeeze.

"Hey, no fair! How can I concentrate?" Casey laughed, splashing her with a skip of her hand across the warm water.

Rebecca got out of the tub, padded dripping wet over the tiled floor across to the wall and pushed the button to activate the electric covers for the windows. They were designed to leave the overhead dome free to let in the starry night sky. The soft whirl of the motor started up, releasing the stiff fabric that effectively kept out the winter cold. And peering eyes, if Miranda was right.

"Say, what do you know about the Masonic Temple, the one that housed the Old Spaghetti Factory for a few years?

Is it true they're renovating it again?" Casey asked her crew. Rebecca turned her head toward her, cocking it to one side, listening. *Vested interest.*

"Yeah, it's going to be turned it into a dinner theatre. I think it'll be good for the downtown core. Add some culture," Elin said.

Rebecca wrinkled her nose. "Not certain I like the idea. It's such a wonderful example of early Winnipeg architecture."

"Better than a spaghetti joint," Lily added. "Though the food was good."

A muffled noise sounded from outside. "Damn, I'll bet those raccoons are at the garbage cans again. I put it out tonight so I won't have to get up so early," Casey said. *That damn disposal schedule.*

"Maybe we'd better check," Rebecca suggested. "Miranda thought she saw something moving –"

"Are you kidding? And get dressed then undressed? Forget it. My bet is on the raccoons, too. The other day garbage was strewn all over our front driveway. Annoying messy little creatures," Lacey said. "Will, thank goodness, insisted on buying and installing a chained lid system before next week's pickup. All by himself, too, when he could have had anyone do it with the money he's got stashed away."

"Enough boring talking about raccoons and garbage already," Miranda complained. "Did you hear about what happened at Jackson's party on the weekend?"

She paused, obviously waiting for the inevitable chorus of *whats*.

"Hooked up with our Ava," she exclaimed, wiggling her dark eyebrows. "For the entire weekend."

"Not the *entire* weekend, Miranda," Ava protested hiding a look of chagrin at the charges. "Jackson had an early Monday morning meeting and left around three."

"Glad you cleared that up, darlin'," Lacey drawled with a wicked grin.

"So, is he as good in bed as I've heard?" Miranda asked. All eyes turned to Ava who turned as red as the twins' hair.

"Come on, give her a break," Rebecca protested.

"We need music," Casey said impulsively. She reached over and turned on the sound system. The upbeat tones of Carrie Underwood's latest country song filled the room.

Lily groaned, rolling her eyes.

Casey's phone sang a few bars of the Canadian national anthem.

"New rule, no cell phones around the hot tub," Lacey said, frowning at the interruption.

Casey had heard it all before. She glanced at the number. Professor Truman Harrison. *Not him again.* She sighed and rose from the water, picking up a dry towel and tying it around her waist.

"I need to use the bathroom," she said to the crew and watched a few eyebrows rise before she pulled on her flip flops and padded over to the nearby powder room. She slipped inside before answering the call then sat on a stool. The mirror opposite reflected her flushed face as she swept wayward strands of white-blonde hair back from her brow, tucking them into the loose bun piled on top of her head.

"Hi," she said, turning away from the image.

"Casey, glad I caught you. Are you busy?" His low-toned voice strummed a chord she was unaware her brain would enjoy so much. She reminded herself how annoyed she was by his recent set-up. *Better.*

"Yeah, kind of. What's up?" She chewed on the edge of her thumbnail while she listened.

"Have you given any more thought to specifics? Like when you're free to head to Oak Island? I hate to rush you, but I need concrete dates."

Her heart rate sped up at the idea of spending time solving the Oak Island mystery. Set-up or not, easy access only a fool would turn down awaited her. And it wasn't like they'd given her much of a choice.

"I can't do it this weekend. After that." She heard the ungracious tone in her voice but ignored it. He'd more than earned it.

"Good, good. I was hoping you'd say that. I'll book our flights for next week. As the head of our department, I've gotten you some extra time off," he said with satisfaction, either ignoring or obvious to her obvious reluctance.

"That's handy." *At least a suit's good for something.*

"Be prepared for some local opposition. They won't look kindly to our roaming their island. But we have legal access with the permit to lots ten through seventeen just this side of the Money Pit, including the stone cross. It should be enough for us to get a clearer picture. They can keep their flooded Money Pit to themselves. Do you want to tent or motel it?"

"I think we should do both. Set up a day camp with some amenities and sleep in a motel at night, except I don't own one." *Well, not since the last one burned down.* She'd have thought the company would make them fire-proof to avoid such an outcome.

"No problem. I have a sturdy two-person domed affair."

"Fine. I should go. I have company." She fidgeted on the seat.

"Of course, but I want to say how happy I am to have you aboard, Casey Madison." The tone of his voice warmed her as he spoke her name. *Damn, southern gentlemen are good.*

Casey ended the call. She pushed aside any concerns about being on an island with a man who happened to be her boss. She was an expert at handling herself. Besides, he'd made it clear he was only in the venture to look good to the university while writing his book. *Damn suit.* He didn't need to know anything about her ulterior motives. *So* not his business.

Grumbling to herself, she rejoined the Ringers.

"What was that about?" Rebecca asked.

"The new department jackass's doing his best to make my life fucking miserable. Set me up today. I'll never forgive him. God damn it! There's that noise again. I'm checking it out."

Gritting her teeth, she scrambled out of the hot tub. Pulled her robe on and tied the sash tightly. Stormed out of the room to the back door, yanking it open.

"Get away from there!" she shouted, stomping down the driveway toward the garbage cans, clapping her hands loudly, expecting to chase away scavenging raccoons.

But instead of small animals, an aberration suddenly appeared in the darkness. It grew taller, as if rising from the metal containers themselves. Her heart rate increased. She blinked. *What the hell?* The sense of it being an otherworldly creature was not dimmed by the unusual height it finally revealed once fully exposed, its back to her.

It turned toward her as she continued her approach, the duster-length coat swirling around the tall frame only adding to her shock. What was going on?

"Who the fuck are you?" she shouted as she recognized it was a person, a man, a very tall, thin man. She did not stop her advance, preparing to tackle him. *The taller they are, the harder they fall.* Besides, she'd had enough of being fucked with for one day.

She gave chase, but the guy was quick on his feet, racing off, but not before throwing the lid to the garbage can to the ground, making her dodge around it. The clatter it made as the metal hit the curb an annoyance.

Halfway down the block, he jumped into a van. It tore off. *Damn it.* Headed in the opposite direction. Not giving her a good look at the guy who'd run. Or the guy driving.

She stopped, watching the van turn the corner and vanish from view. Was this connected to Soapy's Gold?

Full of questions that needed answering, she vowed to check it out first thing. No one was going to intimidate her and get away with it.

* * * *

Casey crept down the back staircase that led to the museum's basement archives, the odor of musty books and mold permeating the stale air growing thicker with each downward step. With Doris away on her coffee break, she should have just enough time to return Hefty McGee's borrowed journal. She didn't need a repeat of last year's near disaster returning that ship's log thought to be connected to one of Captain Kidd's exploits. Though it had been kind of sweet when the old penny-pinching department head Philips — *thank God he'd been forced to retire in June* — had gotten the boot, when it was revealed he'd been the one responsible for missing items from the museum's vaults. He'd even tried to throw suspicion her way that one time. It still left a bitter taste in her mouth. Made her hate suits all the more. Or maybe that was when it all got started? The door at the bottom of the stairs squeaked open, alerting her to company.

"Casey Madison. What a pleasant surprise. This is fortuitous — you're just the person I was wanting to talk to," Truman said, starting up the stairs toward her. For a second, she appreciated standing so much taller than him, before he drew abreast of her. The old narrow staircase instantly confining. His familiar scent tantalizing.

What was he doing there? Her eyes narrowed with suspicion, checking his hands for any indication of what he had been up to in the archives. Though access was restricted to students, staff and professors had the run of the place. He carried a clipboard, nothing else visible. Perhaps just doing his job.

"Sorry, I don't have time to talk, gal on a mission, you understand, right?" She edged by him, trying not to breathe — or look at him, for that matter. He'd made her so damn angry with setting her up, and, to boot, she had precisely five minutes before the librarian got back. Being delayed was the last thing she needed now. She had such a busy day planned too. And she still had not figured out who had been snooping through her garbage. The surveillance cameras hadn't picked up a darn thing.

"I was hoping you and I could have coffee," he began. "Discuss the timetable."

"Uh, sure, could it wait until later? Just working on a bit of research and running late." She made two whole steps before he spoke again. She sighed.

Tick tock. Tick tock.

"Fine, but I've made a schedule for observing classes for those up for assessment this year. Yours is in two weeks."

"Could you send me an email reminder?" She turned back and gave him the fakest smile possible. Why were suits such an interfering lot? And since when did they have to look like him? All golden with intense blue eyes. Such a stupid waste.

"Well, yes, of course. I just thought delivering the news in person added a nicer touch. If you have any questions about how I go about it and assess your performance, I'm more than willing to have my ear bent."

She licked her lips. *I'll bend more than your ear if you don't stop talking.* Caught him staring at her before she turned and clambered down the last few steps. She opened the door to the sub-basement, the hinges squealing their usual protest.

"Well, I hope you find what you're looking for," he called out before she shut the door, cutting off any further response.

You bet. She *always* found what she was looking for.

She slid the worn-out journal into its slot on the shelf not a second too soon. Her heart beating madly, she turned and faced Doris, who had crept up on rubber-soled shoes.

"Miss Madison," the woman said dryly, her gray hair forced into perfect tight curls as rigid as her schedule and expectations. Her ever-suspicious gaze glanced at the shelf Casey had just slid the tattered volume into. Though she said nothing further, her lips tightened. "I found something you might be interested in on the history of the Knights Templar in Nova Scotia."

"Great! Thank you, I appreciate that." Casey's heart rate jacked up even further. Damn him for delaying her and having Doris become suspicious. The last thing she needed. The library was a treasure trove she depended on.

The woman's face colored with keen interest, her normally rock-solid persona changing right before Casey's eyes. She even fluttered her capable hands to her iron curls as she tucked the rigid coils even more securely into place. "I just met the new Department Head, Professor Truman Harrison. Have you been introduced to him? Such a nice man, so helpful and charming."

Casey frowned. "Yeah, we've met."

Doris apparently didn't pick up on her disinterest as she waxed on. "He went out of his way to help me refill a shelf. Took it upon himself to ask if I needed anything, anything at all? And when I told him I could use some new shelving, why, he said he'd see right to it. Let me know he intends to have it okayed by the comptroller ASAP. We're all so lucky he's come all this way to join us. And so handsome, too." The woman even gave a small sigh. *Good Lord.*

"Yes, aren't we just," Casey said, as neutrally as possible, chewing on her bottom lip, her mind drifting away from the book stacks, praying the fawning would just end. Like five minutes ago.

"And especially after the debacle with Professor Philips retiring early. I can only hope his time here didn't influence others in negative ways. Why, when I mentioned the scandal to Professor Harrison, he reassured me he'd be putting extra checks and balances into place to avoid such an occurrence in the future. Yes, we are darned lucky to have such a scholar among us. Why —"

Casey interrupted. She couldn't take any more of this crap. "Please forgive me, but I must be running along. I have a class to teach. We don't want to disappoint the new head."

"Yes, of course. Would you like to check out that book now?"

"Book?"

"The one I just told you about on the Knights Templar. Are you sure you're okay, Miss Madison? You do seem a tad off today."

"I'm fine. Thanks, yes, I'll take the book." She needed Doris's goodwill. The suits, she could do without.

Chapter Seven

"Life is not always a matter of holding good cards, but sometimes, playing a poor hand well." *Jack London*

"So, how was Dawson?" Truman asked while working with Casey to unload their rented SUV at the campsite on Oak Island. He liked the way she just got into it and didn't worry about a broken fingernail or the like. Though she'd not said two cents' worth on the plane trip to the island, her nose buried in her e-reader the entire time, he hoped to change that.

"What happens in Dawson, stays in Dawson," she quipped as she pulled out the tent poles. Still holding the cards close to her chest. It just made him want to learn more about the intriguing young woman filling his thoughts far more than he would like. He wasn't exactly clear on how they'd gotten off on such a wrong footing. Surely, just doing his job when he'd pressed her to write research papers couldn't account for this much animosity? He wasn't the big bad wolf, after all.

"Wasn't it an all-female road trip? What kind of trouble can a bunch of women get into in a small northern Canadian town?" he pressed. Maybe he'd finally found a topic she had more than a one-syllable answer for.

"Well, for starters, Lacey just about swallowed the Sour Toe," she said with a snort, working to maneuver the tent into an advantageous position on the ground with him holding the opposite end. "Almost had to pay a twenty-five-hundred-dollar fine."

"Sour Toe?" He gave her a quizzical look.

"Yeah, a human toe pickled in Yukon gold whiskey."

"A *real* human toe?"

"Yup. Been swallowed a time or two, in point of fact. They raised the fine to try and stop it."

Truman shook his head, grimacing. "Don't get the attraction," he said as he helped lug the tent to the exact spot Casey was tugging it toward, her pretty face full of determination. No matter, watching her in her snug jeans and T-shirt was well worth losing any imaginary coin toss. "More of a Crown Royal man. And now that I live close to the award-winning source, Gimli, Manitoba, I plan on touring the facility. What's your poison, Casey?"

"Champagne. Love the bubbles, though most times it's just a box of house wine," she said with a gleam in her eyes.

Got it. Alcohol and her friends – both good topics. "I wouldn't trust a man who doesn't drink," Truman said.

She raised her eyebrows, questioning the quote. "A personal philosophy?"

"More like a family philosophy, originating from the more than usual number of carousing relatives. Family gatherings tend to be rather dysfunctional affairs."

"You're going to fit right here in Canada – it's a national pastime. Well, that and hockey and a large double-double at Tim Hortons." Casey grabbed a tent pole opposite the one he was working on and slipped it through the metal grommets, forcing the end into the hard-packed topsoil. They pulled the tent taut between them.

"We're a good team," he said, complimenting her efficiency. "I'm hoping to learn a lot about Canada and Canadians while I'm here. And keep the chancellor happy by writing papers, and my book, of course, the kind that gets academics to sit up and take notice." He gave a wicked grin, acknowledging the sensitive subject.

She pursed her lips in obvious annoyance and he had an urge to kiss them, to see if they tasted as sweet and ripe as they looked. He shook his head to dispel the daydream. He certainly didn't need that complication in his life right now. After all, he had invited her along as his way to help someone under his leadership reach her full potential, his number-one priority. Fine, if he was being totally honest, enlisting her help rated a close second too.

"No university talk while we're here." She frowned, a slight pout making her all the more adorable. Her braid was unraveling. He had the urge to undo it all the way, to run his fingers through the silken strands that gleamed white-gold in the sunlight.

Truman turned back and scooped the folded cot from the SUV. He marched it past her and inside the structure. She stood at the outer doorway as he worked. The first, smaller space at the front of the tent created a kind of foyer before entering the main body. He deftly unfolded and set the cot upright near the back wall. He glanced toward the doorway and found her still watching.

"I'll get the lawn chairs," she said, her cheeks turning bright pink before she zoomed away.

He hauled the heavy cooler into the tent foyer. Filled with ice, refreshments, plenty of food and snacks, it would carry them through the three days he expected to spend pacing out, measuring and mapping the huge stone cross that overlaid the lots he'd licensed. Not to mention investigating as much of the island as Casey thought she could get away with. He understood that much about her already, having read her unusual file at the university. The woman reinvented the definition of human dynamo. Her drive to discover the unknown more than intrigued him—it rivaled his.

Casey dove into the cooler soon as he set it in place, and pulled out a cold drink.

"Thirsty work," she said as she tipped her head back and let the liquid run down her arched throat. Her swan-like neck looked the perfect location to sneak a first kiss. When she pulled the can away, a drop of moisture ran down her chin.

"What?" She noticed his interest.

"You've got some of it on your chin."

She swiped at it. "Want one?" she asked.

"Sure, we're all set up. Let's take a short break and discuss our plan of action."

He snagged a bottle of water and sat on a lawn chair. She joined him and they both took a moment, though the island straddled the ocean floor too low for the view to be much more than trees and bushes with a glimpse of blue water lapping at the cove.

"So, what's the plan, Professor?" she asked, giving him a cool look that said she was there under duress, nothing more. So their little chitchat hadn't accomplished much, if anything.

"I'm hoping to measure out the stone cross. See if Nolan's work was accurate. I'm dedicating an entire section of my book to the subject."

"Okay." She shrugged. "Good place to start as any, I guess." She sounded about as inspired as a man condemned to the gallows.

He finished his water and threw the plastic bottle into the recycling bag set up on a wire device to make disposal easy. "Well, let's get at it," he said, certain she'd come around. After all, he could be damn charming when he wanted to be.

Truman grabbed the bundle of sticks with their florescent yellow flags to poke into the ground as they located all six stones. So far, he'd been an entertaining companion, easygoing and far too charming. Good at hiding his 'suit' nature. It just made her all the more leery. He was not going to get away with what he pulled. No, not in a hundred million years.

"We'll start at the skull-shaped rock, then search for the five cone-shaped rocks as we work our way outward. It's a large feature, which is why its significance is often overlooked. And, of course, many consider it purely a religious symbol. I warn you, the rocks will be hundreds of feet farther apart than one might think. We'll use the measuring wheel after we've located all the rocks and flagged them."

"You expecting any specific distances or numbers associated with the Knights Templar?" she asked. She held enough aces up her sleeve to discuss one. And maybe she could get him to share more. If she was forced to be here because of his so damned important agenda, then she could capitalize on her own desire to find treasure.

"Maybe. Any ideas you want to propose, feel free to share."

How sweet your ass looks in those jeans. Where in the hell did that come from? "Perhaps some number with Biblical significance will emerge. We won't know much until we confirm distances."

He gave an appreciative grimace. "Well, we'll just have to find that out. But I do like the way you think. It's something I've speculated as well. A religious number makes the most sense."

Casey hefted half the sticks and set off, fairly certain that the entrance to the well would be found as part of the equation. *I just have to think like someone wanting to disguise their secret.* Now that she was hot on the trail and away from *him*, she could breathe easier and think better.

It was hard slugging through the thick underbrush and she was sweating profusely by the time she found the first cone-shaped lichen-covered rock an hour later. She could hear Truman off in the distance, making his way toward the other side of skull rock to find the left arm. *Huh.* It was probably not ideal conditions for a suit. The coarse sandstone of the rock she faced had marks embedded in its surface, marks which had obviously been fashioned by man. This right arm of the cross was a huge rock weighing a couple of hundred pounds, slowly surrendering to the corrosive effects of salt and wind storms brutalizing it off the Atlantic Ocean. She could not imagine having to move it to this spot originally. And these rocks were nothing compared to the size of the ones moved to guard Easter Island or shifted to create Stonehenge.

"In the name of the Ringers, I claim you," she said and drove the stick deep into the earth beside it. She drank down an entire bottle of water before taking another photo on her cell phone.

"What the fuck do you think you're doing?"

She swung around to find Mr. Tom Byrne AK John Wayne-wannabe staring her down with hard beady eyes that pretty much looked loaded for bear. *God, not that guy who went ballistic on our official tour of the island.*

"I'm not trespassing, Mr. Byrne, if that is what you're insinuating. Professor Harrison and I have a license to investigate all the lots that this cross stands upon. And right now I'm mapping it for my university course, Mysteries and Lost Treasures of the World, in which the Money Pit will feature prominently. I would think you'd be delighted to have the island known to a whole new generation."

"Like hell I want that!" His already ruddy complexion flushed apoplectic purple.

"Why would it be such a bad thing, being part of a venture that invigorates young minds? Isn't that a little selfish?"

"I believe those young minds you speak of are not much younger than you, girly." His eyes narrowed with mistrust. Lasered a line in the sand. "Don't think you're fooling me, all this snooping around. You're up to something and I, for one, intend to put a stop to it!"

"Are you meaning legal action or something more sinister?" Casey did not stand down to anyone, though at the moment, her bear spray might have proved handy.

"What appears to be the problem, Mr. Byrne?" Truman demanded as he appeared behind the man. The cowboy swung around to face him. Truman's expression was tight with concern, though his tone remained neutral. Byrne stood ramrod straight in his cowboy boots, but still the professor loomed over him. Casey sighed. A difficult man with the potential to spoil all her time on Oak Island if she let him. It was even worse than having to be here at the professor's insistence. It still rankled like hell having been hauled into his office and told what she was going to do. Obviously his trying to be charming earlier had been a devious ploy. *Well, two can play that game.*

"I was telling this young woman here that you're not going to get away with this. That you are both on notice that I am filing an injunction with the government of Nova Scotia against you being here. I expect to hear back any day now and I want you gone!"

"Well, since it's still legal for us to be here at the moment, I hope you'll have the courtesy to give us the space to do our jobs. I did pay a premium to the government of Nova Scotia for the privilege."

With a final glare of disapproval, Byrne spat a wad of disgustingly brown chewing tobacco onto the ground at their feet before stomping off into the brush, his boots noisily snapping twigs.

"You didn't have to do that. I was doing just fine on my own, *thank you very much*," Casey hissed at Truman, to make certain he understood her ability to hold up her end of things. Like he'd given her a choice about being here. If he wasn't her boss…

"I could see that," he said mildly, not taking the bait. "Just wanted to see what his deal was."

"Do you think he'll really get that injunction?" she asked, more worried about that than anything else. She could handle the likes of Byrne. Or a suit. The legal system—not so much.

"Hard to say, but I think we're on notice to get the job done." Truman leaned toward her and brushed something off the shoulder of her T-shirt, capturing her full attention. The intimate action brought them too close. A sudden memory of being pressed tightly against his hard body by the side of the sinkhole made her flesh heat uncomfortably.

"My, the day's getting warm," she said to excuse her sudden blush, fanning herself with her ball cap.

* * * *

"Yeah, right fuckin' now as we speak. Mapping out Nolan's Cross with flags. Got a fuckin' campsite set up all nice as you please." He called the cross by the name of the man who'd discovered it, like most the locals did.

"If you'd desist in the use of profanity, Mr. Byrne, I would greatly appreciate it. It's not helpful to our current situation."

"Fine, fine," Byrne grumbled. "Just this pair raises my ire. Think they're better than everyone else with their la-di-dah university connections, like butter won't melt in their mouths."

"I appreciate your calling me, Mr. Byrne. I do hope that drill was helpful?"

"Yes, it works fine. What do you want me to do about this pair?" He got straight to the point as he laid the high-resolution binoculars on the windowsill. Another piece of equipment provided by his new benefactor.

"Nothing for now. Just keep a close eye on them and call if they do anything out of the ordinary."

"Like what? Dig?" Byrne said with barely concealed sarcasm as he clenched his left fist and banged it against his thigh. He wanted to hit something in the worst way. "That's what they're here for, right? But if you want me to send them packing, I'm open to ideas."

A sigh over the phone line made Byrne's skin crawl. If he didn't need the man's money, he'd tell him to go to fuck himself, as well.

"No need for a shot over their bow just yet, Mr. Byrne, when we have no clear idea of their intentions. Just keep a close eye out. Watch for any digging near the cross."

"Stupid choice to dig way over there — too far from the main pit to be effective."

"Be that as it may, I still want to know if it happens."

"Fine, fine. I'll be in touch."

He stabbed the End Call button on his cell with his

forefinger and shoved the phone back into his shirt pocket. His frown turned to a self-satisfied grin as an idea came to him.

"Mason, get in here!" he shouted out the window at the boy weeding the flower beds recently planted to give the tourists something else to photograph for the price of their tour tickets. He watched Mason spin his head around toward the office, a questioning look on his face. The boy then scrambled to his feet and pulled off his gloves before dusting off his knees and heading in. He knew he had to come when the boss called.

"I have another job for you."

"But I haven't finished—" Mason began to protest.

"Fuck the flowers. Here's what I want you to do."

Chapter Eight

"Three can keep a secret, if two of them are dead."
Benjamin Franklin

"Ready for supper?" Truman asked as he stepped back from forcing the last pole into the ground at the bottom of the cross. The yellow flag hung limply from its mast with no breeze to stir it. The shadows around them were lengthening, adding an otherworldly stillness. Her stomach rumbled making her aware of how much time had passed.

"Yeah," she said. "I could eat just about anything right now."

"We'll leave the measuring until first light then."

The small rustlings of animals slipping through the bush alerted her that she and Truman were not alone as they walked back to camp. The island was so small, less than a mile in length, no spot that far away. Their belligerent neighbor remained absent. *Good thing.* She was in no mood to suffer any more fools gladly.

"'A touch of nature makes the whole world kin'." Truman recited one of her favorite quotes from Shakespeare. *Not going to work, if you're thinking to soften me up.* All day long she'd caught him watching her at odd moments, as if trying to figure her out. She could have told him there was nothing to figure—she was there under duress, plain and simple. Well, that and planning to get her needs met, of course, but that was well within her rights. *Tit for tat, Professor.*

Though as the day had gone by, being outside, learning more about the island, she had secretly enjoyed it more than she'd let on. *Eye candy as compensation.* And unexpectedly, he hadn't complained about the hard labor involved.

"You want to eat here or head into town?" Truman asked as he filled the tin basin with water in preparation for washing up. He snagged a hand towel from his kitbag.

"Here. I'm cooking steak and baked potatoes," she announced. "I'd never give up a chance to eat outside when I'm camping." *No matter who I have to eat with.*

She lit the flame under the Coleman burner with a wooden match, the odor of sulfur flaring sharply before dissipating. The dark green camping stove rested on the collapsible picnic table she'd brought along, a hell of a find at a curbside. Once a year, on a specific day, Winnipeg had a city-wide yard sale where people basically traded items by leaving them for others to pick over. Small city stuff. *The good stuff.* She lit a Coleman lantern, as well, relishing the sense of exhilaration roughing it outdoors always brought.

"I swear to God, food tastes twice as good when eaten outside," Truman said, joining her, wearing a huge grin of satisfaction. "What can I do to help?" His low tone of voice did things to her. Vaguely disquieting things. She hurried to pull the salad fixings from the cooler.

"You can make the salad." She thrust the produce at him.

"No problem. It would be my pleasure, darlin'," he said with a gracious bow. She frowned to let him know she'd heard the *darlin'* and did not approve. He took a cutting board and green salad knife off the portable hanging shelf and plunked down at the picnic table to get to work.

The fragrance of sizzling meat and potatoes, the sight of a good-looking albeit annoying male nearby, the sun setting over Nova Scotia's picturesque mainland and a two-hundred-year old mystery to solve. They all came together as she prepared supper. *Not too shabby.*

"You look like the cat that's swallowed the canary," Truman remarked as their glances locked.

"Camping's all right." She shrugged, turning away to check the meat again. "Ready," she announced.

"Me, too," he said with a cocky grin. She ignored the innuendo. Sometimes he just didn't quite fit the mold.

She used the tongs to remove the meat and foil-wrapped potatoes off the grill, shutting off the flame with her other hand. Setting the fragrant food down on the table made her mouth water as the tantalizing odor wafted her way.

"Let's eat."

Crickets began chirping their eternal song as Casey and Truman ate by firelight.

"You cook a darned fine steak," Truman said between appreciative bites and blissful sighs.

"Thanks, and your salad's—quite edible," she quipped. By this time, the island was in full darkness and the separateness from others was heightened to a sense of being the last two persons on earth.

"Normally, after such a fine meal, I'd reward myself with a cigar and cognac," Truman said, rubbing his flat belly to demonstrate his satisfaction.

Prime physical shape. That was the biggest thing that stood out about him, that he didn't look the part. Hardly fair.

"I bought something for afters," Casey replied, getting up to retrieve a last-minute purchase made before crossing the causeway to the island. She opened the cooler and pulled out the bottle of apricot brandy and two red plastic glasses.

"Dessert," she announced, plonking the sweet liquor on the tabletop. Something to soften up the suit. She broke the upper seal on the neck of the bottle with a quick snap of her wrist, twisting the plastic cap free. The amber liquid gurgled from the bottle into the glasses, the fine fragrance of apricots tantalizing and the humming of busy insects heightening the atmosphere. Casey licked her lips.

"What shall we drink to?" she asked.

"To meeting a fellow explorer. The kind of woman I never expected to find in the wilds of Canada," he said, his glance lingering. Thought he could butter her up, eh? *So not going to work.*

"And to finding out more about Oak Island," she added,

just to be polite. They clinked glasses and sipped their drinks, the atmosphere thrumming around them. Cocooned by nature and the wild call of adventure with no ties to the everyday, she didn't think twice about pouring them a second glass of the heady liquor, with Truman nodding his consent.

"We'll have to sleep here if we want to avoid the possibility of being stopped by the RCMP if we have any more of this. It's got some kick," he announced. "Don't worry, you can have the cot and I'll pull the lawn chairs together out here."

"It's early yet. I'll make coffee before we go. I've been giving some thought to the significance of numbers used in creating the cross." Sitting there with Truman, the zing of alcohol relaxing her, the night's magical properties fueled her imagination. Ancient peoples surrounded them in the firelight cast by the lantern. In days long past, they would have acted out their stories, gathered around the fire.

"Hmm, if what we both suspect is true, I'm fairly confident that we'll find a correlation there somewhere. Got any particular numbers in mind?" His voice reached out to touch her in the darkness. She ignored the sensation and pressed on.

"Well, the lagoon's shaped like a pyramid, the symbol of enlightenment, with the cross perched on top. If we consider that it's truly the treasure from the Knights Templar that lies beneath our feet, then yes, I'm fairly certain one of their significant numbers will emerge as we measure the distances between the stones. The cross is definitely there for a reason."

"Do you have a boyfriend, Casey? I was wondering, as I can't imagine his wanting you to be wandering all over the countryside without his protection. I know I'd have some objections if it were my woman going off with a strange man looking for ancient treasure."

"*What?* I am quite capable of taking care of myself, thank you very much!" And just when he wasn't looking quite so annoying, he came out with that old line. *Came out with it out of the blue, as well. Huh.*

"You didn't answer my question," he said.

"No," she admitted, the alcohol freeing her tongue. "My track record on that score is dismal. Never seems to go past one or two dates. Most guys just don't get it."

"Don't get what?" Truman sat so close heat radiated from his warm flesh. She shivered.

"The last guy I went out with liked ketchup on his steak. Steak that he liked well-done, for heaven's sake! Who burns a forty-dollar steak then puts ketchup on it?" The alcohol loosened her tongue further. "And there was the guy, an accountant, talked about his retirement plans on the first date." Casey snorted. "Oh, and his married brother with their two perfect children. Showed me photos on his Facebook page and everything. He just wanted a wife and one-point-seven children." She took another sip of the liquor to stop herself from going any further. "Sorry, you don't want to hear about my dating woes."

"No, it's quite fascinating, really."

"My bullshit meter says differently," she replied.

"I understand about commitment issues."

"Why, have you been burned, Professor?" Hardly the question she should ask her boss, but he'd started it.

"Yeah, you could say that."

"Care to talk about it?"

"No, done enough of that already," he said, a twinge of bitterness exposed.

"Therapy is overrated. My personal philosophy is 'suck it up, buttercup' and get on with things," she informed him.

It was his turn to snort. "Yeah, well, maybe next time." He got to his feet. "I'd better make us some coffee, darlin'. I'm starting to feel a little too good." He froze. "Did you hear that?"

"What?"

"Something large moving in the bush directly across from us. I'll bet that Byrne is up to something," he said grimly as he got to his feet. "You stay here. I'll check."

"Like hell!" She scrambled off the chair. She'd had more training than him on defensive moves — she'd bet her bottom dollar on it.

He gave her a quick look.

"I'll head to the right. You take the left," she whispered before he could speak. As quietly and quickly as possible, she maneuvered around rocks and debris, making a wide berth into the stand of trees, all senses on high alert. Truman headed in the opposite direction, moving like a shadow. *Not bad. For a stuffed stooge.*

Bright red eyes glowed fiery in the darkness. Casey froze and a twig crackled under her shoe, making her wince. Every sense thrummed on high alert. The eyes were approximately a meter above the ground, the right height for a very large dog or giant wolf.

The head moved slowly as it caught her scent. The piercing eyes bored into hers. *Fuck.* What was it?

She'd trained to ward off humans — but this, this was something else entirely. Her breath quickened. Raspy. Too fast. She longed for full-body padding. A gun. Bear spray. Any weapon.

Calm down.

She racked her brain. It could only be one thing. The Devil Dog.

Legendary guardian of buried treasure. Byrne had to be playing at creating one to frighten them off. It wasn't real. *Can't be real.* Someone in a costume most likely. She took a step closer. Her eyes remained riveted to the spot. She prayed she was right. Because if she was wrong...

The dark shape moved closer. She stood her ground. Swallowed. Hard. Was it going to attack? Her alcohol-befuddled mind froze. Hell, *time* froze.

Then, in a flash, it turned and moved toward the shore, away from them. She heard Truman following as she rushed forward, not worrying about making noise now that whatever it was knew they were onto it.

They reached the beach. Casey whirled around.

Gone. Nowhere to be seen.

"What the fuck!" she exclaimed.

"My sentiments exactly," Truman said, coming up to her. With only a sliver of moon, navigating the beach was difficult, the sand dotted with lurking potholes and large objects. He pulled a flashlight from his pocket and shone it on the ground, looking for prints in the sand. Nothing conclusive.

"Hologram?" she mused aloud. Let out a deep breath. "Laser eyes? Little person in a costume?" Now safe, she could let out the stress.

He gave a bark of laughter at the last one. "Not sure. It moved silently. I wouldn't put it past that Byrne guy, though, to come up with some crazy way of doing it. He wants us gone. He's made that abundantly clear."

"What, you don't believe in ghosts and Devil Dogs?" she teased, her voice strained. "This would be right up Miranda's alley. She studies the paranormal. She'd love to debunk this one. Miranda's like a bulldog herself when she's fired up — never letting go."

"That's quite the group of friends you got there," he said. "How many Brass Ringers are there, anyway?"

"Eight. Lily and Lacey, twin private investigators." She counted them off as they walked back to camp, her nervousness making her talk too much. "Elin, Ufology expert. Rebecca, our storyteller with a flair for research. Ava's the lawyer — I worry we're going to need her services any day now — and Tessa. She's still finishing her graduate studies in music. She's definitely concert pianist material. And Miranda, of course. A more amazing group of women you'd be hard-pressed to meet."

"Maybe we should have that coffee now," Truman suggested as they made camp.

"Yeah," she agreed.

The fragrant hot coffee brewing on the stove and poured into tin cups did help. She took the mug Truman offered, cupping her hands around it, doing her best not to shiver visibly. Who wanted them to leave the island this badly? Was it somehow connected to the guy who'd been snooping around her garbage? Was that connected to the old guy she'd met while removing Soapy's Gold? If so, this was a whole different kettle of fish. Either that, or she had two groups trying to stop her. One from Dawson and one from her new island adventure.

Truman poured more coffee, then a third cup, a quiet and reassuring presence in the darkness. He was rethinking things, too. Good. Maybe he'd get the hint and go home and leave her here. Alone.

"We should be going." She stood. Sober now. *Three cups of coffee and some time will do that.*

"You take the SUV. I think I'd better stay and make sure nothing else happens."

"Do you think that's a good idea? What if things escalate?"

"I want to be here at first light to take the measurements. I regret not doing it earlier tonight." His tone was hard.

"What's really going on, Professor? No one goes to this much trouble to write a book," she scoffed. "You'd think you had a priceless treasure at stake here."

Inspiration hit. Her body stiffened in triumph, energy surging through her bloodstream.

"That's it — isn't it! It's not just about your writing a book or my needing to do research — it's really about you wanting the treasure buried here! You think it's still here! I'm right, just admit it," she crowed.

He hesitated, then his expression cleared as he seemingly made a decision. "Okay. I admit it. You're right. I've wanted a stab at what's buried here since I read the story in an old *Reader's Digest* back issue. I wanted you here to pick your brain. Not just because I want to help you do your job better, though that's a big part of it." He sounded equal parts annoyed and relieved that she'd guessed.

Fuck. A little something in common. With a suit. Who'd have thought it. Casey swallowed. *Time to 'fess up.*

"Let's do it right now, then, 'cause this is why I'm here, too.

Not just for info and photos for my course, but to discover the truth. Let's do all the measuring tonight." Alive with the excitement of the chase. And knowing someone else was in the throes of its sway made all the difference. Now they were on equal footing in this battleground.

"In the dark?"

"We have flashlights. What? Worried about the Devil Dog?" she teased. She threw the dregs of her drink into the bush. This was too good to be true. Too sweet.

"Fine—you're on." Truman got up and turned the burner off, disposing of his coffee as well. Casey grabbed a flashlight, Truman the measuring wheel, and they trooped off into the bush.

The light shone on the first yellow flag. Skull rock. He set the measuring device on the ground and began to wheel it toward the next yellow flag. Too many obstacles in the dark made him stop in his tracks.

"This isn't working—it won't be accurate," he said, frustrated. "We'll need to use a measuring tape. I'll get it." He pulled out a flashlight and vanished into the darkness.

Casey waited, acutely aware of every little noise. Small critters scurried across the ground and crickets chirped. Nothing could bother her now that she'd won a round.

"Okay, take this end," he said, unrolling the fiberglass tape measure from the large spool and holding the metal tab her way. She grasped it and held it steady by the rock. He began to unravel it as he walked toward the first arm of the cross.

Her cellphone rang. She held the tape awkwardly in one hand while digging out the phone. *Rebecca.*

"What's up?"

"I'm so close I can taste it!" Rebecca's exuberant voice sailed across the airwaves.

Casey's heart beat quickened. "For real? You're close to knowing the magic number?"

"Yes! I've got my hands on a very, very, very old manuscript written about the Templars back in the thirteenth century. So old I'm using cotton gloves to turn the pages for the translation I'm working on. It's written in an archaic version of Latin—interesting and challenging in about equal parts. Borrowed the book from my uncle who got it from the old Masonic Lodge they're renovating downtown. He's a Grand Master of a local lodge and really knows his stuff. Wasn't too thrilled, secrecy and all that, but I'm his favorite niece and I worked that angle for all it's worth." She sneezed as if to confirm the dust mites the old tome contained.

"Bless you," Casey said automatically. "So, we're close to having the number for the dimension of our equilateral triangle. Sweet! Haven't had a chance to inspect all the rocks yet for the symbol. Hopefully tomorrow."

"How's it going?"

"It's going. The fabled Devil Dog visited earlier, but he wasn't looking for a bone."

"Really? How did that happen?"

"The islanders—I shouldn't say that, it's not all of them, just a jerk manager by name of Byrne seems to find us lacking."

"You be careful."

"Of course. Got my handy dandy bear spray in my pocket now. He'll never know what hit him." At least she hoped it was Byrne. And not the unknown parties from Winnipeg. She could handle the first easily enough.

"Good. Just remember that stuff's illegal to use on people. Just threaten him with it—should be enough to do the trick. How's it going with the professor?"

"It's going better than expected. Turns out he's wanting to find the treasure if it's still here as much as me. He's an interesting man." *And a hell of a lot more man than I gave him credit for at first.*

"All right. Good. At least that clears the air and should make your job a whole lot easier."

"Yup. Catch you later."

Truman came back into sight as she tucked the phone

into her pocket. He was rolling the tape measure back onto the device with the hand crank provided on the side, concentrating on the action.

"So?" she asked. Not that it mattered. Her mission to find the stone inscribed with a symbol used by the Templar Knights would be up to bat soon as Rebecca found her the correct number.

"Three hundred and sixty-five feet. I would imagine the other arm will measure out about the same distance. Depends if the ground has shifted more than anything."

She nodded.

Truman headed off in the opposite direction and she was left with too much time to think. And seeing the boss in such a different light wasn't something she wanted to ponder. Raised too many red flags on the play.

Truman came back again. "Three hundred and sixty-five. Seven hundred and thirty in total. Almost the same as written in Nolan's report. We're just out by a few feet. Could be accounted for by ground shift—this island is riddled with holes, making it somewhat unstable—or he measured from a slightly different spot. Now for the longer distances of the center stones. Let's start with the bottom section."

"My turn," she piped up, not wanting to be left to her own thoughts for one more second. And she ached to walk and observe the distance, figuring the secret society of the Templars, like most, had a thing about the Tree of Life and the importance of the roots. The most likely spot for a hidden well was the bottom of the cross. Maybe she'd see something that would help. Who knew how long before they were booted from the island? Too many games were being played.

"I'd rather it was me—"

"I'm quite capable of doing it," she objected.

"Okay, but watch your step. You don't want to sprain an ankle."

Her hackles rose. "I'm always careful." Who did he think

he was? She'd spent plenty of time alone in the bush and in faraway places and always made it home.

She stomped off, unrolling the tape as she went. At a depressed area in the land that bore more checking out, she stooped down and stuck a piece of yellow fabric under a rock with the color just peeking out around it. Straightening, she hurried to finish her task. Big mistake.

"Fuck!" She slammed into the ground so hard it drove all the breath from her body. Her ankle was caught in a tree root, trapping her foot.

Truman rushed up as she was trying to untangle herself while simultaneously spitting dirt from her mouth. *Un-fucking-believable.*

"You jinxed me! 'Don't sprain your ankle,'" she mimicked, gritting her teeth against the pain as he kneeled down. Of all things, she hated being helpless the most.

He ignored her temper tantrum, making her angrier. "Can you get up?"

"Of course!" she muttered while letting him help her to her feet. Her right ankle buckled.

"God damn it!" she cried as he stopped her to keep her from tipping to the ground again.

"Nice talk from such a lovely young woman," he chided. And most unwisely.

But though she wanted to lash out, she bit her tongue instead, drawing blood. Added a piquant metallic flavor to the dirt. *Yuck.*

"I apologize for having you do this in the dark and jinxing you," he said as he untied her hiking boot, easing it free from her foot. He checked her ankle, looking for the source of the pain.

She winced when he found it.

"It's already starting to swell. I'm carrying you back to camp, no objections. We need to get it elevated and iced right away."

"No way! Just let me lean on your arm. I can do this."

"You want it getting worse?" he asked. Before she could

object further, he picked her up.

"Put your arms around my neck. It'll make it easier."

For who?

They were too close. She breathed in his intoxicating fragrance with the underlying male musk. No choice really. She was pressed tight against his hard chest, could even hear his strong heart beating under his sweatshirt as he bore her through the bush.

"You caused this with your talk," she said, not letting it go and knowing she was being irrational. The man had said he was sorry. She swallowed hard.

"Are you superstitious? That surprises me."

"No, I'm not. But a sane person doesn't say anything out loud they don't want to happen. At least according to my Aunt Milly."

"Aunt Milly?"

"A very wise woman," she snapped back.

"I take it you never got a spanking for having a temper tantrum as a child?"

"Put me down!"

"When we reach camp."

The campsite came into view. She scrambled from his arms, hopped to a lawn chair and sat. Inspected her throbbing ankle. Swelling, the skin blue-tinged. *Just great.*

She took the ice wrapped in a dish cloth from Truman and tied it around her ankle. He hefted a flat rock about six inches high and a foot square and maneuvered it into position in front of her to elevate her foot. The rock looked heavy.

"Thanks," she said.

"Now that's a nice word," he said. She gritted her teeth.

"Coffee?" he asked.

"No, just water, thanks."

"That's fast becoming my favorite word," he said and retrieved a bottle from the cooler, handing it to her. He poured himself a cup of coffee and sat on another lawn chair.

The silence stretched.

"I'm sorry I was so hot-headed earlier. I do appreciate your help."

"Thanks just became my second-favorite word. How's the ankle?"

She ignored his dig. She took the ice away and inspected her ankle. "Not bad. The ice is helping."

"What do you want to do? Sleep here or head back to the mainland?"

"Hmm, not sure. Maybe lying in a hot bath would help or maybe I should just stick with the ice. Let's give it a few more minutes."

Casey naked in a bathtub, water flowing over all those sweet curves—fuck, that was way more than he wanted to envision. Should envision. The thought made his groin tighten and his mind freeze-frame on the image. Just minutes before, she'd been pressed to his chest, him breathing in her clean, flowery fragrance. So much passion lay within that tiny, compact body that he wanted nothing more than to seek its depths. Relief filled him that he'd shared the secret they shared the same goal. Maybe now they could work together with less animosity.

"I think we should get you back to the motel room soon as you feel up to it," he said. *Where I can close the door, have a long ice-cold shower and get that image out of my head.*

"I'm all better. Let's go."

"Uh-huh," he said, pursing his lips in an effort not to smile as she gave him a wide-eyed innocent look. "I can see that. No, keep icing it." The look he earned was priceless. The woman hated to be told what to do. Probably been given her way all her life. Did that also apply in bed? His groin tightened. Again.

Chapter Nine

"The only really indecent people are the chaste."
J. K. Huysmans

Stupid ankle. Infuriating man. Probably damn fine in bed. Loves to give direction there as well, most likely. Well, that she wasn't about to find out. She ignored the twinge of regret.

"You have someone special back home, Professor? Quid pro quo. I mean, you asked me." She shrugged.

"Yes, but we've parted ways. It was a lot of things, really, and happened before I decided to move to Canada. She's in publishing and wanted to stay near the action."

He turned silent, studying the coffee in his cup, and it made her wonder. Who was the woman? Casey sensed more to the story.

"Still on the rebound?"

"No. Definitely not on the rebound. It's been quite a while since we've even seen each other."

She pressed her lips together. "I'm going to test my ankle's stability. The swelling's gone down." She gingerly to her feet. It could take her weight. "The ice appears to be the cure."

"Good. A day off it and you should be good as new."

"No way! I'm not giving up a whole day."

"I'm in charge of this expedition. You will take the day to ensure you don't come to any more harm."

Loggerheads.

She gritted her teeth so hard her jaw ached.

"Then I might as well head home." She winced. Hearing the words hurt worse than saying them.

"Fine."

"Fine."

"Except you're not traveling until that ankle's better."

Fireworks lit up the inside of her brain. "Then I'm staying here all night and icing it. I'll be fine by morning. Guaranteed."

"Maybe. But I'm staying as well."

"I'm not a child."

"Then quit acting like one."

Dead silence.

"Look, Casey, I don't want to fight with you, but I don't want you to come to any harm. I know you're a damn fine explorer, a risk-taker like me, but I can't have something happen on my watch. It might mean my job."

He had her there.

And he thought her good at exploring. Sweet to hear, the commitment ran so deep in her veins. *All the way, baby, whatever it takes,* was her motto.

"Okay. We'll reassess in the morning."

"That's all I ask." He looked relieved, even a little boyish with his golden hair disheveled from running his hands through it. *Getting under his skin, eh?* She favored him with a grin. The ability to forget an argument so quickly was thanks to her sisterhood. And now she would share his company all night long. Further scratch her itch of curiosity. Only for the sake of learning, of course.

Truman reached over and rubbed her cheek.

"You've been eating too much dirt lately, darlin'," he said.

She snorted.

"Hell of a shock to have a mouthful of dirt. Exploring in the dark sucks. Ever had a situation develop while exploring, Truman?" His name rolled off her tongue easily — it suited him to a T. A true man.

"Of course. Want more coffee?" he asked. "Because I have tales to share. One in particular comes to mind."

"Rather have a beer."

"Me, too," he said and retrieved a couple of cans of Coors

Light from the cooler. After pulling the metal tab off the top of the beer, he handed it to her.

"Thanks."

"Third time lucky."

"Sorry?" she queried, confused.

"The thanks. It quickly becomes addictive, eh?"

She dropped a punch on his upper biceps. It was hard as steel. *So* not an empty suit. But maybe even more dangerous. And he was still her boss. *Get a grip.*

"You must work out a lot." She took a swig of the cold beer, her mouth gone dry.

"It's important to stay in good physical condition to explore. The nature of the game. You lift weights?"

"I have a schedule for staying strong. It's vital, in my opinion, as well. So, this tale you want to share. Can't wait to hear it." She adjusted her ice pack and lay back against the lawn chair. Shivered. The night was growing colder, the air damp with moisture as the salt-laden breeze drifted off the North Atlantic. And the ice pack sent cold blood snaking up her body.

"I'll get you a blanket." He went into the back room of the tent and emerged a few seconds later with a distinctive black-striped-patterned cover. He leaned over, deftly maneuvering it around her body, coming too close for comfort as he tucked it around her top half. A slight brush of her breasts. She licked her lips. He looked different to her now. Prime alpha male. *This is not a good idea.*

"There you go," he said his bright blue eyes locking for a split second with hers.

"Thanks. Yeah, I know. Number four." She made the joke to hide her enjoyment and slight embarrassment at his being so close and thoughtful. And for misjudging him.

He sat beside her again and took up his beer, taking a gulp.

She looked up to the heavens. The stars gleamed and twinkled brightly in the clear night skies above the dark tree line, defying all human exploits. She soaked in the wonderment. Here and now. It mattered. As much as any game plan. Aunt Milly knew that. It bore remembering more often. What was that line? *Yeah, the doom of man is he forgets.*

"Okay, share." She gave him her full attention. The alcohol was easing the slight pain that lingered. And being a fast healer didn't hurt.

"Well, let's see. I guess I'll start at the beginning. I was born thirty-five years ago in a New England hospital after forty-nine hours of hard labor to Joyce and Henry Harrison."

"Not that far back!" She swatted at his arm again. "But really, wow, forty-nine hours. Bet you heard about that a lot growing up. I know I would use it to keep you in line."

"Oh, yeah. She had need of it at times — can't blame her for that," he said ruefully, running his hand over his chin.

"When did you move down south? Hard not to miss your accent. I like it, by the way." Wow, she was actually saying nice things to the former stooge.

"By the time I was five we had moved three times. Fortunately, my parents decided to stay in one place after that to ensure I got a good education. But that's old history. Now, I'm going to tell you about my experience with the Lost Dutchman Mine while I was still in college," he said, his eyes twinkling mysteriously.

"Oh, the Lost Dutchman. This I've got to hear." It was refreshing to be this much in sync. Been through a lot of stress of late. Oh, hell, she thrived on it.

"You know the tale? About Francisco Vasquez de Coronado leading his conquistadors to find the Seven Golden Cities of Cibola? They were warned by the Apache of their Thunder God taking revenge if they dared to trespass on the sacred ground of the Devil's Playground." Truman paused to take a swig of beer.

"Superstition Mountain," Casey mused, sitting up straighter in her chair, riveted.

"Yes." He nodded. "Men began to vanish from Francisco's group, later to be found mutilated, with their heads cut off, which is what began the legend. Eventually, the Spanish fled. It wasn't till a century and a half later that a Jesuit priest found the gold. In retaliation, the Apache began to prey on all trespassers."

Casey shivered. "Hell of a cost for finding gold. Losing your head."

"Wait—it gets worse. In 1846 four descendants of the original land grant showed up in Sonora laden with gold, bragging they'd found the gold mine. One of the men, a guy called Pedro, went back for a second year to get all he could before the land became part of the United States. That's when the trouble really began. Word got out that the Apache were planning an attack. Pedro hid the entrance to the mine after his men took all they could and loaded it on mules and wagons."

"They didn't make it back to Mexico. The Apache attacked," Casey remembered.

"That's right. The gold was scattered to the winds. Another attempt was made years later to locate it and all but one of the four hundred men in the column succumbed to an ambush on that mountain. Hell of a thing. The land they died on is now called Massacre Ground. Dead *burros* have even been found over the years on that mountain, their packs laden with gold." Truman shook his head, his eyes darkening.

"And yet you went there," Casey said.

"Actually, a guy I went all through school and college with talked me into it. I didn't know all this history at the time, just thought it was a summer lark. But the tale gets an interesting twist long before Sean and I got there. A doctor who had helped the Apache was actually taken there, blindfolded, as a reward for helping tribal members. He was allowed to pick up all he could carry and became a rich man as a result."

"Nice to be rewarded and not lose your head," Casey said.

"The legend just grew from there. One poor native woman even lost her tongue for revealing the location to her German husband. Another man who knew the location had a stroke. Decades of bad luck. Worse than the legend of Oak Island. By the time Sean and I got there that summer to investigate, the place was considered haunted by all the tortured spirits. Of course, I don't believe in ghosts, at least not guarding treasure. However, I do believe in rattlesnakes being on the rather dangerous side."

"Rattlesnakes. You're venturing into Indiana Jones territory there."

Casey finished her beer and held it out to him, wagging it entreatingly. *Hmm, how lovely to have such a handsome waiter and fellow adventurer.* Medicine for her pain. Truman got up and fetched them both a second one. Handed her one after popping the top.

"So, what happened with the rattlers?" she asked as he sat back down, crossing his legs toward her.

"We were fairly certain we'd found the mine's main entrance when just inside we came across a nest of them. Damn things were guarding it—seemed like." He shuddered at the memory.

"Did anyone get bitten? Did you find anything?" She was envisioning the moment, the suspended sense just before finding a huge cache of gold. Soapy's stolen hoard had spoken to her, given her heart palpitations days in advance. As good as the real thing. Almost.

"No, they drove us off. We didn't have the resources to deal with dozens of them. I'm no snake wrangler. Then our time was up. I never went back. Got busy with school and the like. I think it's the memory of the camaraderie Sean and I shared that summer that meant the most to me. A special time of being with my best friend and having a case of gold fever. I treasure the memory of that more than any treasure we could have found. Camping and tall tales. Heady stuff."

"What about Sean? Did he go back?" Truman had a look on his face she'd not seen before.

"He did," Truman said. Cleared his throat. Began speaking in a quieter, more reflective tone. "He died on that mountain two years later. I should have been with him. Maybe I could have helped him, stopped his fall. A terrible tragedy. I don't know why I'm sharing that part—about Sean. But most people don't ask about him and I just share my knowledge of the history of the find and my disgust with snakes. That's generally enough."

Casey awkwardly lurched forward in her chair, spilling beer onto her T-shirt where the blanket dropped away.

"Oops." She ignored the spill, letting the beer sink into her top. "I'm sorry to hear about your friend. Horrible tragedy." She shook her head. "You shouldn't blame yourself. He knew the risks. We all do. Can't go after treasure without encountering them. I mean, look at who's trying to stop us from finding anything here, doing their best to drive us away. We make our own choices of our own free will. I'm sure Sean would tell you that himself if he could."

"Let me get that." Truman grabbed a towel and began blotting her shirt front. His touch, his closeness, his scent flowed all around her as he mopped diligently at the beer. She reached upward without thinking, placing her hand behind his neck, leading him downward in the vicinity of her mouth. The pull of his tragedy spoke to her on the deepest level, brought the magic of the moments they were sharing on Oak Island to the forefront. Made her grateful for being alive. Treasure hunters understood, perhaps more than most, the call.

He took control. Accepted the invitation. Kissing her back with a fervor that defied the chilly night and tales of terror.

She moaned. Under the slightest pressure from him, her lips opened. The kiss. Hot. So much hotter than expected. Or imagined. Fierce passion exploded.

He blocked out the stars as he captured her lips, pressing softly at first, then firmer as she raised no objections. He tasted of apricots and beer, his mouth commanding. The kiss stirred her emotions, leaving her breathless. An excellent kisser, he slid his tongue across the seam of her lips, seeking the warmth within. Her body tingled with excitement, the darkness a catalyst for letting go. His tongue stroked hers as she opened her mouth. So fine.

She moaned. A real kiss. A man's kiss. It stirred something deep within. Pressed against his chest, she forgot her list of objections, all the rules and the reasons, everything but the spontaneous combustion.

He kissed her harder. A kiss fueled by intensity and passion. An unexpected yearning overcame her doubts and she let him in across the divide that normally kept her separate and free. Her body took control, nipples tightening, an urgent need flaring within. It awoke greedy, wanting everything. Now.

Truman pulled away.

Don't stop.

"Did you hear that?" he asked, peering into the darkness, his hand still grasping the back of her neck. She liked it there. Warm and firm, his touch made her want to purr like a kitten, rub against him.

"What?" Her body, swimming in sensations, grasped at his meaning.

Wild howls echoed softly in the far distance, the sounds flowing into their camp on the freshening night breeze.

"Sounds like a pack of coywolves."

"Coywolf?" she asked, intrigued by the term, though annoyed by the interruption.

"The Eastern wolf is a mix of gray wolf and coyote, often referred to as coywolves, though Nova Scotia has four times as many coyotes. Sheep farmers hate them with a passion. But we don't have anything to fear." He put his arms around her, hugging her close. She snuggled against him, sharing the warmth.

"Hmm, you feel mighty fine, Professor Truman," she said, the invitation clear in her voice. They were standing on the brink of something huge.

"I think it's time we called it a night. You're tired and you've been through a lot today. We both have," he said, pulling away.

Shoot. Hearing wolves had changed things? *This much?* Disappointed, she pulled away, as well. Then sucked it up. He was right. It was far too soon. And how had she forgotten so quickly who he was? There was a solid rule against dating the boss. For a good reason.

It could only lead to trouble.

Chapter Ten

"Treasure! It's out there. It's whispering to me."
Anonymous

The morning light filtered through the large screened tent window, waking Casey. She yawned, snuggling under the blanket, reluctant to leave the warmth of the cot. Her breath rose, visible in the chilly air. Smiling ruefully at the memory of the night before, she tucked her chin back into the sleeping bag. Had last night really happened? Had she really found a fellow adventurer in Truman? A sweet dream come true. Life's infinite possibilities beckoned, thrumming through her bloodstream. Today the key number would be revealed. She just knew it. Excited, she wormed her way out of the covers and off the cot. First order of business — coffee.

The campsite appeared deserted as she exited the tent, the blankets Truman had made use of lying neatly folded on a lawn chair. Idly wondering where he had gotten off to, she went about making the coffee. Excited to see him this morning and yet nervous, too. Things were changing rapidly between them. As big an adventure as finding the treasure. That surprised her. *Keep in mind he's the boss, Casey. Best to let this big fish go.* She frowned. Trust her goody-goody conscience to quash her excitement.

The heavenly odor of dark roast coffee tantalized her taste buds when a cell phone chirped nearby. Mystified, as hers was quiet in her pocket, she searched around the area. In the grass about twenty feet from the tent, she tracked it down. She picked it up, noting the name of the caller. *Hailey*

Sinclair. The last name decided her, curiosity overcoming her better judgment. She answered the call, knowing damn well it was Truman's phone, most likely fallen out of his pocket last night chasing the Devil Dog. "Hello."

"Truman?" A woman's voice, soft and southern, slowed time down. To. A. Crawl.

"No, but I can get him for you." Her heart began hammering. Bad ideas abound on spur-of-the-moment decisions.

"Excuse me for asking, but who might you be?" the sugary voice asked, its underlying stiff spine coming through loud and clear. *Sweet magnolia my eye.*

"Casey Madison. Who are you?"

"Hailey Sinclair. Truman's wife."

Truman, the man of the hour and creating what could only be called a charming picture if she wasn't breathing dragon-fire, strode into camp.

She marched right up him as he emerged into the clearing, watching his eyes change from soft blue to dark and wary in a matter of a split second. She thrust the phone at his chest, nearly stabbing him with it. "You wife wants to talk with you."

"What?" he replied, looking more confused than anything.

"You heard me." Casey turned and kicked a lawn chair out of her way. Hurried into the trees heading for the shoreline. Took out her phone and dialed Rebecca. Then hung up before the number engaged.

Truman caught up to her as she sat on a stump by the water in Joudrey's Cove, mesmerized watching the ocean waves sway endlessly back and forth on the rocky beach, a soothing sound for the ravaged soul. Nature's lullaby. Until a brutal winter storm hit the island. The metaphor did not escape her current condition.

"Casey, this really isn't what you think it is," he said.

"Classic response," she replied, directing her anger and hurt toward him.

He kneeled at her feet and tried to take her hand, but she

held it stubbornly frozen at her side. "No. It isn't. Hailey's my ex-wife. The divorce was final over a year ago. I have no idea why she said that to you. Jealous is my best guess. I took her to task for it."

"Why didn't you tell me you were once so serious about a woman that you married her?"

"I didn't think it mattered that much and I guess I was reluctant to mention it. It was such a special time between us last night, so fragile and perfect. I should have told you—you know—before we kissed. I'm truly sorry. It was inexcusable."

"You didn't think it mattered!" A shorebird squawked and flew away at her rising tone of voice, obviously not up for the duel.

"Okay, I'm sorry, bad choice of words. But you have to believe me, Hailey and I are not together any more. And I have no intention of getting back together with her. Ever. It's over. The ink's been dry for a year. Last night—" Truman hesitated and thrust his hands into his hair, pushing it back from his face, obviously looking for the right words. "Last night was special. I don't know what this is that's just beginning between us. I don't know where it will lead, but I want time to find out. Please, forgive me my transgressions. I'm really sorry. I care about you, Casey. I want time for us to get to know one another. Can you give me that much at least? Put this mistake aside? Give us a chance? See where this leads us?"

Her anger dissipated. His expression, his abject posture, his eyes, all suggested how sincere his feelings were as he tried to take her hand again. This time, she let him. Perhaps she was a fool. She didn't want to know what the Ringers would say—they'd most likely crucify her. But this wasn't their deal. It was hers. Alone.

He took her hand up to his mouth and kissed the back of it, keeping his lips pressed warmly against her flesh. Faint tingles of pleasure rippled along her arm. Her jangling nerves relaxed. He tugged her toward him. They hugged for a few seconds, letting the doubts take wing. After all, she was the one he was with, brought to Oak Island on an adventure, not Hailey Sinclair. *Why do exes always conveniently forget to use prefixes?*

"Another thing." She pulled back and looked him right in the eye. "The name. I don't suppose...but is she by any chance one of the Sinclairs connected to the Templar treasure? One of Prince Henry Sinclair's descendants? Does she also believe the Rosslyn treasure was reburied here on the island?"

"Yes. You're dead on the money there. More than you know. She has a keen interest in the outcome. Her and her father, Alec, are obsessed with anything connected to Oak Island. Alec has been a mad bear about it for years. And Hailey's a real Daddy's girl. She'd do just about anything to win favor with the old man. That's the only reason she called. She heard about what I was up to from my parents. Hailey and I — we haven't been in touch in months."

Makes sense. And the jealous angle also rings true.

"I really don't want my past to change one thing between us. I promise. I will do my level best to be straight with you from now on."

"You'd better be, or so help me God, I'll be kicking your ass from Oak Island all the way back to Winnipeg!" She exhaled a deep breath along with the warning.

He gave a rueful grimace. "I hear you loud and clear. Ready for coffee?"

"Oh, yeah," she replied. Her stomach rumbled. "And bacon and eggs. Plus, I need a shower in the worst way." Was this just a momentary connection like all the others, she wondered? *It would be for the best. Just one kiss, nothing really. Then why does it feel like so much more?*

"I'll rig up the portable one while you cook." He caught her pained expression. "Or vice-versa. Whichever you like." He helped her to her feet. "How's the ankle?"

"Much better."

"Great. You need to take it easy today."

"I know how to be careful, Truman."

"I know. Just sayin'."

She cracked a smile. "Sorry, still a little testy."

"Do ya think?" he replied, softening his words with a grin.

"No other surprises? No children in the woodwork?" she asked as she worked to put up their portable shower. They'd tossed for the choice of tasks. Truman lost.

"No, that was one of the reasons for the break-up. I wanted children and she didn't, among other things."

"You didn't sort that out before you got married?" she queried.

"Okay, this is going to sound so chauvinistic and make me look like a bigger fool, but I just assumed."

"She didn't even hint about it?"

"Well, yeah, but I just thought—being a woman and all."

"Oh, man, that is *so* bad. You've got a lot to learn about women."

"I know, I know. I'm hoping you might assist me there. Give me an introductory course. Like Understanding the Modern Woman 101. Most men are still Neanderthals in that regard."

"That's been done to death, Prof. Men-are-from-Mars-women-are-from-Venus kind of books abound and yet the sexes still excel at misunderstandings." She turned her attention to her self-appointed task, her stomach complaining loudly. Too hard to think on an empty stomach. "Is that breakfast nearly ready? I'm *starving* here."

"Just another minute. Can't rush perfection."

"To hell with perfection—just feed me already!"

He grinned and plated the meal. They ate in companionable silence. First one. She ignored the significance and enjoyed the food.

"Not bad."

"What? I'd call this bacon done to perfection!" He gave her a look of mock horror.

"You want to use the shower first?" she asked as she

gathered up their breakfast things.

"No, you got ahead. I have someone I need to see."

"Be careful. He's a loose cannon," she warned. "Wait, I just had a sudden thought. He was talking about an injunction yesterday. I could text Ava. She's a good lawyer. See what she can dig up."

"Sure, wouldn't hurt to get an expert opinion. I'll catch you later." Truman gave a small wave, striding off toward the office.

Casey hurried through her shower, finding the portable plastic set-up somewhat challenging as it constantly clung to her wet body. She'd bought the cheaper version. Big mistake. She'd better be careful or she'd turn into a bigger hoarder of the gold than Soapy. Money was meant to be enjoyed, at least according to Aunt Milly.

She finally gave up on the monster and toweled off. The gravity feed was adequate, if limited. She grinned. Truman's larger body would overwhelm the confined space and give him even more grief. Bigger mistake. *Don't envision the boss naked, even if he's hotter than hades.*

She wove her damp hair into a braid and tied the end. There. Time to finish the measuring. And maybe, just maybe — her heart rate sped up — she would have her answer today.

She sent a brief text to Ava, having promised Truman, but her friend texted right back before she could get on with things.

No worries. Blustering. Injunctions take time. Stay safe.

She texted back.

Thanks. You, too.

Her skin itched to get at it, look for evidence of the Devil Dog. Something to shove into that manager guy's face.

She thrust the phone into her pocket and headed out to search the bush.

She followed the trail they'd tramped down with their boots the night before, eyes peeled to the ground and foliage for proof. Just needed something. Anything.

Aha!

Something sparkled in the sunlight. Triumphantly, she bent and picked up a red crystal stuck to a maple leaf with a clear plastic glob of glue. Most likely applied from a hot glue gun. She envisioned the device in her mind. Red crystals glued around a black mask. That would do the trick. She recognized the ruse from the Amazon jungle adventure she'd shared with a shaman. He'd emerged from a blast of gunpowder thrown in the air to conceal his change into a fertility god. Cheap trick. *That bastard Bryce is behind this.* Fucking with them. She tucked her find into her pocket, wrapped in a bit of tissue. She'd share it with Truman later. He might be a department head with all the paperwork in place, but she'd bet the farm she'd outscore him any day on field experience.

* * * *

"I'm looking for Mr. Byrne. Is he around?" Truman asked the young man who'd given him and Casey the guided tour. He was busy restocking the shelves of the office that pulled double duty as a gift shop. "Mason McGinnis, right?" he, added, recalling his name.

Mason nodded. "Yeah, he's out back. Working." His eyes narrowed. "What do you want him for?" Apparently, Byrne had shared his thoughts about Truman being on the island and the review had not been positive. *Figures.*

"Just wanted to have a talk." Truman kept his tone level, not wanting the bad-neighbor label added to reported misdeeds.

The door opened. In walked a pair of identical women who just about made his mouth drop open of its own accord. Mason had no such qualms—his jaw had gone slack and his eyes were bugging out. No wonder. The pair were as out of place in the office as a pair of mermaids at a ballgame. Truman took in the long, luscious flame-red waves curling to their waists, the porcelain skin with the red painted lips, breasts spilling out of low cut tops, tight jeans and red leather booties. Sex personified.

Say something. "Good morning, ladies," he said.

They eyed him, giving small smiles with their full lips and sashaying farther into the cramped space. The room had been spacious enough before they showed up.

Mason appeared frozen to the spot, his arm raised to place a trinket onto a shelf, completely useless.

The door opened again, and in trooped Byrne. Truman was gratified to watch the man's expression change from one of aggression to one of full-on wonder and amazement in less than a second. Gobsmacked, like his assistant.

"We're here for our friend, Casey Madison. Any of you cow pokes know where she can be found?" one of the women asked, raising a suggestive eyebrow above a bright emerald eyes. Her piercing glare appeared able to see right through a man.

"She's with me," Truman said evenly, enjoying the discomfort of the other males immensely. Luscious as these women were, they didn't hold a candle to Casey. The woman with the face that could launch a thousand ships. Not to mention enough attitude to power those same exact ships.

"Ah, Professor Truman, we've come to see you, as well," the woman said, narrowing her eyes. She flicked the other woman a quick glance.

"And who might you be?" he asked, knowing full well he was asking for the other men, too.

"Lacey Cameron and this is my twin, Lily. We're very good friends of Casey."

"Nice to meet you." He moved forward, offering his hand.

Lacey took it, but Truman could not miss the slight hesitation. What was her problem? She was one of the Ringers Casey had mentioned. He recalled the names, wondering if appearing so protective of their friend was their normal MO. Lily shook his hand as well, murmuring a quiet greeting.

Byrne stepped forward, having pulled his jaw off the floor and regained some of his usual bluster.

"Welcome to Oak Island, ladies. I'm Tom Byrne. Anything you need, I'm your man."

"Thank you, Mr. Byrne. We just need to see our friend. ASAP."

"Please, call me Tom. Follow me. I'll escort you to your friend." He hitched up his sagging jeans and slicked back his hair with a quick gesture.

"That won't be necessary," Truman interjected, earning a black scowl from the man. "Casey's with me. I can take you to her right now, if you want."

"That would be good." The pair about-faced. Byrne made to follow. Truman blocked his path.

"I know what you did last night and I want it to stop."

The man had the grace to look guilty, though he blustered through a denial. "What are you talking about? I was on the mainland last night. You can ask anybody."

"You know exactly what I'm talking about, Mr. Byrne. Just see it doesn't happen again. I'm not the kind of man who takes it kindly when his friends are threatened." He got a return glare free of charge before striding off after the twins. He left Mason standing stock-still, watching the tableau unfolding before him with all the innocence of a deer caught in the headlights of a Mack truck. Truman inwardly chuckled. That boy would have his mind full of racing thoughts all day long and be hard-pressed to concentrate on chores and business.

"So, ladies, is Casey expecting you?" Truman asked as he directed them down the narrow path to the camp site. With the island being so small, no destination was far away.

"No, but we had some fact checking to do in Halifax for a client. Then we learned things she needs to know, which is why we're here. Actually, all about you, Professor," Lacey said, with little grace.

"That's taking a lot on yourselves. What did you find out that's so all-fire important you feel a need to interrupt our work?" Nothing bugged him more than well-meaning friends. Were they suggesting he wouldn't treat Casey well?

The woman pursed her lips, giving him a look. Anger stirred at her lack of regard for him.

"Have you shared your marital status, Professor?"

"Yes, of course."

His answer took some of the wind out of her sails, but she pressed on. "And did you share that you pulled a Jerry Lee Lewis of *Great Balls of Fire* fame and married your freakin' second cousin? That she's one of the Sinclair clan — a woman with a vested interest in the outcome of this venture?"

No. That tidbit he had not shared. Guilt struck. And damn, now they had the ammunition to cause further work interruptions for him and Casey. Lacey's smug look told him that was exactly what she'd intended to do. They rounded a corner and found Casey just tucking her phone away. She gave him a look he couldn't discern and approached the twins as he walked over to the cooler and pulled out a bottled water. Thirsty as hell.

"Casey! We've come to rescue you," Lacey exclaimed, hugging her friend as if her life depended on it. Lily also hugged her and the trio faced off.

"Rescue? Why on earth would I need rescuing?" Casey asked.

"We've found out things about Professor Harrison," Lacey began.

"Yes, I know. He's married to one of those Sinclairs!" Casey said with mock-scorn.

"And it doesn't worry you? He's also related, you know. Married his second cousin," Lacey said, her expression equal parts mystified and horrified.

She stopped. Slanted a look at him that would freeze ice in a barrel. "No, he didn't share that gem." Casey chewed on her bottom lip. The same lips he had so enjoyed kissing.

He prayed that it wasn't going to be the only time he felt their plushness.

"Sorry we have to tell you this, but it's our job to make certain you're okay. The university wouldn't be looking that deeply into his personal situation when they vetted him—just his professional one," the other twin piped up.

Truman chugged the water in short order, throwing the empty in the recycling bin.

"Can I get you ladies anything?" he asked, desperately trying to ignore the tension building around him. "Water? Coffee? Beer or liqueur?" Maybe alcohol would soften them up. Lacey ignored him but Lily came closer. "Water, please."

He fetched her one and indicated the lawn chairs. "Have a seat. Are you hungry?"

"No, thanks, we ate on the plane." She settled on one of the chairs and uncapped the lid. Taking a swallow, she used the bottle to indicate their surroundings. "So, have you learned anything yet?"

"Yeah, be careful of well-meaning friends."

She blushed, her cheeks nearly matching her hair.

"Yeah, I'm sorry about that, but it's in our blood. And for the record, it's not against the law to marry a cousin. And yours is a distant relationship—so it's not as bad as Lacey makes out."

"Casey said you were P.I.s. Business good?" he asked while watching Lacey working on Casey. He shouldn't interfere. She was Casey's friend and deserved her say. Then maybe things would settle down. *Yeah, and I have a bridge to sell you if you believe that.*

"Yes, as a matter of fact, it's very good. We're especially good at digging up all the dirt. If you have anything to hide—anything at all—we'll sleuth it out, that I can promise you."

Her grim tone sent a frisson of concern through Truman. This wasn't the weaker twin, after all. Damn it, why hadn't he thought to tell Casey he was a Sinclair, too? And more importantly, how was he going to get her trust back after this?

"Anything else you want to share, Professor?" Lily gave him a look too piercing for comfort. As if she could actually read his mind. He worked to keep his tone level as he answered her, knowing the women were most likely trained in lie detection.

"Nothing comes to mind. Sounds like you've uncovered all my deep, dark secrets. Besides, my mama always told me it's best to keep your cards close to your chest until you're certain of the motives and intentions of the inquisitors. And, please, call me Truman. No formalities when we're in the field."

"I assure you our motives are pure. We care very deeply about our Casey. We don't want to see her hurt. In fact, we'd do most anything to prevent that outcome."

"Then you have nothing to worry about. I only have her best interests at heart, as well. I want to see her advance professionally and get a better hold in the university. That is, if we can get the time to explore this island without interruption."

"Fair enough. I'm willing to give you the benefit of the doubt—for now."

"How do any of you get second dates if the vetting process is this stringent within the Ringers? It's worse than what I went through to get the job at the university."

She hid a smile. "Well, we normally know the man. And it's not like Casey goes on many dates—far too busy globe-trotting for romance. Yours is a different kind of situation—an adventurer from another country who'll be going home at some point. Am I right? You're just here for a certain period of time?"

"That can change. What will the future bring? I can hardly make all my choices based on the unknown. As for Casey—we just met. I think it's a bad idea to get so far ahead of ourselves."

"And I agree," Casey walked over and gave Lily a stern

look, almost as stern as the one she glinted at him. "I know you mean well, but time to butt out of my business. I'm a full-grown woman and know my own mind."

Lacey followed closely on Casey's heels. "What say we all head into town tonight and get to know one another better? Break the ice. Have some fun."

Casey just shook her head. He recognized the stance. Hell was about to break loose as soon as her friends left. He needed to do something right now to earn her approval. Against his better judgment and reluctance to take time away from work, he gritted his teeth. Went for it.

"Good idea," he said, earning a smile of delight from Lacey. *Obviously, following the advice, keep your friends close, but your enemies closer.*

"So, you conveniently forgot to mention you married your cousin," Casey said as the pair left, promising to call them later with the place and time.

He winced, even knowing it was coming. *Just when things were improving.*

"I'm sorry about that. It literally escaped my brain."

"Yeah, right." She crossed her arms over her chest. "I don't see how I can trust anything you say, Professor."

This was bad. Trust issues struck at his core. He'd been on the receiving end and it hurt to think he was now the one at fault.

"No problem. I'd like to get to know your friends better. It's not every day a man meets such unusual women."

"What's that supposed to mean?"

He groaned. He couldn't step right for stepping wrong to save his life. "Nothing bad. But you have to admit, they're not your normal females."

"And what do you know about so-called normal females?"

"I know that you're not one," he said. "With your lovely face that could launch a thousand ships and your amazing skills in the field."

"Not going to work, so don't bother complimenting me."

"I understand. I am sorry, very sorry. I should have mentioned my heritage sooner. But the compliments are sincere, just me speaking the truth of things."

Though she still looked angry, she wasn't breathing fire anymore.

Focus on the work. Casey dug out the bit of tissue from her pocket. Still angry, she handed him the tissue for inspection. Time to show him a thing or two.

"Where did you find this?" he asked, holding the red crystal up to the sunlight.

"It was stuck to a patriotic maple leaf. Obviously part of last night's disguise. That damn Bryce pulled an old trick, gluing these to a facemask and putting it on a dog to try to scare us off. I saw a similar ruse perpetrated by a shaman in the Amazon rainforest of Brazil to turn himself into a deity to the local tribe. He was trying to get one over on his neighbor. Happened on the bank of the Negros, near Manaus, nicknamed the Jungle City. Worked like a charm. Lots of amazement. Bigger show, though, with the gunpowder explosion fireworks. Quite amusing. Far more than what we were exposed to here."

She thoroughly enjoyed the way his eyebrows rose higher and higher as she spoke her piece.

"I tend to forget your adventures have taken you to locales that most archeologists could only dream of."

"It's not all about paperwork."

"Yes, I can see that."

"But be careful at the university—it can be a minefield. They have a notorious old boys' network that might not see things your way. You don't want to lose your job. Mine's been on the line a few times. I don't always live up to their ivory tower standards." She waited for it, expecting him to take the bait. He had to know about what the last stuffed suit had done to her chances of getting tenure, right? Making all her exploits seem to conflict with university policy.

"Don't worry. I get more than you can know how difficult

it is for you trying to get ahead there. The mind games played. Unfair. But I can play the game with the best of them—the southern way learned at the breast, as natural as mother's milk. Which reminds me—we'd better get to work."

Good. Some things were getting sorted. But trusting him entirely was off the table until she was dead certain he wasn't holding anything else back. Satisfaction that she was doing the right thing in holding back a key fact or two offered its own reward.

"You go ahead, I'll have the world's fastest shower and meet up with you," he said, obviously in an effort to be helpful.

"Fine."

He approached the shower stall and stepped inside. It was indeed a tight fit trying to wet all of his body. He could only do a part of it at a time. The sides of the tent kept sticking to him, causing frustration in getting all the soap off. Finally, he emerged and was busily drying himself when he heard a cry of outrage followed by a loud thump coming from nearby.

Casey!

He wrapped the towel around his waist and charged toward the sound.

Chapter Eleven

"You have power over your mind — not outside events. Realize this, and you will find strength." *Marcus Aurelius*

Casey stood by one of the boulders they'd flagged and kicked at the empty space where the stake had been. She should have known better, gotten the job finished last night and not twisted her damn ankle. And now all their work had been undone. *Damn it.* This hurt far more than that stupid Devil Dog costume stunt. This was their actual work someone was fucking with. She took a deep breath. Someone had gone too far this time and needed to pay up. Big time.

Truman rushed up. "What happened? Are you okay?"

She stared at him covered only in a bath towel tied around his waist, broad, tan chest bare and sparkling with drops of water that formed diamonds in the sunlight, sculpted abs rising above the trail of scant hair down the centerline of his body. *Uh. Wow.* She swallowed hard and forced her mind on the task at hand.

"Yeah, I'm fine, but somebody needs to pay for this crap! They pulled out all the stakes during the night. Now we've got to do it all over again." She carefully kept her eyes diverted away from him. Hell of a lot easier to stay mad away from that vision.

"Don't worry. It won't be as much work second time around. We know the area much better. If you're okay, I'll get dressed and grab my gear."

She nodded. He'd taken it better than she'd expected. She watched him turn and leave, her mouth gone dry. *Such a nice ass.* Too bad he was such a jackass at times.

She set to work in an effort to clear her mind once he was out of sight. The work took over as always as she focused. Truman had been right. She had replaced two of the stakes by the time he rejoined her and they finished up the preliminaries in short order.

"Take this end and we'll have this bad boy measured in lots of time to get to the motel before we need to meet your friends."

"We don't have to do that. There's so much to do here. I can call and cancel."

"Let's see how the work unfolds. See how much we can get done. I'm already off to a bad footing with them and I don't want it to get any worse."

She shrugged. "Okay." She liked that though he was obviously as driven by his work as she was, he still knew the value of friendship.

They had nearly completed their calculations and still she hadn't found the symbol. Or was it hidden under the boulders? Because if it was, she was out of luck. No way could she move one of those babies without a sturdy backhoe. Unfortunately, she did not have one of those in her back pocket.

The last distance to measure loomed, the bottom rock of the cross up the center line. She held the measuring tape for Truman as he walked away. She worked her hands over the rough-hewn granite surface, searching with her fingers for any indent. All the boulders were manmade, their shape conical and pointing upward at the sky. She methodically checked from top to bottom. Near the bottom edge under the grass her fingers sank into a sharp impression. Her heart rate jacked up. She pulled the grass away and took out her water bottle, dribbling water on the spot.

The liquid ran in and around the marking, making it clearly visible to the eye, approximately a three-inch equilateral triangle. A triangle with a distinct *G* carved inside. *Oh, my God. I've found it!* She sat back on her haunches, thrilled, relishing the moment and the discovery. Her research had finally paid off. *Proof. An ancient symbol of the Knights Templar. Their symbol for the all-knowing God.*

She heard Truman's boot steps and stood, uncertain. Should she share this new knowledge? It was his family, after all. But also his ex's family and that fact cut to the bone. Would she be sharing in this find, a full share with someone not even here and doing the hard work? That would suck, big-time. She'd never done that before. Or worked with a partner.

She needed time to think. Shoving grass and soil back against the boulder with her boot to hide the find, she stood.

"Find anything interesting?" Truman asked.

"Nah," she said, not looking at him but concentrating on watching him jot down something with a mechanical pencil in his small black notebook. He kept it at the ready in his back pocket. It might not be high tech, but it would work if a battery failed.

"Okay. So, what have we learned?" she asked, leaning in for a view of the page he was scribbling on.

"It confirms what we know. The cross exists and conforms almost exactly to the distances recorded by Nolan. Now we need to check each rock thoroughly for markings."

Casey's pulse instantly increased tenfold. "I'll check this one first," she volunteered, hoping she wasn't being too obvious.

"I was thinking we should check each one out together. Two pairs of eyes being better than one."

"Yeah, but won't that just take a lot longer?" she asked, biting her bottom lip.

"Best to be thorough. Always saves time in the long run."

"Okay, but I don't think it's necessary." She sank down on her haunches and pretended to get right to work, her mind feverishly trying to come up with a plan. *Damn.* Nothing was coming to mind. Was she better off just 'finding' it, being the heroine of the story and getting on with things?

The Sinclair clan, including Truman, didn't have all the facts and she could keep secrets as well as him any day. She pushed away a frisson of guilt. His secrets were worse than hers. The strong drive to be first had always been her number-one priority. She'd never made any secret of that.

"Hey, I think I've found something!" she exclaimed to cover up the falseness.

She watched as Truman discovered it, his eyes glowing with excitement as his strong fingers traced the carving dosed with a second splash of water. Under the warmth of the sunshine, she experienced a moment of true clarity. An epiphany. It wasn't worth it — this hiding information from someone. Looked what it had already fucked up today. And last night's kiss had been so damn good…

She gave a heavy sigh. Loud enough that he turned to lock eyes with her, his deep blue ones questioning.

"I have a confession," she began, fidgeting with her thumb nail, biting and clicking it against her front tooth.

"What? You found this already and wanted to hide it from me?" His precise reading of events knocked the guilt clear out of her. "No surprise in that, darlin'. Don't all of us hunters have this code that we hide all we can? Keep our secrets close? I knew how your mind worked the moment you wouldn't share your moose story." He chuckled. "I still want to know all about that. I'll bet it's a doozy."

"You — you!" she sputtered, not coming up with a big enough word for him and his utter gall. All her good intentions flew out of the window and off the island.

"I should think you'd be pleased at my understanding. Gives us a chance to start over. Make a pact to never withhold the truth from the other. What do you say? Want to take a blood oath?"

"A blood oath?" she asked with confusion, her emotions all over the map.

"Yes, clans — and there's no reason why partners can't follow suit — swear an oath of loyalty one to the other."

"I'm already sworn to a sorority of sorts," she

harrumphed, clenching her fists at her sides so tightly her fingernails bit into the palms. Just when she'd been filled with good intentions. This was why she normally did a dig alone. Unfortunately, he'd brought as much as her to the table with his digging lease. And exactly what choice did she have with the damn chancellor pushing it?

"No reason the two should not co-exist. But if you aren't willing to, I can't force you," he said evenly. "In the meantime, this is a good discovery. Proves the Knights Templar were here and buried treasure at some point in their history."

Off-kilter, Casey silently watched as Truman waxed on about the find, his hands animated as he explained, demonstrating his theory. She forgot her anger as listened to him. His keen mind demanded admiration. She reluctantly admitted he knew as much as she did about Templar history.

"Okay. Let's head to town." He got up from the ground and dusted off his jeans.

"Aren't we going to check the other rocks?" she asked, confused, the tape measurer idle in her hands.

"No need. Only one could hold the key."

Damn. He knew that, too. *Quid Pro Quo, Casey.*

She hurried to keep up with him as he strode through the grass, a man on a mission who knew exactly what his next action entailed. She had to know what he knew to see if it lined up with her own knowledge.

"This blood oath, how does it work?" she asked.

He turned to look at her. "You ready to tell me all you know about the cross? And the moose?"

"Maybe. You ready to share what you know about it? And the details of the side deal with your ex-wife?" She threw in the last request. She had to be sure.

"Okay. But if one of us breaks the pact, legend has it bad luck is soon to follow."

"I didn't take you for being superstitious, Professor. It doesn't mesh with the image I have of you."

He shrugged, not concerned about the charge. "Does one ever really know another human being until tested?" He stopped and gazed off into the distance, his face gone thoughtful. "I've experienced the frailty of human loyalty — seen it dissolve under pressure. I swore I would be a better man than that. Live up to the history of my clan that paid dearly for its loyalty in keeping its word to bury Robert the Bruce's heart in the Holy Land."

Casey knew a little about his family's history. "They were buried in Rosslyn Chapel — where the Templar treasure was taken for safe keeping after the torture and burning of the knights."

"Yes." He turned and grasped her shoulders, gazing into her eyes as if he could see inside her mind. "I believe such loyalty matters as much today as then. Maybe more. I promised myself, after the divorce — " His face twisted with raw emotion. "That I would surround myself only with those I can trust. It's fine if you don't want to go that far with me, Casey. I will understand. I enjoy spending time with you — our banter — it's been great this last while when we aren't at loggerheads. Don't ever stop being who you are. Don't let anyone take that away from you."

The depths of Truman astonished Casey as she stood there and returned his probing glance. She had to live up to such honesty.

"It's a lot to take in. I need to think about all this. What it is that you're asking for — it's more than I expected. Not sure I'm ready for a blood-brother kind of commitment." She said the last in a lighter tone. This true sounding of his character spoke to her on a level that she needed time to sort. Hell, was she even capable of such a thing — with a man? The gal who could not even get to the third date without getting cold feet? Yet, deep down, something stirred. Awakened.

"Of course. I don't know what came over me." He dropped his hands from her shoulders. The modern Truman was back and the ancient clansman consumed by the call of loyalty was gone. "In the meantime, let's go to town and howl with your friends. And you could start with at least sharing that damn moose story that's been plaguing me all to hell."

She laughed aloud, relief making her almost giddy. "Okay, okay. On the way to town. I promise. Cross my heart." For good measure she made the sign of the cross over her heart. A flock of birds rose from the trees and bushes as she made the gesture, taking flight.

He smiled as he watched the lighthearted gesture, pleased she was coming around again.

"Maybe I can use the story for my own book," he teased.

"No way in hell! I promised the story to a friend." She pretended to thump his chest hard with her fist. He grabbed her hand and raised it to his lips, kissing each finger tenderly.

Lust stirred. The very forest hushed as if anticipating a momentous event.

"Guess we'd better get a move on it," he said, then noted with gratification the instant look of disappointment she tried to hide. He didn't want to rush her, having learned about her track record, but he didn't want to disappoint, either. Neither of them moved.

"I thought perhaps in the name of science we could check to see if last night's kiss was a one-off?" she suggested, sending the air rushing from his lungs. A woman who said what she wanted so forthrightly—a rare find. He'd had enough of female games to last him a lifetime.

"Well, in the name of science, I'm more than willing to sacrifice my body."

"Kissing me is a sacrifice now, is it?"

He chuckled at her look of outrage. Reached out and ran his fingers down her braid, enjoying the silky touch. "Last night's kiss was amazing, darlin'. Yes, I do think we need to make sure we weren't just imagining it. How sweet and fine your lips felt—"

"For heaven's sake, kiss me already—"

He leaned in, silencing her with his mouth. He gently pressed his lips to hers, the second touch of her soft lips even more mesmerizing. Her lips parted wonderfully under his, so warm and responsive. She held nothing back. His body roared to life, instantly needy. Though she looked like fine china, she was all woman in his arms.

He pressed harder against her mouth, seeking entrance. Her breath fragrant and warm against his. The instant she softened in his arms, he tugged her closer still. Her full breasts pushed against his chest, nipples tight as buds. His groin thickened in response. He groaned.

They were headed into dangerous territory. Lust filled him. Drove him. He wanted this woman. More than he imagined possible. So much it caused him to hesitate. The last thing he wanted to do. But he also didn't want to lose her by rushing things. By pressuring her. The peace between them—was so fragile.

"What's wrong?" she murmured, her clear eyes, so free of artifice, coming up to meet his own. A man could get lost in those liquid pools all day and not miss the rest of the world. It was new line of thought for him. Usually it was all about work. But today he'd set it aside. He wanted more. Hell, by even trying to get along with her friends.

"I don't want to rush you," he admitted, while wishing she would do just that.

"I'm a big girl. I know my own mind."

"Of course, but we've just gone from not agreeing on much to this." He tried to explain what he was feeling. "I don't want to ruin things. I've had far more time to think about this than you have. I've wanted you since the first moment I saw you standing over the pit, looking as amused as all get out. But I've sensed you've been trying to avoid me since then. That I've angered you by making you come to this island. Even though I was doing it mostly for you— to be with you. To spend time with you. Then I angered you even more by my memory lapse today."

"Kissing's not going to ruin anything, I promise you. Unless you got more secrets hiding in the woodwork that doesn't involve our work here. Sure, I was a tad put out by your insisting I come here, but it's working out just fine. It truly has turned into a win-win." She smiled at the memory. "And, yes, I was instantly attracted to you. I want to find out what it means, too."

She held her kiss-reddened lips upward towards him in such a sweet curving way, a definite invite to kiss her again. Torn, he groaned with desire.

"You're killing me here, darlin'. I think we'd better stop. Give you time to think about this to make sure you're ready for us to go further. If I kiss you one more time, I don't think I can stop myself so easily. We should end this for now. Take a break and head to town."

* * * *

"So, ever heard of Jefferson Randolph Smith, AKA Soapy Smith, and his legendary shell game?" Casey asked as Truman started the engine.

"A confidence man who worked the miners and citizens of Skagway, Alaska during the Klondike Gold Rush— murdered on the wharf by the city engineer after a vigilante meeting." Truman flashed her a grin, deftly turning the SUV onto the causeway that led to the mainland and the motel.

"Right. Well..." Casey filled him in on her adventure. She savored the moment his eyes lit up with the knowledge of what she'd accomplished all on her own. Just before they darkened with a deeper realization that she'd tried her best to make it sound more a lark than dangerous.

"But you might not have made it out of that cave alive, Casey. When I think of what could have happened — oh, my God, you have to promise me not to take such chances. How can I protect you if you run around and take on such dangerous undertakings?"

"I don't need protection! I'm right here—safe and sound," she sputtered.

"Calm down," he said, placing a hand on her forearm. "I'm just concerned for your welfare is all. You know you could have been hurt, right?"

She took a deep breath. This trying to navigate whatever it was that was beginning between them seemed a worse minefield than being out in the thick of things. "Of course, but that's not going to stop me from going after what I want. I want to live this life, not be shut away worrying about breaking a fucking fingernail." She rolled her eyes for emphasis.

She could see him suppressing a grin as he pulled into a parking spot at their motel.

"You are some woman, Casey Madison," he said, turning off the motor of the purring SUV and leaning over the center console to kiss her. Her anger vanished as his lips lingered on hers. Damn, but he was a good kisser. If she were a referee she'd call unfair on the play.

"And you're some kind of man," she murmured against his mouth.

"I could kiss you like this forever," Truman spoke softly into her ear, kissing her sensitive neck with his hot, trailing lips. Chills ran down her spine. She swallowed hard, the arousing fragrance of sex rising between them.

"Forever is a long time, Professor." Reluctantly, they broke apart. He was right—she needed to think about this more. Things were heating up so fast it made her head spin.

She escaped the vehicle, heading to one of the pair of motel rooms they'd booked. Truman dug out the key, manipulating the lock and shoving the door open with his shoulder when it stuck. She laughed at his caveman tactics.

"I'm going to take a shower and check in with the twins. I'll let you know what time we're heading out," she said.

"Good. I'm got some work to do, anyway." He lightly kissed the end of her nose and let himself out.

A knock a few seconds later made her smile broadly as

she threw open the door.

"Back so — ?"

Her two Ringers stood there, silly grins covering their gorgeous faces, bottles of champagne in Lacey's hands while Lily's held a make-up case and an outfit encased in dry-cleaning plastic. They were even hotter stuff tonight. Both made up and dressed to the nines.

"No time to lose," Lacey announced pushing her way into the room, a cloud of expensive perfume trailing her. "We're giving you a complete make-over."

"But — "

"No buts. We can tell you really like this guy from your last text and we don't want you looking less than your best." Lacey took charge. "Shower, then the transformation begins. We're going to see to it that we knock off the locals' socks tonight."

"Is this strictly necessary?" Casey wasn't all that much into getting fancied up. She'd come to the area to work.

"Oh, yeah, it most definitely is. You don't play enough, girlfriend. You need to experience some local color." Lily added her two cents.

"Okay, then." She gave up and trooped to the shower. Some things just weren't worth fighting over.

Fifteen minutes later, she was perched on the bed and the twins were attacking their project with gusto.

"Hmm, you're glowing, my friend. This island adventure is agreeing with you. Something to do with a certain department head?" Lily suggested, waggling her eyebrows at her.

"I'm glowing from just having had a damn shower," Casey grumbled.

"Right!" Lacey snorted before getting down to serious work, applying make-up and fixing her hair into a mass of soft waves with a curling iron. They were good at it, knew their stuff, having practiced on each other over the years.

"Okay, put the outfit on and you're ready to go," Lacey said with satisfaction as she stepped back and surveyed the results. She was definitely the bossiest of the pair, born three minutes, twenty seconds sooner. Apparently, that mattered.

Casey sighed. "Yes, mistress." She gave an eye roll. That was before she caught a glimpse of her reflection in the mirror.

"Wow, nice work, guys."

"I know! Now, get dressed."

Casey smiled and tugged the clothes out of the plastic. "Kind of skimpy."

"That's the whole point. You're going dancing. You don't want to get too hot and have bulky clothing in the way of a good time, right?"

There was nothing remotely bulky about the sleek red dress that emerged from the cover. Casey threw off her robe and pulled on fresh underwear from the carryall bag she always took with her when traveling. She unzipped, pulled the dress up her thighs, tugging and smoothing the sparkly spandex fabric into place with both hands. Lily zippered her up

The mirror over the dresser demonstrated the dress's effect. *Oh. Boy.* "Uh, guys, I don't think —"

"If you can't wear something like that now, then when?" Lily asked with an innocent grin as she trampled on Casey's concern. The twins were dressed in matching tight dresses, one in black with royal blue inserts and the other in emerald green. They suited the look, used to dressing in such a way as to distract men into making mistakes when in the field. Herself — not so much.

"Okay, but for this part of the world?" Her tone was skeptical. "Do you think we're heading out to a nightclub? I don't think we're going to find one anywhere around here. And why are you both wearing cowgirl boots?"

"We've discovered something better," Lacey said, her eyes alight with good humor. "Besides, you're headed out alone with Truman. We're bowing out as of now. Here's the information." She handed Casey a piece of paper.

"Lunenburg County Center's holding a dance less than half an hour away. The place that epitomizes the term *Bluenose*. Lily and I are hot on a case, so, no, we can't go with. And the boots are for flavor." Oh, yeah, the bossy one, all right.

A knock at the door. Casey rushed to open it before one of the twins could.

Truman stood there, dressed up, his dress pants and charcoal shirt making his blonde good looks even more seductive.

"You look amazing," he said, apparently unable to stop staring at her curvy body encased in its tight red dress and her hair curling enticingly over her bare shoulders in soft waves. She grinned. *The power of looking good.* Too bad he was her boss.

"And tonight, I want you to forget I'm your boss, got that?" he said as if he could read her mind.

"Aye, aye, captain!"

He laughed out loud at her antics. "No, seriously, there's no protocols against our dating. We're colleagues after all."

"If you say so." A relief to have the last barrier removed. *Exit stage right. Together.*

Chapter Twelve

"The best-laid schemes o' mice an 'men; Gang aft agley."
Robert Burns

"You're in luck. House bankin' and figgy duff are on the menu tonight for a proper taste of Nova Scotian fare, especially since you're all from away. We can serve that up quick as a wink, if ya like." The waitress gave them a broad smile as she took out her pad and pencil, obviously pleased with her restaurant's selection that evening.

"Does it come with a side order of lassybread?" Casey asked, earning a blank stare from Truman and a quick nod from the waitress.

"You betcha," she confirmed. "You got Bluenose relatives, dear?"

"No, but I've been looking forward to visiting."

Truman's lips twisted into a sly smile as he pulled out his laptop and booted it up. "Someone's been studying the local lexicon, smarty pants," he teased and turned to the beaming waitress. "Sounds good. Make that two orders and I'll have coffee as well."

"Lassybread's made from molasses," she told him, a twinkle in her eyes. Every time he took in how amazing she looked tonight he started to get hard, diligently trying to keep his eyes averted from the dress's plunging neckline and the sleek thighs exposed by the eye-catching hem.

As soon as the waitress set off to order their meals, he placed the laptop at the head of the table so she could share the screen. Once he had her attention, he cleared his throat and began. "If you take a look at the measurements I've added for the stone cross today, overlay them on the most recent geological survey of the area, you can see where the most likely spots to dig are located. The overburden is shallower at theses points—only between fifteen and twenty-five feet deep to bedrock. And they all fall in the bottom coordinate where we found the signature markings on the rock. My best guess is it does point the way."

"Hmm." Casey leaned forward across the table to study the 3-D diagram he'd been manipulating in real time to show the area from different angles. He swallowed hard, unable to avoid glancing down the valley between her perfect breasts. It was like looking at the sun—too much for his eyes to handle. He swore his retinas were burning.

"This helps a lot." She gave him a winning smile. "Figure out the number—find the treasure."

He suspected she knew more than she was saying, but held his tongue. They were partners and she would share when the time was right. At least, he hoped she would.

The waitress bustled up with their food on a large tray. Truman packed up his laptop.

"Here ya go." Her cheerful tone was endearing as she set their meals before them.

"Yum!" Casey said, returning the hard-working woman's wide smile in spades. "If it tastes as wonderful as it smells, business must be good."

"Could be better," the woman said glumly, concern in her eyes. "But people do travel from miles around to eat here once they know about this place."

"You should be showcased on that show—what's it called? Oh yeah, something like *Diners, Drive-ins and Dives*," Casey said after trying a bite and expressing her satisfaction with the mouth-watering quality of the potatoes and herring. The boiled pudding studded with raisins was up next.

"This ain't no dive!" The woman's expression turned to one of horror.

"Sorry. I meant no disrespect. It's a fun show about great casual places to eat across North America. I thought the PR would help," Casey reassured her.

"Maybe," the woman said pursing her lips. "I'll ask the boss what she thinks. Might be something in it." She finished serving them and hurried away.

"According to the tickets, the ceilidh starts soon and it's twenty-five minutes away," Casey said, stuffing her mouth with lassybread. "This is *so* good."

Truman enjoyed watching her eat. She lit into the food with the same passion she showed for everything else.

Within a short space of time Casey put down her spoon after consuming the last rich morsel of the pudding. "I'm stuffed. If I eat another bite, this dress is going to rip open at the seams."

"Can't have that—it looks too good on you," he said, enjoying the smile he received in return. "I'll take care of the check." He rose from his seat, picking up his laptop case by the handle.

"I'm leaving the tip and paying to get into the ceilidh then," Casey announced, pulling open her change purse and leaving a few bills for the waitress.

"We make a damn fine team," he said, placing his hand on her lower back to assist her. Her flesh was warm and her fragrance so fresh and sweet that he wanted her. To just bend her over a table and ravish her—fuck the real world. He held himself back with difficulty, having to be content with their slight connection as they made their way to the front, heading for the cash register. Out of the corner of his eye, he spotted a man watching them. Truman noted that he was by himself, dressed all in black. And far too interested in them. He narrowed his eyes at the man in warning, letting him know he saw him. A pre-emptive strike.

The man looked away when he realized Truman was checking him out. But as they exited the building, Truman's neck tingled, as if warning him of further surveillance. He didn't like the unusual sensation but dismissed it. He was most likely just imagining things after the problems with Byrne on the island. Why should anyone else care about what they were up to? It was more likely the man had been admiring Casey. God, she was looking good tonight. He swallowed, his skin heated just thinking about her.

Crossing the parking lot, he dug out his keys for the SUV, looking forward to the rare evening out—minus the twin tornadoes.

The beauty of the small seaside town was not lost on Casey as they drove through it searching for the community center. It should be easy to spot. Weren't all such centers ubiquitously Canadian, with their flat, squat appearance clapped in boring beige siding?

"It should be around here somewhere," she said as Truman watched the road.

"I miss my GPS device."

"There it is!" Casey pointed out of the front windshield.

He made a quick, efficient change of lanes to the right to make the sharp turn into the parking lot.

"Nicely done, Professor."

He smirked, pulling the SUV into a vacant parking space. "I've had to make a few fast maneuvers in my day."

The two of them, alone on this glorious night—pretty cool. Even the moon had cooperated, coming out in all its full glory. "This should prove interesting," he said as they disembarked. They walked up to the entrance doors with their homemade sign that spelled out the words *Old-time Dance Tonight with the Cape Briton Fiddlers* in crisp block lettering. One side of the beige double doors opened at that moment, revealing a large man who gave them a wide infectious grin.

"Wellll-come! Come on in!" he cackled in enthusiasm.

"Thanks," Casey murmured as she scooted by the man, heading for the open bar with Truman at her side. It was always nestled in front of the kitchen in every community center she'd visited, with Lunenburg's no different.

"First drink's free for the pretty lady," the red-plaid-shirted waiter assured them when Truman beat her to the punch, pulling out a twenty-dollar bill to pay for the two vodka and orange juices, the best bet on the very limited drink menu of local beer and spirits.

Casey turned to watch the musicians tuning up on the raised stage at the front of the hall. The Cape Briton Fiddlers. And they had a drummer and guitars. Hmm, did *those* musicians mind being kept out of the billing? The hall's long banquet tables covered in white paper, typical for a social in Winnipeg as well, were placed all along the perimeter and already filling with a few hundred people, some still milling around, most looking their way with keen interest.

"Let's find a seat," she suggested, wanting to sit down and get the hell out of the limelight.

Most seats were taken, but Truman cleared a path and located two plastic orange chairs together near the back, facing the stage. The other people already at the table invited them with a smile and a nod as they sat with their drinks. Everyone had a similar red plastic cup, white inside, common to every social event ever hosted in Canada in the last twenty years.

Casey's cell phone dinged and she checked the text.

Truman's hot.

She turned it off, not needing to answer that sophomore remark from Lacey.

"Tastes good," Casey said, sucking back more of the sweet orange drink. It was strange to be here, out of her element, and yet Truman looked quite comfortable sitting back in his seat and surveying the crowd. Soon their glasses were empty and he headed back for refills to the now busy bar. She sat and waited, wishing she were wearing jeans and a shirt when a nice looking, well-dressed man approached.

"I hope I'm not out of line, but could I ask if you'd save a dance for me?"

"Ah, I'm with someone, but sure — what the heck — later."

Casey changed her mind as she watched the man's earnest face fall. She understood how hard it was for a man to just go up and ask a stranger to dance.

Truman came back and set their drinks on the paper tablecloth. "What was that all about?"

"Just a guy asking me to save a dance for him. Of course, I said I would. Not an easy thing to ask a stranger."

He frowned but didn't say anything.

The squawking squeaky noise of the microphone being tested made her wince as one of the band members — a middle-aged man dressed in the same black and red western shirt as the others on stage — poked at it with his finger.

"I'm Daniel King and I'll be your caller tonight. I'll explain the dance moves which Paul and Linda Parker have volunteered to demonstrate, first with a walk through, then with a bit of music. After that, you're all welcome to join in. Enjoy your evening, folks.

"The Schottische is an open dance with the partners facing away from each other and going around the room in a circle. It's heel, toe and one-two-three. Into the room with your right foot, then out again. Then switch sides with your partner and do it again in reverse. When you get to the end of the hall, come back up the middle. And that's all there's to it."

"The steps look easy enough, even for a man with two left feet. I'm game if you are?" Truman asked, turning to her and offering his hand.

"It ain't rocket science," she teased, to hide her nervousness. This was turning into an actual date. So far, she could find nothing seriously wrong with him if she forgot how they had come to be on the island and his need for secrets. Of course, it mirrored her own if she was being honest.

"You don't have two left feet. You've done this dance before," she said, as he expertly led her around the dance floor.

"How's the ankle?" He looked down at her, holding her lightly, his strong body touching hers occasionally.

Oh, boy, those blue eyes could do a number on a woman if she let them. She swallowed and looked away. *Don't let them — too soon.* "No worries. I'm wearing flats even though it horrified the twins."

He chuckled, spinning her around at the end of the hall and leading her up the middle. They fit together perfectly, bringing its own special magic. The air vibrated with anticipation, flying as they were in orbit, like a satellite soaring above the other couples of Nova Scotia. Magical. She could dance like this with Truman all night. Just. Like. This.

"I'll bet the twins haven't passed a shoe store leaving their credit card unscathed since being teenagers," he said.

"You're right — not in a month of Sundays!" She laughed, enjoying the sensation of being in harmony with a man. *This man.* Awesome. Breathing in his fragrance, tingles of pleasure broke out, flowing down her body. The heat of his kiss alive in her mind, she imagined him kissing more of her, working his way to discover all her sweet spots. What else could he do with that talented mouth? *Oh, bad idea — breaking out in a hot sweat here.* Hell, even her panties were dampening. *Steady.*

The dance ended. Another began immediately.

Blue eyes smiled down at her. "Care for go again?"

Against her better judgment, she nodded. How could she not? *Heavenly* about summed it up. As near to having sex as the law allowed. Maybe the Puritans were right. This could lead to far more dangerous moves.

Oh, boy. A waltz.

Truman pulled her in closer, one arm holding her tightly around the waist while the other took her right hand in his far larger one. He directed their flow around the room, dream-like, the spell of being so safely held in his strong arms intense. Their thighs brushed through the thin material

133

of her dress. Their groins touched, making her breasts swell almost painfully and her nipples tighten. She wanted to rub against him in the worst way. Naked. *And now would be best.*

"Are you all right?" he asked as a groan escaped her partially open lips.

"Uh, yeah, fine." *So lame, Casey. Just breathe.* But he smelt so good, the heat rising off his firm flesh from the dance only adding to its intoxicating edge.

The dance ended and she reluctantly moved away a few inches. Truman kept his warm hand on her back, heating her further as they stood side by side to discover what came next.

"Time for a butterfly dance, folks!" the caller shouted with glee.

The man who had asked her earlier for a dance instantly showed up.

"May I join you in this dance? I mean, it takes three people."

Truman frowned at the man as if wondering where the guy got the audacity.

"Sure." She could be gracious.

Truman's lips tightened. "Perhaps with your sore ankle—"

"Oh, it's fine. I can manage."

"Great!" the man said. "I'm Connor, by the way."

"Casey and Truman," she said, when Truman didn't take the initiative.

"Nice to meet you." He moved to her other side in preparation for the music to begin and she was sandwiched between the two men. An awkward silence fell.

The dance floor was flooding with people eagerly lining up, itching to get into the spirit of a dance that involved swinging each of the partners around in a full circle with linked arms. A lot of hand clapping and foot stomping fun was guaranteed, not to mention the odd spill. Not for the faint of heart. Or the poorly coordinated.

"No throwing me about willy-nilly," she warned the pair.

Truman's face darkened. "If you think I would take a slight chance with your health, you are entirely mistaken."

"I'll be careful," Connor promised with a wide grin.

"See that you are," Truman said, obviously smoldering.

She gave him a warning glance. *Play nice.*

The teeming dance floor turned out to be the best antidote to anyone getting carried away—it was absolutely packed. She took a deep breath, telling herself to relax and soon the rhythmic beat of the simple music, the much practiced and easy movements, the enthusiastic crowd, all combined to free her mind. Sailing around the room, being spun around by the two men—too much fun.

The dance ended and Truman had put a branding arm around her shoulders, about to lead her away when Connor spoke up. "Would I be out of line in asking for the next dance? Then I promise to leave you alone."

Obviously, Truman thought so by his instant frown, but she quickly intervened.

"Of course, I'd be delighted," she said, the imp in her rising. And it would give her a break from the smoldering sexuality firing on jet engines between them. A moment to catch her breath and get back to reality. Much needed.

Truman watched the interloper move Casey around the dance floor, his hands on her. her head thrown back, exposing the delicious column of her neck, her generous mouth wide in a bright smile, shimmering white-gold curls flying as she exuberantly followed the dance steps. It did nothing to ease his state of mind. The flash of jealously as unwelcome as the black plague. And just when they were getting along so well. Bob Seger had it right. 'Heaven was opening doors where angels feared to tread'. He pressed his lips together, imagining her wild spirit in his bed. That delectable body spread out under him, hair spilled on his pillow, all pink and golden. Her mouth smiling just for him. God, he needed a drink. He swallowed the last of his vodka and orange and went in search of more alcohol.

Arriving back at the table, he set the drinks down and joined Casey just as her new friend blew her a kiss before striding back in triumph to his table. Truman's jaw ached as he gritted his teeth

"What, your partner found greener pastures?" He hadn't meant to say that.

Casey narrowed her eyes. "Don't take that tone! I thought you weren't the boss of me."

"You don't know that guy from Adam. He could be a damn serial killer for all you know."

Another person at the tightly packed table snorted loud enough to gain both their attentions. "That's Connor McGovern. He's about as dangerous as a lap dog. He just likes to dance with all the pretty ladies. Especially the ones from far away."

Truman swallowed hard. Now he was making a spectacle of himself. This was why work was the better choice. That he understood. *Women? Never.* Maybe they were just too different. Then what about that opposites attracting nonsense?

She laughed out loud. "You're jealous — admit it!"

"What?" He looked into her clear blue eyes, the merriment riding high in them. He took a deep breath. *Calm down. Don't fuck this up.* "Okay, you got me." He'd much rather be on the same page with her. She might not think another book was needed to understand the sexes, but right about now, he'd like the operating manual for Casey. And especially the chapter with instructions on how to get her into his bed.

Casey shook her head slowly. "You'd have made a great puritan, Professor, if you think women shouldn't be dancing with anyone but the one they came with."

He leaned over and whispered in her ear. He didn't need all their nosy neighbors butting in. "Long as I'm the one you go home with."

The hot breath near her ear woke all the sensitive nerve endings in her neck. An erogenous zone she had been blithely unaware to be quite so effective. Till now. She chewed her bottom lip, tucking it under her top teeth. Considered.

"Perhaps we should call it a night." She leaned closer to him as she spoke, kissing the edge of his ear softly.

His eyes locked with hers as he swiveled his head around. Very interested. As though she was the last woman on Earth, he gave her his full undivided attention, tucking a lock of hair behind her ear.

"I'd like that, darlin'," he said and stood, leaving his drink untouched. Escorted her out of the door, hand to her lower back, and into the vehicle in a heartbeat.

The clear night sky of the countryside allowed for a perfect viewing of the stars as they drove back to the motel. The same ones she enjoyed while camping away from the lights of a big city. Casey glanced at Truman.

"Thanks for going along with taking me to the dance. I know the twins can be bossy and direct things their way all too easily."

"My pleasure, darlin'," he said easily, turning a charming smile her way. Was he just being a southern gentleman, or did he really mean it? He was unlike any man she had met before. She sensed his strength. His moral compass was as strong as hers.

"I understand how much work matters to you, Truman," she said, savoring his first name. "How much you hate for it to be interrupted. I get that. I can be driven to distraction when I'm on the case."

She glanced at him again, saw he was intently listening as he expertly drove the SUV through the countryside of Nova Scotia, focused on getting them back safely. A quality he certainly didn't share with her friend Lacey.

"Yes, sometimes I become obsessed with work. But I'm glad we took a few hours tonight to get to know one another better. In a different setting. You look beautiful in that dress, by the way. Like an angel. I mean it when I say you have the face that could launch a thousand ships."

"Well, tonight I got fixed up. I hardly look like this sweating and digging on a treasure hunt."

"Don't shortchange yourself, Casey. You're just as beautiful as Mother Nature intended. You don't need to fancy yourself up on my account. Just be yourself. Warts and all."

"Warts!" she teased, blushing at the wonderful compliments he was paying her. Her entire body thrummed with interest. What was going to happen when they reached the motel?

"I mean it. I like you in jeans and a T-shirt just as much as a fancy dress."

All too quickly, they pulled into the parking lot. Truman shut off the motor. *What now?*

He leaned over the seat and took her face gently between his hands. His eyes appeared darker in the overhead lights from the motel, intense and smoldering. Hot. Her whole body tingled with anticipation.

"I don't want this night to end," he said simply.

"Neither do I."

He kissed her. Soft at first, then harder. A promise of endless passion sparked between them. *Fire. Playing with fire.*

"Do you want to come to my room?" he murmured against her lips, sliding his tongue over the seam as he spoke, making all the nerve endings soar to life.

She nodded, clearing her throat. "Very much."

He got out and went around to help her from the SUV. He embraced her, holding her tight. She savored the feel of the full-body hug, his interest becoming clear as they pressed harder against each other. Her whole body flushed with excitement, her groin naturally fitting into his.

"Let's go inside," she suggested. They pulled apart to allow him space to find the room key in his pocket.

"*Truman!* Oh, *Tru*-man!" a voice called out of the darkness. Casey turned to see who was there.

Truman looked up in the direction she was staring. A woman was crossing the parking lot towards them, calling out his name.

"Truman! Thank goodness I caught you," she said breathlessly as she came up to them, her hugely pregnant belly obviously the reason for her shortness of breath. Her bump pushed out her sweater as if she'd swallowed a watermelon. He couldn't stop staring at it. Dumbfounded.

"*Hailey?* What are you doing here?" He dropped his keys on the parking lot from fingers suddenly gone completely nerveless.

"Hailey! As in your ex-wife Hailey?" Casey's words made him glance toward her and he caught the look on her face as it filled with shock, hurt, then deep disappointment once she grasped the situation. It cut him to the bone.

"What are you doing here?" he repeated, more sharply as Hailey moved in closer, reaching up on tiptoe to kiss his cheek. He took a step backward and nearly stumbled to keep from touching her belly which pressed into him. Casey reached down and grabbed the keys off the ground. She didn't hand them over but stood biting her lips.

"I'm here to see how your exploration is going, you silly goose. And to share my good news, as it affects you," she said lightly, the tone belying her sharp eyes as she took in Casey's appearance. "I see you're paying close attention to our family business." Her disapproval was apparent in her dry tone.

Remembering his manners, he swallowed hard. "Casey Madison, Hailey Sinclair," he mumbled after clearing the sudden lump in his throat so he could speak.

The women did not shake hands.

"You said you had good news? About the dig, you mean? It must be important for you to come all this way," Truman said, baffled.

"It is," Hailey said, seeming to pause for effect. "You're about to be a father, Truman. It's definitely yours, since you were the only one I've been with since the divorce."

A few seconds of dead silence.

"I'll catch up with you later," Casey said in a strained tone. "I can see you two have a lot to talk about." She walked away, leaving him staring at her rigid back.

"Casey, I—" he said, wanting to stop her but unable to explain what he didn't understand. What the hell was going on? He hadn't seen Hailey in over seven months and she showed up in this condition? And blaming him?

"No need to explain, *you silly goose.*" Casey threw the words back carelessly over her shoulder as opened the door to her motel room.

Exit stage left. Alone.

Chapter Thirteen

"I am never more alive than when I am on the hunt."
W. C. Jameson, Treasure Hunter

Casey pursed her lips, fisting her hands together to stop the tremble as she leaned against the inside of the motel room door. *Damn it.* She wanted to kick something or thump the lights out of the punching bag at the gym. A tear escaped. *Stop it. Don't start crying. It wasn't a huge love affair you're giving up. It was just the beginning days. Hours really.* But her heart hurt, nevertheless. A part of her had thought this was the real deal. And all that talk about a blood oath and paying her such sweet compliments. She dropped her face into her hands. And to think she was about to wave him into home base. A single sob escaped.

She blinked the accompanying tears away angrily. No way was she giving in to this. She pushed back her shoulders. She was Casey Madison—female adventurer extraordinaire. No time for theatrics. *Neither a buttercup nor snowflake be.*

She tore off her dress, pulled on her robe and re-braided her hair. She had notes to go over, things to study—anything really to get her mind off what was happening right next door. She turned over the pages of the thick file she'd studied numerous times before. She glanced at the obscure reference to an 'Island of Oak' and a 'Cross made of stone' suggesting it represents 'the days of the years and the four seasons'. *Hmm, each arm of the cross is about three hundred and sixty-five feet. Right. Good omen.* She turned a page and studied the shape of the cross of the Templar

Knights, noting its different shape from the Christian cross — the shape of the one on the island. Inspiration hit hard. How had she missed this?

"I get it! You just got to square it off!" She said it aloud, startling herself, remembering the triangle. "Then go for the spot that hits dead center of the equilateral triangle like the pictograph. Add the instructions from the Templar book Doris found for me in the university archives, 'look to the roots for the answers you seek on the right-hand side of God', the bottom right corner, squaring the number and dead center is the place to dig. It can't be that easy."

Casey let out a deep breath. Maybe not, but she'd bet a few shekels on it. She might even have walked over the top of the well's entrance today while they were busy measuring. And — this was the best part — it was most likely only hidden by a couple of loadstones under a few feet of soil, easy once she knew where to look, just like the other two wells of history. She'd need to take a good sturdy pry bar instead of a backhoe. The excitement caught up with her at that moment. She let fly a fancy Highland jig, pretending to dance over imaginary swords crossed together on the motel room floor, turning in a few circles, feet flying in all directions, making her laugh aloud with giddiness.

She hurriedly yanked off the robe, dragged on jeans and thrusted her arms through her sweatshirt, pulling it down to cover her torso. She had work to do. She was already back on Oak Island in her mind, watching herself discover the entrance and going down deep underground. And discovering its secrets…

A knock at the motel door stopped her cold. She swung around. Who was it? She ventured closer, standing on tiptoe to peep through the eyehole to see who was about to invade her space. Lacey and Lily, looking very pissed off. *Good. They could help.* She didn't know what she would have done if it had been him.

"We just found out," Lily said by way of explanation, her face distraught.

"How?" Casey knew they were good, but this?

"Friends of friends saw her arriving at the airport late this afternoon."

"The bastard!" Lacey summed it up.

"Glad you're here." Casey didn't waste any time. Last thing she needed was any kind of sob-fest. "I'm calling favor." Favor—meaning no questions could be asked when one Ringer needed something badly. "We're driving back to the island tonight—strike while the Sinclairs are busy with family problems. I believe I know *exactly* where to look."

"Okay, but in the dark?" Lily asked.

"Yes, in the dark. I have plenty of flashlights."

"Can we at least change first?" Lacey asked.

Casey shrugged. "Sure, but hurry."

"I've got clothes in my bag," Lily suggested.

She nodded. "Get them. It'll save time. I want to be out of Dodge before morning."

The twins wasted no time and soon the trio left the motel, taking Casey's belongings and leaving the hotel room key on the table for housekeeping.

With them discussing logistics, it was only a short while before she was parking the vehicle on Oak Island. Casey jumped out, then quickly led the way down the path to their camp.

The site was still deserted. She breathed easier. No Sinclairs to deal with. She scrambled around to find everyone a flashlight, picking up the handy-dandy measuring device.

"Okay, let's make this quick. I want to be out of here well before dawn. One for all and all for one."

"One for all and all for one." The twins repeated the Ringers' code. They fist-bumped to complete the oath.

"Be careful, guys. The ground's uneven in spots," Casey warned, not wanting anyone to experience a twisted ankle or worse. She clenched the flashlight harder, along with her teeth. The memory of being in Truman's arms just hours before hurt like hell.

"Okay, three hundred and sixty-five feet." She called out the magic number and marked the spot with a yellow flag. The easy part behind them, finding dead center lay ahead. Two hours plus later, after many calculations, much stomping through the bush, swearing that would give a salty pirate pause, and fortunately no interruptions, their mission was nearly complete. Casey put on work gloves, then got down to basics, busily using a sharp machete to hack away the last of the thick bushes and brambles that obscured the area.

"Aha, there!" She pointed with deep satisfaction at a large rock. Was this it? Using a pry bar, she worked the stone from the ground, looking carefully for any pictographs.

"Look!" she exclaimed, running her hand over the impression, her fingers beginning to tremble with excitement. "It's the same exact symbol. The triangle with the G. We've found it!" She sat back on her heels with supreme satisfaction, the machete forgotten at her side.

Untold treasures lay beneath her feet. *Awesome.*

Then she remembered Truman's troublesome sinkhole. She scrambled off the top and beyond the reach of the well suddenly opening up beneath her feet. Falling down a deep well would be brutal.

All three of them stood silent around the perimeter of the rock, looking at the ground as if endowed with X-ray vision and they could peer through the soil, down the well and to the treasure beneath.

"Group hug," Lacey demanded, breaking out in a huge goofy grin, her arms flung wide. Lily and Casey stepped into them, careful to avoid the spot, embracing her tightly.

"So, what's next?" Lacey asked her as they pulled apart.

"It'll take time to dig it out and that's one thing we are quickly running out of. The sun will be up soon and I want to be far away from this place when — well, you know why. I say we come back when the Sinclairs aren't scheduled to be here and dig up the spot in daylight. Cover it up for now. The chances of their finding it are very slim. They don't have access to the same information I've compiled."

"Makes sense. Besides, we got that appointment with Miranda's ghost. That promises to be fun," Lily said.

"More like a drink-fest," Casey snorted, remembering notorious past events and the waiting that had gotten out of hand when no ghost had the simple decency to appear per request. But it would make for a good diversion.

"Okay, let's hide this sucker," Lacey agreed, donning her work gloves. Paying careful attention to detail, within the half hour the three of them had totally obscured the area, leaving no trace of human intervention.

Tired, Casey led the way back to camp. They packed up the last of her belongings and trekked them back to the waiting vehicle, making a couple of trips to finish the job. She kept seeing Truman about the island, his golden looks and special ways of doing things. She shook her head to dispel the now painful memories.

"We've got Will's plane on standby at the Halifax airport," Lacey said with satisfaction as they climbed inside the SUV in preparation for leaving. Lacey driving, Casey content to sit back and rest on the way. The night had turned from exhilarating to exhausting. She'd gotten answers, but, oh, the cost.

"Thanks," Casey said, giving her friend a grateful smile. "That's a big help. I don't say it enough, but you guys are the best."

"Ah, shucks, it weren't nothin'," Lacey said with a grin, deliberately gutting the English language.

"That's where you're wrong. It's everything."

As they turned onto the narrow causeway for the final two-hundred-meter distance to the mainland, a car turned onto it from the opposite end. *Truman.* Through the windshield, he appeared alone, giving off an unearned golden halo. Casey had a sudden thought—he might not be still sleeping with the ex. He hadn't looked too pleased to see her. In fact, he had looked pretty darn shocked, too.

Lacey didn't stop or back up but drove determinedly

down the road that only allowed the passage of one vehicle at a time, making Truman have to exit. Or begin a Mexican standoff.

He kept coming, the expression on his face as determined as Lacey's. *Oh, boy.* The two reminded Casey of a matador and a bull facing off in a Spanish ring. She shook her head, began biting her fingernails. The vehicles came together in the center of the causeway of course, stopping mere inches apart. Given a plow on the front of the SUV, no doubt Lacey would have pushed Truman right down the road and back to the mainland or into the water. Casey sighed, unbuckling her seat belt.

"I'll talk to him. It's my problem." She eased the passenger door open, mindful of the guard rail nearby that could ding the paint.

"No! Wait—"

She closed the door. Drawing a deep, steadying breath into her lungs, finding the salty sea air mixed with a fishy odor oddly bracing, she walked around to the back of the SUV, waiting for Truman to join her. The seagulls squawked nearby, adding their two cents.

"Casey," he said, his voice strained.

She looked up at him, noting how pale he was, the tension lines around his eyes that had not been there while they'd worked together.

"I'm so sorry," he began. "I had no idea she'd show up out of the blue like that."

"Must be a dream come true. You said you wanted children." She could not keep the bitterness out of her tone. She cringed inwardly. She was better than this.

"No. It's not what I wanted. If the baby's mine—it's not what I wanted at all. Divorced parents." He shook his head with sadness.

"Maybe it's not too late. Is the divorce totally final?"

"Yes. And there's no going back. A child can't fix what's wrong." He stopped and ran his hands through his already disheveled hair. "This isn't coming out right—what I wanted to say — what I rehearsed in my mind."

"Well, spit it out. I have a plane to catch."

"It only happened that one time. Not long after the divorce was final. We were just lonely, I think, or maybe checking if we had really done the right thing — I don't know. Apparently, it's not uncommon among divorced couples — at least according to the therapist I searched out for a while to help me make sense of some things. But I swear by all that I hold dear that it meant nothing to me. We parted and I haven't seen Hailey since. Not in months. An uncle who's stayed in touch with her told her what was going on here at the island. I let him know that I'm not thrilled about his intervention, but it looks like the damage has been done. I moved out of the States to get away from stuff like this. And now it comes home to bite me in the ass. I'm truly sorry, Casey. Can you forgive me?"

Could she? He made it sound so reasonable. But if the child were his, no doubt he would be involved in its life. Did she want to be involved with the difficult path that lay ahead for him? It would complicate a beginning relationship to the friggin' nines.

She let out a deep sigh.

Listened to the squawking seabirds, watched them flying in circles over the foaming waves as they lapped at the rocky green shoreline.

She glanced up at Truman, his eyes filled with sadness.

Looked into her heart.

This was a turning point. Never experienced before.

She could smell his desperation. His unhappiness.

She swallowed hard, trying to find the right words. "You're going to have a hard go of it until you know for certain if the baby's yours. Is there a paternity test planned?"

"I will insist. Soon as possible. The not knowing — yes, it's going to be hard."

"And if it is your baby, it's going to get much, much harder, that's a certainty."

"I know. But if you could just forgive me, at least it's a

beginning. A light to help me find my way."

"I can't be someone's compass, Truman. Hell, I'm an adventurer. A woman who can't stand to sit still."

"I don't want you to be anything but yourself."

Casey couldn't look at him.

"If I had known about this before—I wouldn't have dragged you into it. But I didn't, and I can't—I won't regret our time on this island. It was the best it's ever been for me. Finding a fellow adventurer. You know what that means to me? Everything."

He continued with even more passion vibrating in his voice. "I want a full life, not a woman content to stay home and raise children and give up all her dreams. Unless that was her dream. I love that you dream of adventure. I do, too."

He swallowed hard. She watched his Adam's apple move up and down before her glance traveled farther upward. His eyes searched hers, locked with hers, a plea for understanding clear in their crystal-blue depths.

"I don't know what you want me to say, Truman."

"All I ask is, please. Please don't end it right this minute. Just give me the time to handle this situation first before deciding anything."

Casey watched a seabird grasp a choice morsel in its beak off the rocks by the water, then fly away quickly as other birds tried to snatch it.

"We haven't really started much. Shared a few kisses."

"Is that what you really think? That it meant nothing to me?" he asked, his confusion clear. "Did it mean so little to you?"

"I didn't mean it quite the way it came out. But what I feel—way too soon to know. I did feel a connection." He was being honest with her. She needed to do the hard work as well. "But what it means—I don't know yet."

"Then don't say. Wait. Give me a few weeks. I will sort this thing out."

She hesitated. Her brain demanded she end it now. Her

heart, far less certain.

Her heart won.

"Okay. We can stay friends. But we wait to be anything more until you've sorted things."

"You drive a hard bargain, darlin'. But yes, I'll take it. Can you stay? Continue our work?"

The mood shifted instantly as hope stirred the air around them. But she wasn't going to be taken in by it. She shook her head.

"No. I'm sorry, Truman. That's far too much temptation. Being alone in the tent again—you know darn well what could happen. And it wouldn't be right." The slight hesitation in her tone bugged her. She was stronger than this.

"You asking me? I would vote for any kind of time spent with you." He leaned in for a kiss. The horn honked loudly. Casey nearly jumped out of her skin.

"Damn it, Lacey! What's the big deal?" she shouted in her exasperation, banging on the back of the vehicle with the palm of her hand.

Her friend's head popped out the side window. "Sorry, my bad!"

"I gotta go," Casey said. "I've got this thing to do in Winnipeg tonight. I promised a friend I'd be there." She couldn't believe she was considering staying.

"I wish you'd stay. But I understand." This time his kiss landed. A gentle kiss turning more passionate as he pulled her into his arms. He held her tight against his chest, whispered in her ear, "Wait for me—for us, Casey. I'll sort this out. Please."

"I'm sorry. I can't promise you anything."

A lump tightening her throat, she slipped from his arms and hurried to get back into the vehicle. Truman waited a moment before walking over to the rented SUV and getting in the driver's side. He twisted around to look out of the back window to the mainland, his arm along the top of the seat, and managed to back all the way off the narrow land bridge and out of their way in short order

Lacey drove ahead, quickly bypassing Truman as he sat in the SUV by the side of the road. The last view of him was him watching intently through the front windshield before Lacey cranked the wheel to the right and onto the road that led north to the Halifax airport. And home.

* * * *

"Yeah. There was three of them, trooping all over the damn place in the middle of the fuckin' night. Crazy shit. And three women. Don't that beat all!" Byrne raked his hands through his hair then yanked his Stetson back on, chomping down on his unlit cigar, the memory of the twins fresh in his mind. His groin tingled with the image of the two of them tending to his special needs.

"What section were they most interested in?"

"Bottom right hand side of the cross. Doing all kinds of fancy-smancy measurements. No idea what the fuck they think they're going to find there." Byrne snorted with disgust.

"Thank you, Mr. Byrne. That is most helpful."

"How helpful?" he taunted, scratching an itch under his arm as he came to the reason for his phone call. He prayed the interlopers would cause problems while at the same time he wanted them gone. Not a quandary he liked or would spend any time analyzing. That was for pussies.

"I'll have funds transferred to your account within the hour."

"Looks like the women have left for today. Just that Truman asshole left at the campsite. Want me to keep an eye on him?"

"Of course."

"Okay, I'll be in touch. Leave you alone to send me that money." Byrne gave a dry chuckle and ended the call.

Chapter Fourteen

"Walking with a friend in the dark is better than walking alone in the light." *Helen Keller*

"Genghis Khan or Don Juan DeMarco as played by Johnny Depp?" Lacey asked, her eyebrows wiggling upward with speculation, sipping her third margarita. She perched on the end of the Fort Garry hotel room bed, waiting like the rest of them for Miranda to finish fiddling with the controls of her recording device designed to catch EVPs. It was part of the chain of evidence required of a paranormal investigator and she was nothing if not thorough. They were all busy playing a favorite game comparing two famous men. Simply titled *Who would you do?*

"Genghis Khan, of course. Who can resist a warlord? All commanding and stuff," Miranda surprised them by answering first, her violet eyes glinting with speculation as she went about her self-appointed task with a silly grin.

"No way! It would be one of those annoying slam, bam, thank you, ma'am kind of experiences. I want the more sensitive type, a man who looks like he'd take the time to go downtown—if you know what I mean," Elin said, her Scandinavian beauty on full display tonight in her sky-blue robe. A recent acquisition was opened on her lap—a first-hand report of the man involved in the Falcon Lake incident. Ufology was her constant passion. Of course, Casey couldn't say much to her about the obsession—any clue about finding treasure would turn her head in a second.

"How about you, Casey? Which would turn you on?" Rebecca asked, her husky tone capable of sending delicious thrills down anyone's spine — including most females.

"I think she's too fascinated at the moment by one particular professor who shall remain nameless to make a rational choice," Lacey said, her tone edgy.

"So not true." Casey denied the charge, refusing to show how much Truman had managed to get under her skin. "Give me the warlord. I'll have him tamed in no time."

"Oh, right! I'd pay to see that," Rebecca chortled, nearly spilling her cocktail. She sprawled on the other side of the queen-size bed in Room 202 — the famous haunted room of the hotel — a nest of pillows supporting her back. Lily and Ava were enjoying the tenth-floor spa, the famous wellness center aptly called just *ten*, that had helped bring the old hotel back from the brink of bankruptcy. Casey stretched out her toes, admiring the rare pedicure she'd indulged in an hour ago. *When in Rome, right?*

"Too bad Tessa couldn't make it," Rebecca mused. "That girl drives herself too hard."

Miranda chortled. "Yeah, right! She's not the only one around here."

Casey laughed. "Okay, so we're all OCD. What's the plan, Miranda?"

"You guys all know the story, right? About the honeymooners?" Mirada poured herself a diet soda. She always abstained from drinking when hot on the evidence trail of a haunting.

Rebecca shuddered. "To think she died right here in this room — in the closet over there." She pointed at the closed door and everyone turned to stare at it, likely seeing the image in their mind's eye. Casey swallowed hard. This part was too real.

"She hanged herself after she found out her husband was killed in an accident getting her headache pills." She shook her head. "Such a horrible tragedy."

A moment of silence followed Rebecca's words. Tribute to the dead.

"Did you guys know that the original planner of the

hotel, Charles Melville Hays, the guy that built the Château Laurier in Ottawa, died on the Titanic? Spooky or what? A watery grave has got to be the worst." Casey added her bit.

"I agree," Miranda said, her usually animated face solemn.

"This is too maudlin," Lacey complained. "I need another drink. Anyone else want one while I'm up?"

A chorus of yeses made Lacey laugh. "You can all get your own," she declared. They dutifully trooped to the makeshift bar and refreshed their drinks. Nothing much would happen that night, was Casey's best guess. Too much estrogen floating around. Any sensible ghost would stay clear.

A loud knock sounded at the door.

"Crap! That scared me," Elin complained as she spilled some of her drink on the rug.

"That must be the cots," Miranda explained, answering the door.

"You ordered extra beds, ma'am?" A young man stood there with a portable cot in his possession, another one leaning up against the wall.

"Yes, I did," Miranda said with a grimace, obviously distressed at being called ma'am.

The man's eyes widened as he took in the women lounging about the room.

"One in here and one in the adjoining room," Miranda instructed. She'd booked two side-by-side hotel rooms for the seven of them, but everyone was crowded into 202 and would be until the revelry died down. And that wouldn't be happening anytime soon if this was a normal Ringers' gathering.

Casey's cell phone dinged with an incoming text.

Truman.

Her heart leaped uncomfortably. She could sense the women staring at her as she read the brief message.

U busy? Back in town.

Casey used her thumbs to text back one word.

Yes.

Ok. Need to talk about Oak Island.

Tomorrow. After lunch.

Thanks. Looking forward to seeing u.

None of the women asked, though she could see they were dying to. The hurt was still so fresh she didn't want to talk about it. Maybe she was making too big a thing about his ex? About the baby? Envisioning a life unencumbered for years yet, maybe forever. No idea what she'd want in ten years. But hooking up with Truman now — great as that would be — came with a lot of unexpected baggage. Plus, he needed time to digest things and decide what he really wanted. The future of a child lay in the balance. She turned her mind away from the awkward dilemma and gave the women a brief smile.

"I'm good. He just wants to talk about Oak Island."

"Yeah! Good stuff," Miranda's eyes lit up with excitement. "Rebecca filled me in on what you've achieved there. When's the dig?"

"Soon," Casey promised and got up to fetch another cocktail. "But right now, I want to forget all about Oak Island and ex-wives."

* * * *

Hours later, the rooms quieted as all the Ringers snuggled down and found a place to sleep for a few hours. Casey lay on her back and watched TV, the sound on mute, but with the caption option turned on so she could follow the plot of the movie. She couldn't sleep — any distraction was welcome.

Suddenly the back of her neck tingled. Something had

changed. She looked around the room but couldn't see anything different. Then back at the TV. The image blurred into a haze of grey with a black section right dead center. The darkened area contained white lettering, taking up half the screen.

The message was simple. And terrifying.

Death awaits you on Oak Island.

A slight muffled sound. Outside the room. She jumped up and raced to the door. Yanked it open. A figure was disappearing around the corner. She ran. All-out. Damn it, no one got away with threatening her.

She caught up with the guy at the end of the hallway. She didn't run laps at the university track for nothing. He tried to open the stairwell door, but she attacked. Clicking into fight mode.

"What the fuck do you think you're playing at?" she shouted at his back. He spun around to face her. What she lacked in size, she more than made up for in self-defense strategies, thanks to the courses offered at the local YMCA.

"Lady, I'm not fighting you," he growled, his head covered in a black hoodie in an effort to obscure his appearance, sunglasses also hiding his eyes.

"Oh, yeah?" She zeroed in on her target, knee ready to strike a soft spot.

The man shrank back, locked on the wicked gleam in her eyes that told him what was happening next. His eyes shifted to her right. The alert came too late. A shove from behind. She went down. He yanked the door open and vanished down the stairwell, her attacker right on his heels, their boots echoing on the stairs. *Damn it.*

"What is it?" Miranda woke up groggily as Casey came back into the hotel room. She sat up on the cot, looking over at Casey. The bed covers slipped down, revealing she was fully dressed and ready in case something untoward happened. *Good call.* Her biggest complaint — nothing

155

exciting ever happened. That had just changed.

Casey pointed at the screen, but the movie was back on, no message. Had she imagined it? She'd been half-asleep. And obsessed by the place. "There was a message on the screen. A warning about Oak Island."

"What! Nothing there now," Miranda said, staring at it.

"I swear. I chased a guy down the hallway just now."

"You okay?"

"Yeah, but they got away."

"Cheap trick," Miranda said, putting her arm around Casey, giving her a sideways hug. "You really okay?"

"Yeah. More angry than anything else. Who do you think it was? The ex? Playing some kind of sick game?"

"Kind of extreme, even for an ex," Miranda said, pouring a glass of water for Casey and handing it to her. She added, "I'll ask the twins to investigate her just in case she's a wing nut, to be on the safe side."

Casey snorted. "I'm sure they're already on the case. You know they investigated Truman, right?" She downed half the glass of water and set it down on the bedside table.

"Good," Rebecca said, chewing on her lip as she considered. She'd woken up as well. "You need to know who you are working with — and falling for."

"I'm not falling for the guy!" Casey said a little too loudly. *Stay calm. You don't want to wake everyone and have them in on this.* "I need to see him — warn him. He has to know what's going on. This is too important to discuss over the phone." She stopped when she realized both women were staring at her. "What? You don't think this is a game changer?"

"You're going to see him — *now*? In the middle of the night? Is he even home?" Miranda asked.

"Yeah, he's home. I got a text earlier."

"What if his ex is there?"

Casey hesitated, but only for a moment before ducking under the edge of the bed in an effort to locate her shoes. She'd run out without them. "I don't care. This takes precedence. He deserves to know what's going on." *What I can't say is that I have to see him, to know for certain if he's okay.*

A bad sense of impending danger was driving her. The walls closing in, she searched for the offending runners that'd somehow managed to work their way out of sight. Finding them, she then yanked them out and thrust them onto her feet. She hurriedly picked up her belongings, turning back at the hotel room door.

"Don't worry. I'll be fine."

"Just be careful. We don't know what's going on yet. I'll investigate at this end and let you know what I find out. Get the twins right on it," Miranda promised.

"Text and let me know you arrive safely," Rebecca demanded as Casey hastily opened the door and stepped out into the extra-wide hallway designed for days long past, when women in colorful ball gowns and men in tuxes needed to pass by one another without the concern of their clothing actually touching. An elegant era that normally spoke to her in volumes. Today, she just wanted to get to a modern taxi stand and hail a cab. Walking toward the grand staircase, she chose to descend the broad steps over the elevator. Less confining. She checked the app on her phone for Truman's address.

Twenty minutes later, the bright yellow cab pulled up in front of Truman's upscale condo on River Avenue. She paid the driver and got out of the vehicle. Taking a deep breath, she hurried up the sidewalk to the condo's entrance. A doorman opened one of the large front doors and she slipped inside. The building housed a number of condos and the tenants most likely pooled their money to pay for maintenance and security, an arrangement common in Winnipeg in renovated apartment blocks.

"May I ask whom you're here to see, miss?" the middle-aged man inquired as he escorted her, his eyes tired but his tone polite.

"Of course. Professor Truman Harrison." Casey looked around the foyer as the man buzzed Truman. All glass and chrome, the area was spacious and rather industrial.

Casey liked the look. Simple and easy to maintain. Just like she wanted her life to remain. Then why was she here? Just common courtesy of course. And that bad sense of foreboding that still had a grip on her. He needed to know what was up, for his own safety.

It took a few rings, but someone finally answered the security-guard-slash-doorman's call. They spoke briefly before the uniformed man turned to her, sliding the phone back into his suit pocket. His name tag read *George Gallagher*.

"He's on the twelfth floor. The penthouse. Go right up, miss—he's expecting you. Elevator's over there." He pointed to a bank of elevators on his right, neatly hidden behind a mirrored front.

"Thank you, Mr. Gallagher."

"Please, call me George. Everyone does," he said with a gracious smile.

"Thanks, George. I won't be long," she promised over her shoulder.

"Stay as long as you wish," he said. An unexpected twinkle appeared in his eyes that Casey caught just as the elevator doors closed, blocking him out. *Great. Now someone think I'm a booty call.* Chagrined by all the recent events, she got off the elevator in a less than amiable mood.

Truman was in the hallway waiting for her, hastily dressed, hair disheveled, looking endearing and annoying all at the same time. The sight of him brought an instant lump to her throat.

"Casey," he said, rushing to her and pulling her into his warm, safe arms and against his rock-hard body. As she felt his closeness, heard his heart beating, she forgot why she was angry with him. Her deep sense of foreboding vanished. She stood there for a moment, breathing in his intoxicating fragrance that sent her body thrumming, needing him so much after the last couple of days.

"What's up?" he asked. "Why are you trembling?"

"I'm fine. Your doorman thinks I'm a booty call." She pulled away.

"You're anything but. I'll straighten George out in the morning. You didn't answer my question."

"The craziest thing happened tonight and I have to tell you—you need to know." Tears pricked behind her eyelids and she pressed her eyes tightly closed to drive them away. She smiled up at him to hide her weakness. Inexcusable.

"What? You're driving me crazy here!"

"Tonight was Miranda's show at the hotel Fort Garry—you know, Room 202 stuff. Most of the Ringers were there as witnesses. It was really more of a lark than anything, though Miranda takes it seriously. All her equipment set up to test the place. But the rest of us were having a mini-vacation. Drinking and having fun. Then just around three a.m. the TV turns up with a message—*Death awaits you on Oak Island*. Some kind of sick prank. I heard something outside my door and gave chase, but they got away." No point in telling him she'd been shoved from behind. She was no wimp. "But I've been racking my brain as to who would go to these lengths. Surely, not that Byrne guy, right?"

Truman's face darkened as thunderclouds appeared, his eyes glinting sharply. "My God, if it's him, he's a dead man! To think you were exposed to such crap. You could have been hurt! I'm so sorry, Casey. This was never meant to happen."

"It's not your fault," she said.

"It's inexcusable. What kind of person tries to scare a woman off from a harmless dig?" Did his anger at the perpetrator demonstrate how much he cared?

"I thought you should know, so you can keep an eye out. I should go now…" Her brain said, *go home, be safe*, but her feet remained planted. Frozen.

"Come inside. I'll make us something hot to drink. You're trembling," he said with genuine concern and took her arm to direct her to the door. Her feet found it rather easy to unstick now and move in the direction of Truman's condo. Maybe she was really being just a booty call? No way. She cared about this man — wanted him safe. *Warn him about the threat. That's all.*

She perched on a kitchen stool and watched Truman bustle about making fresh coffee. The L-shaped room doubled as a dining room and faced the Assiniboine River. The drapes were pulled back, the view very different from hers on the opposite bank. Her home was nearly right across from his condo — she could see her boathouse with its solidary spotlight shining down on the flagstones. She wished it was daylight to see it all better. On Truman's side, a couple of street lights lit up the steep embankment that led down to the water behind the visitor parking lot. Peaceful. And pretty.

Relaxing for the first time since she'd read the message, she accepted a hot cup of coffee with a grateful smile and took an appreciative sip.

"It's good. Thanks." She sat and waited while he joined her at the island, sitting on a matching stool, coffee in hand.

"I put a shot of whiskey in it," he said, sipping his coffee.

"I can taste it."

"You hungry?" he asked.

"No, I'm good."

"That you are," he complimented her with a generous smile. The sudden urge to run her hands through his hair and straighten the wayward locks nearly overcame her. He was looking too boyish and charming, irresistible really. How had his ex-wife let him go?

"Not that good," she retorted.

"I didn't mean anything by it except that I want to set the record straight."

"Not tonight." She looked away, staring out across the river in an effort to keep her mind clear.

"If not now, when? I'm so sorry about what happened on the island. I can't apologize enough. Will you ever let me off the hook? I truly had no idea."

"All of it? You're sorry about all that happened?"

"No. Of course not. Just the last part. The part I'm not

supposed to talk about."

She rolled her eyes. "Okay. We have a pact then. No talking about stuff out of our control."

"But I am worried about this shit that went down tonight." He shifted gears and she took a deep breath, turning her mind to their more immediate problem.

"Crazy all right. Who would go to such lengths?"

"I think we're too close to revealing the island's true secrets and someone wants to stop it in its tracks," he said, expression earnest, both hands embracing his coffee cup. "I think it means that what's there is very important — maybe more important than we figured on. More than treasure must be hidden there. I'm thinking something beyond price. Something ancient."

"The Templar treasure from Rosslyn Chapel that the Sinclair family guarded so well," she confirmed with a nod. "Perhaps the Ark of the Covenant or the Holy Grail," she added in a whisper, the image sending chills down her spine.

"Maybe. It's bloody well possible." Their eyes locked. The excitement quickened the beat of her heart. She wanted to go back to the island. Find the treasure. Right now.

The mood shifted. She swallowed. Hard. Glanced at his lips, then back into his eyes. He was such an expert kisser — the memory of his kissing her into a pool of want of physical desire impossible to ignore.

"What's going on in here? It's the middle of the night for heaven's sake!"

A high-pitched voice broke the mood, startling them both and Hailey Sinclair stood there in all her proud glory, stomach protruding through her pink flannel pajamas with their Hello Kitty logo. Casey's heart sank.

"Go back to bed. I can handle this," Truman said. The woman raised her dark eyebrows with derision, giving Casey a sharp look before turning and leaving the room, damage complete.

"I'm sorry, Casey, I meant to tell you, but I was so caught

up in things. She needed a place to stay for one night and I couldn't just throw her out on the street. What kind of monster would do that? She's eight months pregnant for heaven's sake," Truman's tone sounded apologetic and frustrated as he tried to explain.

"I need to go."

"Casey! Please, don't leave like this. We need to talk," Truman pleaded.

"I can't right now." She yanked open the door and raced down the hallway and into the elevator. She stabbed the button for the lobby with her forefinger, cursing when her fingernail snapped under the pressure. The door closed on Truman's stricken face as he watched her from the hallway. She fought a terrible urge to go back with nothing but an extreme effort of willpower. She had to do the right thing, stay away. What had she been thinking, showing up like this? Pure insanity.

Casey spent the short taxi drive trying desperately to ignore the recent shot to her heart, chewing a thumbnail down to the quick.

Crawling into bed twenty minutes later, Casey stared at the ceiling, counting the titles, trying not to focus on the scene with Truman and the ex. *What grown-ass woman wears a child's logo on her pajamas, anyway? Beyond weird.* Her cell phone chirped on the bedside table.

Truman.

She turned her cell off without answering it. *Let it go.* Obviously there was more going on. The woman had already flown across the country alone. *Surely staying in a hotel is not beyond reason for one night?* Disgusted with her uncharitable response, Casey focused on what was her life's blood. Hunting treasure. She needed to focus on it and rethink all her calculations. Excitement bubbled as she made plans.

Chapter Fifteen

"If you love someone set them free, if they come back they're yours; if they don't they never were." *Richard Bach*

Truman poured another cup of coffee, sans whiskey, and slumped onto the stool where just moments ago Casey had sat, lighting up the room with her special aura. He took a deep breath. A faint trace of her flowery fragrance lingered in the air, making him acutely aware of what he was missing. Why did Hailey have to show up now of all times? Just when he was getting his life back? Casey was the one for him. Every time they were together, she made him want to be a better man. His heart dropped. A better man would let her go. Leave her alone until this was all sorted with Hailey. Could he do that? Maybe, if fate quit pushing them together. That was an unfair enticement.

"Truman." Hailey's voice entered his consciousness and he looked up to see her coming toward him, clad in a fluffy pink robe. "I'm sorry my being here is causing you trouble." She sat heavily on a bar stool and sighed as if all the weight in the world were pressing on her slender shoulders. The sight of her discomfort made him wince. Guilt struck. Hard. The baby looked so huge. *God, please don't let it be twins. And please let her be okay.*

"It's not your fault. I'm to blame, as well. To think making one misstep could lead to all this. Why didn't you come to me sooner?" he asked, shaking his head at the irony of how one bad choice was fucking up so many lives. He thought this problem was for teenagers. He'd insisted on a condom even though she assured him she was on the pill. She liked the regular periods they assured in her busy professional life. And yet here they stood. About to be parents. At the worst possible moment.

"I couldn't tell you at first. I was so confused, and I thought I could do it all alone. But I can't, Truman, I'm not that strong. Was it really? A mistake? You said you always wanted to have children. I wasn't ready before, but now, now that I am, it's not too late for us. We could still salvage a life."

"I've promised to help you support the child. To help you until the baby comes. But after that, I don't see a future for us. The divorce is final. I don't want to revisit all that pain. I can't handle betrayal again. You cheated on me — lied to my face many, many times by your own admission. I can't go there." He shook his head, his stomach roiling with the bad memories.

"We could go to counseling again. Get some better professional help. Those other charlatans need to have their licenses revoked for all the good they did." She chewed on her bottom lip as she pleaded her case, scorn for the failings of the therapists clear.

"We did that. Remember? It never helped. No, Hailey. It's really over. I think you should go back to bed. It's late and it's not good for you or the baby. You need your rest. I'll take you to the airport in the morning."

"About that." She paused for a second and his heart lurched. *Please, please don't let her be changing her mind.* "I'm thinking I'm going to stay in town for a while. There's an author I want to meet who sent our publishing house a manuscript we're very interested in. A Rebecca Fairfax."

Truman swallowed. He knew that name. *God, let there be more than one Rebecca Fairfax in Winnipeg.*

"How long will you be staying?"

"Just a few days. But if it's too inconvenient, I can move to a hotel." She smiled, eyebrows raised with all the innocent charm he remembered vividly when he was pretty certain he was being manipulated. He swore he could hear a death knell ringing in his ears. A warning of things to come. But his southern training kicked him in the butt. Kept him from doing the prudent thing.

With a smile pasted on his face, he offered to do the right thing.

"Why, thank you, Truman. You are such a gentleman. Daddy never understood that." Hailey rubbed her stomach as she smiled softly.

"Is the baby kicking? Can I feel?" he asked, surprising himself. He didn't want to think about her rich and powerful father who'd been such a fucking pain during their entire marriage, demonstrating time and again that he felt Truman beneath his precious Hailey. *Guess he's trying to make up for years of neglect.* But right now, with her insisting it was his child, he felt the urge to be a part of it, even in some small way. Maybe then it would feel real. Because right now it sure as hell didn't.

"No!" Hailey hastily shrank back as if he had active leprosy that would contaminate the child. "I'm sorry, I'm just kind of self-conscious about the size of my belly."

He frowned. Didn't pregnant women normally like to share such things? He cleared his throat. "Okay, well, you should go back to bed. It's very late."

"Yes, that's a good idea." She agreed and slipped off the stool, scurrying away. Or as least as quick as her heavy belly would let her.

He watched her go. What was going on? With Hailey, he never knew for certain. Even the four therapists they'd gone through during the demise of their marriage had thrown their hands up trying to explain her behavior. And it wasn't just the affairs or the lies she'd spun. She had had to be the one in charge. No one else could do it right.

He should have seen the red flags right from the beginning, but he had been blinded by her beauty and charm. And as one therapist had pointed out, she was very good at mirroring what the other person wanted when she wanted the same thing. But when it clashed with hers, she had no coping skills for compromise. Temper tantrums, tears, threats—whatever it took to get her way. There was no peace until the other person agreed with her. God, he wanted his life back. Desperately. Before it was too late.

* * * *

Casey took a deep breath and pushed open the door to Truman's office. After a night of soul searching, she wanted to make herself clear.

Truman looked up as she entered then slid onto an office chair, smoothing her skirt down. She liked the flattering outfit, though it rode up her thighs. Her heart squeezed. Dark shadows lay under his beautiful blue eyes. She glanced away and out of the tall window behind his desk watching the Winnipeg Blue Bombers practicing on the grassy field.

She cleared her throat. "I wanted to see you to let you know that it's best we keep this strictly professional between us from now on. You don't need the gossip this situation could create when it's discovered your pregnant ex is in town."

"I'm a big boy. I can handle myself and I can assure you I've had far worse. This is academia, after all, where slings and arrows are a daily pastime," he said, frowning.

"It's a minefield all right," she agreed, uncrossing and crossing her legs, unable to get comfortable on the chair. She saw him glance down. The skirt was now exposing far too much thigh.

"Oops, sorry." She blushed and straightened the fabric out.

"I'm not," he said with a smile. "You have beautiful legs. In point of fact, you're beautiful inside and out, Miss Madison. I'm a lucky man you even noticed me."

She swallowed, her mouth gone dry. *Stay on task.* "We need to talk about what we're going to do about Oak Island."

"Hmm, yes," he said, his brows knitting together, his

hands tented on his desk.

"Miranda says someone patched into the electronics of the television to send the message. Nothing paranormal about that," Casey said ruefully, shaking her head. "Not that she's ever found much over the years that can't be logically explained. She's dedicated to exposing the truth."

"But that means someone knew you'd be there and knew how to get to you. I don't like this at all. These could be dangerous people we're dealing with. To lay such a threat out there—it's pretty clear we have to be more careful. I think it's best we just let it go, Casey. I don't want to see you get hurt in any way."

"No way!" She sat up straighter in the chair. "And it's too late for that. I'm not going to let them get away with that kind of crap. I don't scare easily and I don't back down."

"I figured you'd say that," he said with a wan smile. "But I'm going to try to appeal you as a man who cares very much for you. Please, please don't do this. Stay smart, stay safe."

"That sounds like an advertisement for a condom," she quipped. She clamped her mouth shut in horror. "I'm sorry, I didn't mean—"

"So, we can talk about it now? The thing we're pretending's not happening?" he asked.

"No, let's not," she exclaimed, the image too raw. She stood up. "I have to go."

"Casey, please. Promise me one thing. That you won't go back there—to Oak Island—at least not until we figure things out. Until we know who or what we're dealing with."

She shook her head. "I'm sorry, I can't promise you that." She made her escape before he could say anything else, closing the door behind her.

Chapter Sixteen

"Find a place inside where there's joy, and the joy will burn out the pain." *Joseph Campbell*

"For our first class, I've put together an overview presentation. I hope it inspires you to delve into imagining the life of these adventurers as they go about their normal business of discovering how truly awesome our world is — what literally lies beneath our feet, undiscovered until some bold soul decides to investigate." Casey's heart rate sped up as she mentally flashed on Oak Island and the impending dig. Not helping that the class was being observed by Truman when the chancellor had ventured in to speak with him. The two were thick as thieves, whispering together at the back of the theater.

"You can't just dig anywhere you want — right? Not anymore," a student challenged, calling out from the back of the room. The large arena held hundreds of student bodies and today it was packed for Mysteries and Lost Treasures of the World. First day of class always went like that before students starting jostling around to find an easier or more interesting course or professor. Trick was to keep the interest. Hard work. Casey loved the challenge almost as much as treasure hunting.

"No. And you make a good point."

Her positive comment was met with derision as another student shouted out, "Don't encourage him! His head is already big enough."

A few nervous laughs accompanied the words and the chancellor frowned as he looked up to watch how she would handle herself. She took a deep breath, wishing she had the stress ball in her sweaty hands.

"I always encourage student questions. No question is too silly or too complicated or too quirky. If there is any time in life when you can speak freely, this is it. At this bastion of learning. In fact, I insist. If not now, when? Be unafraid and ask away. Catching me after class is also another option." She stressed the important point. More students got into trouble for not asking than anything else. "Getting permission to dig is something I will be delving into in more detail in the days and weeks to come. There are permits and licenses and written permission to have in hand before you dig."

"Wouldn't it just be easier to get in and out by stealth, than be denied access?" another student asked, making a few heads turn.

"No, that can have consequences, as well. Fines and penalties and perhaps worse." Oh, boy, now she was getting into hypocritical territory. Wasn't that what she planned for Oak Island? And how she'd gotten Soapy's Gold?

That reminded her — she had an appointment later tonight with George after the pawn shop closed to dispose of the last of the gold. Smarter to do it one chunk at a time — she didn't trust George any farther than she could throw him. The guy had to weigh close to three hundred and fifty pounds. An image of the man who'd been introduced to her through a friend of a friend, one who had no problem buying black market gold, came to mind. Shiny black hair slicked into a skinny rat ponytail and a love of gaudy jewelry. Three ex-wives kept him in line. She mentally about-faced and brought her mind back to the present and off ex-wives. Her mental lapse seemed to have been noticed by the men observing, making her focus harder. Random thoughts were not a brilliant idea at the moment.

"What could be worse than the authorities taking all the treasure and imposing fines after you went to all the trouble of obtaining it? Kind of greedy," a student asked from his seat nearer the front, his lower lip pushed out with thought.

"Yes, I get where you're coming from. It hurts a lot of adventurers when they go to all the work then the government swoops in and take it all. Says they have to keep it for a year before they can give it back—then never does!" Oops, she'd said too much, even if it was true and had happened to her on one horrendous occasion. She was still waiting for the treasure she'd located early on at the upper end of Pitt Lake—Slumach's Gold—in British Columbia to be returned to her. People shouldn't write books about where the treasure is hidden if they didn't want Casey Madison to find it. Now Truman and the chancellor looked to be arguing. *Focus, Casey.*

"There is a lot of treasure is to be found in dangerous places. Across the border in Mexico, for instance." Casey hadn't been planning to get into this so quickly and wanted badly to backpedal out of it, though it was a subject that deeply interested her. "If you're digging on disputed land, someone could actually shoot at you. People have been killed for less. Remember, we're talking about millions of dollars in gold and silver stashed away in some cases. Always best to get a permit before digging. Okay things with the authorities."

God, she hoped she'd dug herself out of that hole. The real world versus academia—worlds apart. She constantly rode the razor's edge between the two.

That shut everyone up, as some heads nodded sagely and eyes grew larger with concern. A few faces lit up with excitement—adrenaline junkies. They were the ones who needed the course the most to keep them safe. But there was time to fill them in, give them some direction, before the term was complete. *And yeah, just like I used the information to stay safe.* If a person was going to go for it, they'd say fuck it to the risks. She got it—first-hand.

"Okay, let's move on. Here's a recent shot of Oak Island. I toured and took a series of photos just for you."

A few cheers greeted her words as she launched into her

lecture.

The timer rang on her desk, announcing the end of class while she was mid-stride. Timing had never been her strong suit and she needed the reminder to wrap up the lecture. Another frown from the chancellor suggested he was not overly impressed with the crutch. She braced her hands on the lectern, asking the good Lord for strength, as the students filed out.

The chancellor's face hardened as Truman continued speaking, looking like he was trying to make some kind of plea to the old man. Finally, the chancellor strode away and the sound of the theatre door closing behind him echoed loudly in her ears.

"Before you start in, I want to say I don't have time for this." Casey made a pre-emptive strike.

"No time to discuss your overloaded class? And the fact that I just backed up your play with our esteemed chancellor? Got him onboard. Explained with times changing, it was better that students be aware of what truly happens in the real world and that you're just the person to instruct them. That your knowledge is an asset, not a problem. Which is why they flock to your classes. That they recognize the real deal when they find it, just like I do. And here I was thinking to offer you more help, darlin'."

"Oh." She colored. "That's different then. What kind of help?"

"A teaching assistant for marking all the papers you're going to be flooded with, leaving you no time for anything else. I have a list here of potential candidates. Any preferences?"

"How come I rate this treatment? You must have pulled some strings."

"I just made the case that with your extra-large classes it just made sense. Give you time to write all those research papers they're always harping on."

She took the paper and ran down the list with her finger, trying not to look at him and hiding a smile at his self-deprecating joke. The pull of him, the need to be close, to touch him was strong, strong enough to give her butterflies in her stomach. And the fact that he'd backed her with the Chancellor spoke volumes. He didn't have to do that. "Amy Gering would be a great choice, or Samantha Taylor. When do I have to decide by?"

"Today would be best so I can arrange things. Other professors will want help, as well. With impressive numbers like you've been inundated with today, you get first dibs."

"Either would be great. Check with Amy first and if she's too busy, call Sam." She ventured a glance at him, instantly wishing she hadn't. His eyes were shadowed and carrying a burden that bothered her. Damn it, she was not the one responsible. But maybe he wasn't, either. The woman had just showed up out of the blue. Didn't change things, though. The fact was he had a lot to figure out and should be spending his time doing just that. Give him space, much as it hurt. Much as she longed to be held in those strong, incredible arms. No point in daydreaming or wishing for something that couldn't happen.

"I have to go. I have something important to do."

"Please, just give me a moment. I need to explain things."

"No need. Actions speak louder than words, Professor."

"You did a really good job today in class handling all the students," he said, changing tactics.

"Thanks. I enjoy the students."

"It shows."

"I really gotta go!" She turned and he laid a warm hand on her shoulder. She wanted to snuggle up against it but kept herself still.

"I'm sorry. Perhaps I can call you later?"

She turned back around, giving him a level look, her heart beating far too rapidly. "When you've got things settled, yes, call. Until then, keep your distance. Get things figured out." She bit her lower lip. The sadness in his expression. Too much.

She fled.

* * * *

"Yes, it's important to be constantly checking the GPS," Casey said. She loved being in the field with her students. Today was one of her favorite ones—sending her graduate class on a 'treasure hunt'. Whoever put the clues together first and discovered the few grains of gold got to keep them. With gold going for over twelve hundred dollars an ounce, a few specks were all she could afford.

It was an urban treasure hunt through the wilds of downtown Winnipeg. She'd hidden the gold the night before when visiting George at his seedy pawn shop. She chuckled inwardly. If only people knew it was a cover for his far more lucrative black market trade...

Casey's cellphone chirped. She looked around checking. The students were all busy. "Hey, Rebecca, what's up?"

"Oh dear, um, I don't know how to say this—"

"Just spit it out."

"Ah, Hailey Sinclair called."

"What?"

"Yeah, she represents an important publishing house, one I submitted my first manuscript to a few months back, and they want to talk to me about it. Well, specifically, *she* wants to talk to me."

"*Fuck.* Really?" Casey took a deep cleansing breath to get her thoughts in order. She couldn't let down one of her best friends over a man. "Okay. Here's the thing. You have to go and see her. It's your dream come true. Don't let the other stuff going on affect it for you, Rebecca. I couldn't stand it if you lost your chance because of me. No way, girlfriend. Call her back. Set a time. I'm fine with it."

"Are you sure? Really sure?"

"Yes, I'm certain. But I appreciate your telling me first."

"Thanks, Casey, I won't forget this. Catch you later."

"Miss Madison, I was wondering if I could have a word?"

She spun around—she knew that voice.

Damn. She hated being right. Unbelievable timing—she'd

give her that. "Ms. Sinclair," she said, as neutrally as possible given the circumstances. The woman, perfectly groomed today, stood peering down at her from atop her spectacular high heels. How did she manage with such a large object to balance? Casey suddenly felt dowdy, her hair twisted into a braid and a navy-blue hockey cap keeping the sun off her sweaty face.

"I think you and I need to talk."

"A little busy at the moment, if you hadn't noticed."

"Surely, you must take a break. There's a coffee shop on the corner. I'll wait for you there." The woman turned and marched away.

* * * *

Arriving at the Tim Horton's entrance thirty minutes later, after her class finished and all the students had dispersed, Casey took a deep breath and pushed the heavy glass door open. The fragrance of coffee and tasty food assailed her nostrils, making her stomach grumble. She'd skipped breakfast in her hurry to arrive for the field class in time. Well, at least she was in the right place to fix that.

As she stood at the counter waiting to be served, she glanced around and spotted the ex waiting at a corner table, busy on her cell phone, still looking composed and in charge.

She asked the server for a large coffee, three creams and a raisin-studded scone then moved over to the side to wait for her order to be filled. It took all of thirty seconds. She expressed her thanks and carried her food over to the corner table.

She set it down just as the woman looked up. The fake smile plastered on her face — not a good beginning.

"Ah, Casey, how good of you to join me," she said in her lilting southern voice.

"Well, I do believe I was invited."

"Of course. I think we need to have a little talk."

"Hmm — what about? I don't think we have anything in common, quite frankly."

"That's where you're wrong. We have two things in common. Truman and Oak Island."

Casey's hackles rose. The woman wanted a piece of both! Which would cost Casey more, losing Truman or Oak Island? Honestly, losing him forever was impossible to accept. There were other treasures, but only one Truman.

"You know, Truman and I go way back. Our families have been entwined for generations."

"But divorced, right?"

The woman grimaced like she had a bad taste in her mouth. "Yes, unfortunately. But things are looking up in that direction now." She patted her stomach in satisfaction. "And with our son coming in a few weeks, it can only bring us closer. Surely, you can understand that."

Casey bit the inside of her mouth, drawing blood. *A son.* Hailey Sinclair held all the cards. Damned if she'd get all the treasure too. But wasn't it also Truman child's birthright as well? *Fuck. Life can get complicated.*

"So, and I'm only telling you this for your own good, it's time you backed off. Gave Truman and I the space to fix our marriage. Your being in his life right now is not good for him. He needs to focus on more important things. His family. And you should also be aware that the treasure is destined for our family, that you have no right to it. I heard that you've been threatened. I think you should heed those words and get yourself to safer pastures, you know, for your own good." Her eyes flashed darker as she finished her spiel. Was the woman threatening her? Casey bit her lips, considering her answer, the urge to go off half-cocked difficult to fight.

"I think you're taking a lot on yourself. Truman has assured me he's finished with his marriage. That he has no intention of getting back together with you."

The woman's lips thinned, her hatred clear. Casey didn't need a course in understanding human reactions to read

175

that emotion.

"I think you have more to do with that than you realize. You're in the way, Miss Madison. A dangerous place to be." The woman's eyes glittered dangerously.

"Are you threatening me? Because if you are, I assure you, I do not back down."

Her phone rang. With numb fingers she held it up to check the number. *Rebecca.* Any interruption was welcome at this point, what with the conversation going so refreshingly well.

"Casey, thank God! You've got to come home right now! Someone broke into your house. Stole some stuff. They took that valuable manuscript we were working on together to correlate with your research material. I just came by to collect it and found the house in a total mess," Rebecca near shouted over the line.

"You okay? You weren't hurt or anything?" Casey's hand went to her throat.

"No, I'm fine. Just upset. The police are here now. They asked me to call you. You have to come home. Now, Casey. See what's missing."

Casey ended the call and shot to her feet.

"I have to leave. My house has been broken into."

The woman grimaced with distaste at the interruption. *What did Truman see in this woman?*

Casey hurried to her vehicle, threw her stuff into the back and got into the driver's seat, barely managing to remember to buckle up. She careened through the streets. Was Rebecca really okay?

A City of Winnipeg police car was parked in the driveway, lights flashing. She ran to the house, opened the back door that opened onto the kitchen, and, finding no one there, rushed to the living room where voices could be faintly detected.

"And you're certain? That's all that was taken?" A tall policeman, outfitted in Winnipeg Police service gear, stood near the fireplace writing in a small black book, shaking his head. A second policeman, ten years younger and twenty pounds lighter, stood nearby. Casey surveyed the huge mess on the rug, books and papers strewn everywhere. Rebecca sat on the sofa, arms crossed over her chest, paler than usual. The only bit of cheer in the room was Howard and his ornament.

Casey rushed to her side. "Are you okay?"

"Oh, I'm fine. But they got that priceless manuscript," Rebecca said with a hitch in her voice. "The one my uncle lent me. What's he going to say? I didn't keep it safe."

"He's going to say Thank-You-God his favorite niece wasn't hurt, sweetheart." Casey sat down on the sofa and put her arm around Rebecca, hugging her.

"I should have put it in the safe. What was I thinking?" Rebecca lamented.

"It wasn't your fault. How could you know some idiot would break in and steal it? In Winnipeg, of all places. Maybe in New York or London, but our overgrown prairie town? It's crazy!"

"Can you think of anyone who would want that particular manuscript, ma'am?" the taller officer asked respectfully, addressing Casey now.

"No, I'm sorry, I can't think of anyone who would do such a thing." Was Byrne up to his antics again? Hard to imagine — he lived so far away. Or was it somehow connected to Hailey Sinclair? The woman was seriously in their business. No. She was eight months' pregnant, though she what she had said was a definite threat. *Hmm...*

"We did have another incident recently," Rebecca began, her face turning thoughtful, taking Casey away from her pondering.

"Yes?" he prompted.

"At the hotel Fort Garry." Rebecca went on to explain the circumstances. The expressions of the two men shifted as the information became clear. A ghostly warning on a television screen? Sounded like a college prank.

"It seems someone wants you to stay clear of Oak Island," the tall officer said, tucking the notepad into his breast pocket. "Probably good advice, considering the circumstances."

Casey's vision narrowed. *No fucking way.*

The doorbell rang at the back entrance. A prominent sign out front instructed people to use it with care, a legacy of her Aunt Milly. She should change that. She'd meant to for God knows how long.

"I'll get it," Casey said getting up.

She left the room and hurried through the kitchen to the door, not wanting to leave Rebecca alone for long.

She checked through the peephole. *Truman.* She took a deep breath. Opened the door.

"Are you okay? I saw the flashing lights. I was out for a drive," he said. His handsome face was tight with worry.

Tears prickled behind her eyes. Pressing her lips together, she found the strength to answer. Too much going on, that was it. She crossed her arms over her chest and took a step back. His presence was like a force field, sucking her in.

"I'm fine—I wasn't here. Rebecca found the mess. A window was broken in the conservatory. That's where the perp or perps made their way in." God, she was sounding more and more like a P.I.

"Thank goodness no one was hurt. What was taken?" he asked. He stayed standing on the step, likely noting her stiff body language. Far too polite to ask to come in. The sunlight shone on his golden hair, giving him an undeserved halo.

"It's odd—just one important thing really."

"One thing?" His expression shifted to incredulousness. "They must have been interrupted."

"No. They made a hell of a mess. They took a valuable manuscript and some research papers."

"Really? That is odd." He took an involuntary step forward. His fragrance wafted in the air, a tantalizing mix of pheromones and clean male sweat. She took a steadying breath. His presence always helped. She missed that. A few days of pure bliss. Eons ago.

"Yes." She pressed her lips tight together. She shouldn't have made such a big deal of it. He didn't know how much Rebecca had found out in her search. How much they'd been hiding from him.

"What was in this manuscript?"

"Stuff about Oak Island." She didn't want to elaborate, but he did need to know about the new danger. Just last night the bizarre warning, now this. Huge red flags.

"How did you find out about the break-in so soon?" she asked.

"'You always have a green light that burns all night at the end of your dock'," he quoted.

Confused, she stayed silent. He caught the quizzical expression.

"*The Great Gatsby*. I can't believe I'm admitting this, but I can't look across the river without experiencing the intense longing to be on your side of the ocean, holding you," he said. His expression softened and his blue eyes darkened. His speaking from his heart made hers sink into her boots. God, he wasn't making this easy. "And I drove by today just to reassure myself you're okay. I had a sense you might need me — not sure why."

"F. Scott Fitzgerald. The Assiniboine River is hardly an ocean," she murmured, suddenly giddy from a hot sensation that seared her veins as the words hit home. God, he was good, comparing their love story to Jay Gatsby's longing for Daisy Buchanan's undying love. A classic tale, unfortunately also representing the death of the American Dream. Her breath hitched as her mind woke. Life and love. Far too precious not to treasure and honor every minute of the day. *Oh, the tangled web we weave...* "Where are my manners? Please, come in."

He stepped over the threshold.

Chapter Seventeen

"Ever has it been that love knows not its own depth until the hour of separation." *Kahlil Gibran*

"Casey?" Rebecca called out, her voice somehow managing to register past the din in Casey's head. The sound kept her from throwing herself at Truman. Damn, he was unlike any man she could imagine being with. Articulate, intelligent, exciting and romantic. A lethal combination. She needed rescuing in the worst way.

Other voices broke through as the officers came into the kitchen. Rebecca was escorting them to the door, the interview over.

"Well, if you think of anything else, ma'am, give us a call," the taller officer said, handing her a business card. The keys jingled on his thick black belt as he stopped for a moment at the door to answer his radio that was giving loud static barks on his shoulder. He pushed a button and returned a code. Their official presence sent a shiver down Casey's spine.

The second officer gave Truman a speculative look before exiting, right on his partner's heels.

"Why do I always feel like the guilty party?" Casey asked, giving a rueful shake of her head.

"Simple psychology. We all have something to hide," Truman said, sharing a half-smile.

"We do, do we?" she teased.

"Yes, we do." He looked into her eyes. "But I would like to live in a world where it's not necessary. Where we're accepted for who we are and taken at our word."

"Casey, where did you find this guy?" Rebecca asked. A quick glance her way showed that she remained more intrigued than upset by his presence. So, she liked Truman.

"Okay, let me help with the cleanup."

"No, that's not necessary."

"Yes, it is. Just show me what needs doing." His body language suggested he wasn't going anywhere soon.

Her heart gave a little leap of joy. Relieved also that the twins weren't there. *I so don't need their superpowers for sleuthing out what people are thinking. That pair could spot lovers at fifty paces.* They'd both studied the art of universal micro-expression to get at the truth. A valuable ability in their investigations — not so valuable to anyone with something to hide. According to them, the human face showed genuine emotions from one-fifteenth to one-twenty-fifth of a second, regardless of race or culture. As if they weren't in her business enough. A side effect was that making any one of the seven expressions also gave you that exact same feeling, so now she was leaning towards unhappy on the meter. *Just great.*

She pushed the On button for the state-of-the-art sound system in the living room and the upbeat lyrics of *I Walk the Line* flooded the space. Perfect. Johnny Cash and his vow of staying true. *Karma's a bitch.*

Truman pursed his lips but didn't comment on the tune, though he gave a low whistle as he surveyed the jumbled, tangled mess spread over the forty-by-thirty-foot space. He glanced over at the fireplace. A small grin played over the edges of his mouth.

"Lucky moose," he commented.

"Yeah, Howard gets his fair share."

"I'll bet." Truman chuckled. "Yours?" he asked.

"Why, Professor Truman. A lady never kisses and tells."

"We got a hell of a lot of work to do," Rebecca said with a sigh, looking around in dismay.

"Wait. You said the perpetrator broke in through a conservatory window," Truman said.

"Yeah. So?"

"Anyone fixed that yet? Nailed something over it until you can get a glass cut?"

"I'll get right on it," Casey said.

"I got it. You help your friend and I'll take care of it."

"If you're sure—"

"No worries, darlin'." He gave her that kind of look, quickening her breath. "Just show me where it is and I'm on it."

"Okay. Be right back," she said to Rebecca and led the way to the conservatory.

"Damn. There's glass on the tile near the hot tub." Casey surveyed the damage, wanting it fixed right away. Thank goodness it was just the one window. So much fun stuff had happened in this room. Some of which she'd take to her grave.

"Do you have tools? A hammer and nails? Any plywood?"

"Tools, yeah. No plywood, I'm afraid." She shook her head.

"I'll go to the hardware store right now." He checked his watch. "Be back shortly."

"Uh, thanks, Truman. I appreciate this," she began.

"Just so you know, I'm not leaving you alone in this house tonight," he said pointedly.

"I'll be fine." Her heart gave that strange little leap again. "Don't worry about me. I've got the Ringers."

"That's good. But I'm still camping out on the couch right over there." He pointed at the day bed in the corner of the conservatory. "No objections."

He came closer and before she could react, he leaned in for a kiss, planting one on her lips. She enjoyed it. Far too much. "Be back as quick as I can. And just for the record, if you were mine—I'd walk the line."

She watched him leave, thrilling at the reference. Him not being afraid to sound corny only added to his allure. Though she'd never admit it, having him around did make her feel a whole lot safer. She went back to the living room to help.

"Where's Truman?" Rebecca asked, glancing up from the floor.

"Gone to get plywood."

"Nice. I like a guy who can go to the hardware store, a guy who can tackle an entire department at the university, a guy with the balls to hunt for treasure and look as yummy as Truman does. And with a sense of humor. Hell of a find, if you ask me. If you don't want him, I'll throw my hat in the ring," Rebecca said, surprising Casey as she gathered up the textbooks and papers strewn around the floor.

"Sorry, you're not his type. He prefers a woman who rescues wildlife like old Howard here and digs in dirty caves and enjoys poking around islands looking for buried treasure. You know, just your average girl-next-door type."

"Yeah, you're about as average as they come, eh. Being a romance writer certainly can't trump adventuress, to a guy, I guess. But, speaking of poking around islands, what's to be done about our current project? Things have escalated. I'm think we should abort. These people—they're dangerous. We don't know who they are, but they know who we are, and they don't want us tampering with Oak Island. They've made that abundantly clear."

"And let them win?" Casey stood her ground.

"What good is winning if you're dead?" Rebecca asked pointedly.

She had a small point.

* * * *

Truman hefted the third piece of three-quarter inch plywood onto the low-rider cart supplied by the store, leaning it up against the metal bracing bar to keep it stable. The sharp odor of spruce assaulted his nostrils, a comforting smell he enjoyed as it meant a project and the pleasure of building or fixing something. He was wheeling the load toward the check-out till when his cell phone dinged. His spirits sank as he saw the name of the sender of the text. Hailey.

Where are u?

He delayed answering while the clerk dealt with his purchases and he could quickly vacate the busy store. Did Canadians always buy so much lumber in the late morning? What a country. The best part of Canada? It had produced a woman like no other. The amazingly badass Casey Madison. A vision of her, hands on hips with a huge grin pasted across her beautiful face and teasing him about something or other, entered his mind while he pushed his cart across the paved parking lot. He let out a huge sigh. Finished piling the lumber into the back of his SUV. He could put it off no longer. He dialed Hailey's number. She'd been stalking him lately—no other word for it. He'd tried ending this in every conversation they had and it had gotten him exactly nowhere. He was beginning to wonder about her sanity. She answered on the first ring.

"Are you all right?" she asked, her voice rushing over the phone like an avalanche of just-too-much. Every time they talked, he started from square one again. *Lord, give me the patience.*

"I'm fine. I'm busy helping out a friend at the moment. Then I'm going to be standing guard tonight to make sure everyone stays safe. There's been a break-in at her home and I'm partially to blame for an expedition that has put her at risk."

"Is this about that girl? The one from the university? The one who was on Oak Island with you?" Hailey's voice grew more strained with each passing word.

"Yes. And don't expect me back tonight. Are you leaving in the morning? If so, I'll say my goodbyes now in case I don't see you again," he said, hinting as broadly as possible.

Dead silence.

"I had hoped to spend time with you. Mend some fences."

"Hailey, it's much, much too late for that as I've explained numerous times over the past few days. I can stay civil but you and I ever being friends again? It's not going to happen. I'm sorry, that's just the way it is." He would not go into how devastated he was when she'd played him, running around behind his back with a slew of lovers, making a trusting fool of him. How hard it had been to dig himself out of the black hole of depression that had descended. Just about broken him. No. Silence was best. No more blame. He wanted to move on. Embrace a chance at a new life with a wonderfully warm woman who made his heart glad just to be alive.

"Of course, if the child proves to be mine, I will help out all I can. But my life has gone in a new direction," he said, stepping as carefully around the minefield as possible.

"*If* the child is yours?" Outrage burned across the wire and he pulled the phone back a bit from his ear, wincing. "This child *is* yours, Truman. I'm one hundred percent certain."

"Fine. And I have promised to help, financially and otherwise once it's scientifically proven. But I cannot be with its mother. That's just not going to happen. I don't think I can say that any clearer."

"Fine. Call me a liar. Let your family down. Your parents are going to be so disappointed. They're excited about having a grandchild."

"*You told them?*" Now, it was his turn to be outraged. This was the last thing he needed. Pressure from his family. They would be happy about it—too happy and perhaps forget how manipulative and untrustworthy his ex could be. He was becoming more and more certain that the child wasn't his. A gut feeling, really. A sense that something wasn't adding up.

"Of course, I told them! They have a right to know."

"I have to go. I have a window to repair." He looked across the parking lot at a young couple carrying a couple of plants. Even from this distance he could see how happy they were as they talked and laughed together. They stopped at an old red half-ton and he helped her in, handed her the plants to hold on her lap, carefully closing the door for her as if she were his most precious cargo in the world. Simple things. And finding pleasure from just being together. How he wanted that. He'd found it with Casey. He was certain. The knowledge gave him strength.

"Don't make me beg, Truman."

"Please. Don't start. It's over. Truly over. I'm sorry. It can't be fixed, Hailey — it's beyond repair." The words had to be said. Again and again until they sank in, however long it took.

"I'm not just going away. I'm the mother of your child."

He sighed. "I'll be in touch through my lawyer once you're back home. Best I can do."

"You fucking bastard!" she screamed.

He hung up. Took a deep breath. Walked around to the front of the SUV, opened the door and slid onto the driver's seat, then started the vehicle. Things needed to be done. Anything to keep his mind and hands busy. And his heart safe.

* * * *

"Hailey Sinclair's hiding something. Trust me, I can tell," Lacey's voice came over the speaker phone loud and clear as Casey rejoined Rebecca. "I just haven't figured it out what it is that might affect Casey."

"I think we should continue to monitor her," Lily added.

Rebecca looked up from her cell phone, confessing, "I asked them to put my meeting with her under surveillance."

Casey nodded. *Of course. How else can we keep an eye out for one another?*

"I could call your uncle," she offered, giving Rebecca a quick glance. *Note to self: Get the best alarm system money can buy. ASAP.* "It happened under my roof."

"Nah, I can handle it." She sighed. "I guess I'd better make the call," Rebecca said but didn't move. Her expression changed on a dime.

"What?" Casey prompted her.

"In all the excitement I forgot to tell you the good news. I had a breakfast meeting today, just before the robbery."

"And…"

"I need a drumroll!"

"Really, you signed!"

"Sweet! Congrats! You so deserve it!" came from the twins.

Rebecca nodded. "Yes, it's a great opportunity. But—"

"No buts. It's all going to work out just fine."

"I've got to call my uncle now. At least there's some good news to share."

The phone call ended, goodbyes said, Rebecca hurried away and Casey hefted the garbage bag from the floor, heading to the kitchen. She opened the back door and looked around. *No sign of Truman yet.* She placed the bag into a can and closed the lid. She stood still for a moment on the patio stones, enjoying the fresh breeze coming across the river from the northeast, letting it cool her over-heated skin, her eyes closed. The hum of a motor vehicle coming closer alerted her to company. She opened her eyes to the welcome sight of Truman backing up the SUV to the conservatory's broken window in preparation for unloading the plywood.

She waved. When he noticed her, he gave a quick wave in return accompanied by a wide smile. Her heart jumped. She hurried over to help him.

"Hey, darlin'," he said as he came around the vehicle to open the back hatch, all manly and in charge. The sight of him made her want to steal a kiss. Even her toes wiggled in anticipation. Without thinking, she rose to her tiptoes and planted one on his warm mouth. "What's this about?" he asked when she slipped away, obviously surprised by her actions.

"To thank you for doing all this," she said, managing by

the skin of her teeth to resist stealing more kisses.

"No problem. I also want to make an inspection right away. You've probably let security lapse you've been so busy," he said as he pulled her back in for a second kiss.

"Okay, buster, you got to earn the rest," she teased, dancing out of reach of his arms. She swallowed hard. Being so close to him and his animal magnetism, her body kept begging for more. Lots more.

"Piece of cake, darlin'. I'd cross the desert bare for you."

"Ah, Truman, there's something I should tell you."

"Just spit it out."

"Rebecca was offered a book contract with your ex."

She got a glimpse of pain in his expression before he pulled himself together. "I'm going to fix your window, we're taking the day off, then I'm bunking out on your couch. That's my plan and I'm sticking to it. No talk of anything else. Okay?"

"Sure." She liked a good plan. Especially one that just got on with things.

"Okay, grab that end and we'll lean it up against the wall," Truman said, taking the decision out of her hands and gesturing at the plywood. She helped him and together they handled the wood with ease, lining it up on the ground by the broken window. The conservatory windows were huge, a foot from the floor to nearly the top of the first story. Fortunately, they were spaced a foot apart to allow one to be covered and not damage the others.

"I'll get the ladder," she offered. She loved it when things were going smoothly between them. He filled up something she hadn't known was missing in her life. Adding an exciting element that going after a shared treasure intensified. *Fuck. Did I really just think that?*

She sped up her pace, face hot, hurrying over to the garage at the back of the property to retrieve the supplies. Rummaging around in the dimness, acutely aware of a musty odor that suggested the garage needed a thorough airing, she gathered what she needed and hurried back to help. *So not going to think about anything but getting the job done.* Truman stepped forward to help with the ladder.

"You thirsty?" she asked after they'd been working for a while and were nearly finished.

"Yes, thanks, a beer would be great. I'll replace it later," Truman said

She felt him staring at her as she turned to go retrieve the beer. At least her ass looked good in these jeans.

She walked to the refrigerator to check for beer. She dug out two, placed them on the counter and popped the lids, draining half of one in short order. Lifting ladders was thirsty work. Hell, Truman was even thirstier work. She dialed the twins, an urge to talk to a fellow Ringer overcoming her.

"Casey, hey, back so soon? Is Rebecca okay?" Lily asked.

"She'd fine. Do you think people can change, Lily — really change?"

"Hmm. I think so. If the reward's high enough."

Casey stood, contemplating her life. "You know how high I scored on the Risks Attitude Profiler. Through the roof. I need my freedom and my space to live my life as I see fit. This shit — so not me."

"So, you'd give up him? Just like that?" Lily asked. They both knew who she was talking about.

"That's not what I'm saying —"

"Sounds like it to me. Let me ask you something now?"

"Shoot." Casey started in on the second beer. Looked like it wouldn't be her night to go on a beer run.

"What's the worst thing that can happen if you hook up with Truman?"

"Oh, boy, good one." She drank another swig of liquid courage, gathering her thoughts. "Okay, being the wicked stepmother and always being on the defensive with the ex. She's not easy. And other stuff, I guess. Like, what do I know about being a parent? I'd have to change a lot. Learn a lot. Take parenting lessons. Maybe even try to be more careful on digs. It's scary shit. And yet I know Truman will step up and do the right thing, and he's an adventurer first and foremost. Someone he'd manage. He's got the stuff. Do I? Maybe…"

"Okay. Imagine your life without Truman."

"Not fair." Casey grimaced. A bleak scenario, it sucked even worse. Maybe she was changing? "Do you think the ex had anything to do with the break-in? She's got more at stake than that Byrne guy plaguing us on the island. She could have help. Maybe even more Sinclairs hiding in the woodwork? The coincidences today alone stink. Rebecca at a meeting with her, then she comes by my work place, holds me up, and Rebecca accidently ends up discovering the break in when she comes by for the book. Which has gone missing." Casey spoke bluntly. The terrible suspicion that she was on the right track ate at her mind. If she were right, how was Truman going to take it? The mother of his child involved in criminal activity? She suddenly realized he was under more duress than she was. Needed her help.

"Maybe. We're looking into it. If she was involved, we'll be getting Rebecca's uncle's manuscript back, come hell or high water. Hailey's been evasive in the short time I've been observing her, possibly deceitful from the readings we've been getting. I'd need to interrogate her closer to get at the real truth, and unfortunately, that's kind of difficult."

Neither of them spoke the worry aloud. Would it affect Rebecca's future with the publishing house? If they were a good company to work for, it shouldn't.

Lacey came on the line. "Let's switch to FaceTime. I've got some stuff on Ms. Sinclair you should look at, Casey. Rebecca was smart to ask us to put the meeting under surveillance today. This is the whole file we now have on her. With the robbery and all, I completely forgot about it."

Casey set down the beer, fired up her laptop and concentrated on the screen.

"It's her micro-expressions that concern me most. She's hiding something without a doubt. Our video camera captured it very well. Even got some interesting close-up shots of her phone. I've put in several still photos along with some photos taken a couple of weeks back when she was on a film set with an author she's representing. Hey, maybe Rebecca will get a movie deal too."

"Yeah, maybe. Just before the robbery today she met me to warn me to stay away from Truman. And she didn't mince any words," Casey said.

She studied the file and photos on file share Lacey sent. *Hmm.* Something just wasn't quite right. She starred at an earlier photo a tad blurry from the movie set, then back at the one from today in the meeting with Rebecca, comparing them. *Oh. My. God.*

Casey was beyond stunned. Almost unable to take in what she was seeing her with her own two eyes. *Is this for real?*

"What? What is it?" Lacey demanded.

"I've got the goods on Ms. Hailey Sinclair! You're not going to fuckin' believe this! Look at these time-stamped photos from ten days ago and compare it to today's. The woman's guilty as sin."

Chapter Eighteen

"Happiness can exist only in acceptance." *George Orwell*

Truman had finished and was speaking on his cell phone by the time she stomped out to the yard, her laptop in hand. A terrible suspicion entered her mind. Maybe he was just using her? Romancing her to learn all she knew? He knew she'd been studying and researching Oak Island for a decade. She had more field experience. Who better to use? Were they in collusion? Was she even his ex? *No, please God, don't make it the case.* She'd lose her faith in humanity.

"Hey, darlin'," he said, turning to greet her. God, he looked good. Unlike his disastrous, betraying, devious, nefarious, pain-in-the-ass ex. She couldn't come up with any more adjectives at the moment, but give her time.

"Everything okay, Casey?" Truman asked, looking at her more carefully, his beautiful, blue and oh-too-trusting-eyes narrowing.

You could have warned me your ex was Looney Tunes.

"No, it's absolutely not okay!"

"Why? What's wrong?" Truman asked in alarm.

Casey licked her dry lips, watching Truman freeze in his tracks. He was a vigorous man, a virile man and a man with enough baggage to choke a fuckin' horse.

"Tell me!" Truman demanded, his brows knitting into a frown.

"Did you know? Were you in on it?"

"In on what? You're not making any sense here."

"Take a lot at these." She opened her laptop and brought up the incriminating photos side-by-side. Set her computer on the hood of the SUV. Stabbed her finger at the screen. "In this one your ex is at a movie set in Toronto."

"Movie set?" Truman asked, mystified.

"Yeah, taken about ten days ago. Posted on an author's Facebook page. She's the agent for the writer who's having their book made into a movie. It's blurry, but look closely. Now compare it to the one taken today at the breakfast meeting with Rebecca at the Fort Garry."

"Fort Garry?"

"Yeah, Rebecca had a breakfast meeting with her and she had the twins videotape it."

Truman's mouth tightened. "You had Hailey under surveillance?" he accused.

"Damn good thing we did. Take a good long look."

"What? What am I looking for?" he asked, obviously confused.

"Look more closely. Damn it, can't you see it?"

"Two photos of my ex. So what?"

"Look at what it reveals. *The woman had no baby bump on the movie set.* The pregnancy is a hoax. It's fake. She's playing you. Are you playing me? Did you set me up?"

"*Hailey's not pregnant?*"

No one could fake that much shock. Was she wrong? She had no proof he was involved. Just a terrible suspicion. The thought reverberated around her brain, each pinging doing more and more damage.

"You think I'm in on it?" Nor fake the look of complete horror that dawned on his face as realization hit.

She crossed her arms over her chest. She'd cut him to the core. She trembled with emotion, a panicked sensation growing within her. She pressed her lips tightly together. *What a fucking mess.*

"How could you say that? Think that? After all we've been through…" He gave her a bewildered look, searching her eyes for answers.

She needed to explain further. "There's another guy in the first photo, as well—taken on the movie set. He looks a lot like a man from the Fort Garry hotel I chased down the hallway. Then today, the twins taped her while she met with Rebecca this morning to discuss her book and she was obviously hiding something. She made a lot of texts from the restaurant, one to her father, according to Lacey, who got a screenshot of her phone a few times and enlarged them. Technology these days means you can't hide stuff like this for long. She even made a joke about fooling everyone. I think the joke meant her pretending the pregnancy. She wants you back that badly. She's that desperate — that sick."

"No, that's not it." His face hollowed out, staring into the distance. "She's always wanted the treasure. Sees it as her birthright." Then he U-turned back to the worst part. "You think I'm in on this? That I could do that to you — to us? After all we shared on the island — do you really believe that? Because if you do, there can never be an us. I think you'd better go inside before I say something I'll regret." He crossed his arms over his chest, his expression bleak and grey.

"Truman? I'm sorry, I had to ask. I had to get at the truth." She felt things slipping away from her, a huge rent in the cosmos opening at her feet. She couldn't tumble in, she just couldn't. Why was getting at the truth so costly?

"The truth? The truth is you're frightened of having more than two dates with a man. The truth is you're more worried about having your precious freedom curtailed that you'd go to any lengths to find something wrong with the man. *You are not your mother.* You would never sit on a sofa and pine for things you think you've lost out on. You're a strong woman who will walk this earth the way you see fit all your life. No man can take that from you. You'd never let him. And to think I thought we had something special. Something we could build on. No, best to end it now if you think so poorly of me. Just go inside the house, Casey. Leave me alone. We're through. I'm sorry."

The words stunned her. Angered her. He had no right to bring up her mother. She'd told him that in confidence. *I've gone too far – way too far. I've totally fucked this up.* His cold expression stuck a knife through her heart when their eyes locked for a split-second.

She stumbled away, disoriented as her world imploded, her feet disconnected from her brain.

Her footsteps led her down to the river.

She just couldn't face anyone right now. She sat on the edge of the dock, watching the lapping waves of water caress the pilings under the edge. Was Truman right? Was she running so hard to keep from losing her freedom because of what had happened to her mother that she had lost sight of the possibility of love entering her life? From all she knew of Truman, he had never once asked her to stop what she was doing. Just asked for her to do things safely. He'd never keep her from her love of adventure. Hell, he'd go with her. He even accepted her friends readily, her way of living. Perhaps she clung to the Ringers too tightly. She wasn't maturing. Wasn't growing. He saw all her defects and accepted her, anyway. She shook her head. She'd been a fool. He was so much fun to be with, so god damned interesting. As alive and ready for adventure as her. And to think she'd once thought of him as just an unemotional suit. He was a far cry from a suit. He was the real deal. *Oh, God, why didn't I see this in time?*

She swiped the falling tears away. She should have realized that he would *never* do such a thing. She could see his goodness, it shone out from his very pores – how could she have asked such a thing? How to fix this? Was it even possible? She swallowed hard. Truman was worth fighting for. She saw that now. How could she have doubted him? She racked her brain for a solution. She knew what she had to do. Something that would make up for doubting him. Even if he wouldn't listen, she'd do it anyway. At least she could ease some of the pain she'd caused.

Truman swallowed hard. He needed to get this over with. He'd not let himself think about anything else. Betrayal cut too close to the bone. The hurt too fresh.

She answered on the second ring. "Hello."

"Mom," he said, his throat tightening at the sound of her comforting voice. "How are you?" He closed his eyes, envisioning the huge country kitchen with the phone on the wall. His parents were old-school about such things. It only endeared them even more to him now that he was older.

"I'm fine, Truman. How lovely of you to call, dear. How's are things going? Settling in okay?"

She didn't know. He was fairly certain. No inflection of hiding anything in her tone. He let out a deep breath of relief.

"Yes, it's all good. How's Dad?"

"Fine. Busy with his newest hobby. Collecting more junk. I swear that man is going to be the death of me yet. Why couldn't he just take up golf?" She sighed.

"What's it this time?" Truman asked. His father had recently retired and had a lot of time on his hands.

"Drones. He's out there day and night. I'm afraid of what the neighbors will do. I'm expecting pitchforks and torches any day now."

"He always was his own guy. Mom, have you heard anything from Hailey?"

"No. Why?"

"No reason really. Just ran into her the other day and she gave the impression she'd recently been talking with you."

"Strange. No, we haven't heard from her in months. Did she come to Winnipeg to visit you?"

"She was just passing through. But if she does contact you, please let me know. She was acting a little strangely."

"Hailey always was a little strange in my opinion, Truman. I can say that now because you two are divorced and it's a mother's right."

"Too true. Got to go, Mom, love to you and Dad."

He stood and held the phone clenched in his hand, debating. Debating and deciding.

"Everything okay?" Truman asked as he joined her, sitting beside her on the dock. She looked up at him, swallowing hard. She could hardly believe he was there. A golden mirage. She rushed to speak, her words falling all over each other.

"I have to explain. I'm so sorry about doubting you. You can have it all. She can have it all. I don't care about the treasure any more. You were the treasure all along, Truman. I've been such a fool. Please, give me another chance. I can do this. Please, just one more chance, I beg of you."

She let out a deep breath. Gave him a steady look, noting his serious expression. She needed so badly to regain his regard.

"You'd do that?" He turned to look her straight in the eyes, astonishment covering up his recent shock and anger. He looked pale. He'd been through as much as she had. More. She'd questioned his integrity.

"Yes, it's the right thing to do." She said aloud what she'd been thinking anyway. "Plus, if a woman will go to this much trouble to get what she wants, I don't want to take a chance on crossing her. Do you?"

Truman's eyes softened a bit though he still looked wary, choosing to remain silent. A better life hung in the balance. She had to convince him to give her a second chance. Prayed for the time to do it.

"I won't pretend that what you said didn't hurt, it did, very much. But I also know things had conspired to make it all look bad. I could see how someone could jump to that conclusion."

"I am sorry, Truman, for ever doubting you. I was so wrong. Please, tell me how I can make it up to you? I'm working on changing. I get that my thinking was a bit muddled about male and female relationships. I'm probably the one who could use that manual you talked about. I see—"

He looked at her, his blue eyes softening. He leaned over and interrupted her meandering tirade, kissing her long and hard, his lips parting hers and his tongue thrusting inside her willing mouth, making her hungry for more. Much more. The promise of something lay just ahead of them, unencumbered by the past.

Her breath quickened, her arms moving of their own volition, embracing him. He nuzzled her neck. "I was thinking we should spend some time getting to know each other better."

"I'd like that. How about we go inside?" she invited him in a whisper.

Truman helped her up, his arm sheltering her as they headed to the back door.

The kitchen was quiet with everyone gone home.

"Come." She led him up the back staircase and to her bedroom. She opened the door, inviting him inside.

"Are you sure, Casey?" His blue eyes darkened.

She nodded. "More than sure. I want to be close to you. Feel you inside me. I've waited so long already. I can't wait any longer. I need this so much."

Nothing stood between them but fresh air. He reached out and tugged her closer.

"You smell so good," he murmured in her ear, running his tongue lightly along the rim, then kissed the side of her neck. Casey trembled. His warm breath caressed her skin. Seared it. A quick intake of her own breath. She felt his restraint slipping away, joining hers in a heap of baggage on the floor.

She eased up on her toes to bring her mouth within millimeters of his. "We got all night, handsome." She kissed him, hard, on the mouth.

He groaned. Crushed her body against his. "I want you so much. I've been dreaming of being with you for what seems like forever."

His hands swept down her back, touching her, exploring her curves, pulling her closer. He tugged her shirt free of her jeans, caressing the soft skin of her belly. Her blood fired. Her breath quickened.

"I'm not very experienced at this kind of thing, Truman,"

she murmured.

"We've got all night, darlin'. I'll be gentle."

"Not too gentle…"

He stopped for a second to pull her shirt over her head. Her bra came away almost of its own accord. Her nipples pebbled in the cool air before he took them in his hands, tugging on them. She arched her back, her body throbbing, wanting more. So right.

"Yes," she whispered as he sucked long and hard on one nipple then the other, his talented tongue driving her to distraction, the pressure increasing her need for him tenfold.

Her womb tightened, pulsating with acute desire. She wanted this man like she'd never wanted a man before.

He picked her up and carried her to her queen-size bed, pulled back the covers. Laid her down, pulling off her shoes.

"Are you absolutely sure, Casey?" he asked. The expression in his eyes begged her not to stop it. To let them become one.

"I'm not into playing games."

His face took on a new intensity. Passion flared in his eyes. She reached down to help him slip off her jeans. He made quick work of his own clothes and in a few seconds stood naked and fully erect in the soft bedroom light. She pushed her panties down her legs and tossed them on the floor, embracing him as he lay down alongside her. His hot flesh seared her own as they pressed against each other on the bed, caressing, exploring.

He nuzzled her neck and undid her braid, picking up a thick strand and bringing it to rub along his cheek. He smiled.

"So soft and fine, just like you,"

Her hands tangled in his hair as she brought him closer, kissing his face all over, discovering the curves and valleys. The slight day's beard only added to the pleasurable sensations and she murmured soft words of passion, progressing down his neck to his broad chest. A light furring of golden chest hair made her nuzzle him, bringing a smile to her lips.

"Just the perfect amount," she declared and grabbed a handful, tugging gently. She grasped him with both her hands. He reacted with an involuntary thrust of his thighs toward her.

"So fine yourself," she murmured.

He groaned. "You're killing me here," he said, pushing her hair back from her face so he could look into her eyes. Seared her soul with the longing and unspoken love clear in their depths. An unbroken bond just waiting for connection.

"Come here, woman," he said. "I need you now." He got up and retrieved his pants, pulling a condom from a pocket of his jeans. He came back to her. "Ready?" he asked.

"Oh, yes. Beyond ready."

He lay down with her, positioning himself between her wide-spread thighs. He grasped her hips firmly and slid inside her an inch, testing, showing great restraint. Too slow. She wiggled her hips, urging him to plunge deeper.

"Please me, Truman, no more teasing. I'm ready," she urged. And in one steady thrust he fulfilled the promise, driving himself deep inside. Perfect fit. Her world changed at that moment. Deepened. Opened. Widened.

She moaned. Pushed up against him, encouraging him, drumming her heels against his tight ass.

"Oh. God. It's so good. Don't stop!" she demanded hoarsely, short of breath, her passion growing. He obliged, speeding up his rhythm, the sounds of their primal lovemaking filling her ears. The very air hummed with urgency. With out-of-control lust. Perspiration broke out all over her body. He was perfect, filling her up, making her crazy. He pushed inside her warmth, thrust himself into her core, the deepest part of her, over and over. She needed him. Beyond all reason. She screamed her release quite suddenly, came in a blinding rush of light and heat that rippled out from every cell in her body. Bone. Melting. Oblivion. Her heartbeat hammered against her ribs as she tried to draw a full breath. He groaned, gave a final thrust.

"Are you okay?" he asked, pushing the damp hair back from her face. "I didn't hurt you or anything? I'm sorry I was so rough, so needy. It's made me crazy these past days, seeing you, smelling you and not being able to touch you."

"Oh. God. Yes. That was amazing. Beyond anything I could have imagined. And to think I almost lost you," she said as she snuggled along his body, her thigh over his, his arms holding her close. That scared her most of all. More than the threat still out there somewhere waiting for them. She pushed the worry aside. Tonight was about them. Only about them.

Noises in the house a few hours later alerted Casey to company.

"Hungry?" she asked Truman as he lay spent yet again, spooning her close from behind. He reached around to tug at a nipple and she lay her hand over his as he said, "Give me five and I will be, my insatiable beauty."

"I meant for food!"

"Excellent idea. Give me the strength for more amazing exploits." He nuzzled her neck sending tantalizing goosebumps down her spine. Hmm.

"Well, we could go one more round first..."

"Not that I couldn't go another ten rounds. But feed me first, darlin', and you'll not be sorry," he teased, swatting her lightly on the ass and getting out of bed. "I haven't eaten all day."

They dressed and walked hand-in-hand into the kitchen to find two pizza boxes laid out on the large kitchen table and a case of beer opened on the granite counter. *The Ringers have struck and gone.* Casey had no time to ponder what that meant, that her girlfriends hadn't stuck around, hadn't made a fun evening of it, not when the heavenly fragrance of dough and cheese made her mouth water. One need was satiated for the moment—time to indulge the other.

Casey took two plates and opened the pizza boxes. "Vegetarian or meat?" she asked.

"Meat will do just fine." Truman popped the tops off two beers and took a very long swig. "I think I was down a pint of liquid."

"I would imagine that's entirely possible." She grinned at him. "I have been keeping you very, very busy, handsome."

"Handsome, huh? I guess I could live with that. Or stud or cock master or—"

"*So* not going to happen!"

He set the beer down to pull her into his arms. "You have the most amazing laugh. I'm going to work at hearing that sound a lot."

She melted into him, the heat from his body stirring the very depths of her soul.

"Food. I thought you needed food," she teased as he began roaming his hands again. She danced away out of his reach, retrieving the plates of pizza from the counter.

They sat down and ate. Finally, Casey sat back and rubbed her stomach. "I'm stuffed. So, tell me, handsome, what's your favorite tale you'd like to swap for a story of mine?"

"Hmm, another quid pro quo… Ladies first."

"Sure. Let's see, yes, I have just the one for you. History first. Location—Bali, Indonesia, 1459 A.D. Princess Kuta's praying at the altar in the Sakenan Temple for the opportunity to see her true love's face in a special magical bowl designed to show the truth and the future. And to achieve the state of bliss necessary for the gods to answer her prayers, she must show her humility by first being on her knees—"

"Hmm, I'd love to see you on your knees," he interrupted.

She swatted him on one iron-like bicep. "In your dreams, handsome."

"A guy can dream. Besides, darlin', these are early days. Just sayin'. Go ahead. I promise not to interrupt if you don't send me any more of those erotic mind images."

"Men! Okay, we cut to present day and I'm trying to beat a rival to the relic. A Chinese team had a real interest and I didn't want it to fall into their hands as they were going to sell it to a private collector. I wanted this find for the university's museum for everyone to share in."

"Nice."

"I had to go in at night because the temple itself was guarded, though that wasn't where the bowl had been hidden back in the thirteenth century."

He shook his head slowly back and forth. "And I'm wondering if they were armed guards, Casey?"

"Ah — yeah, so, it's not like I couldn't *time* their regimented guard shifts. I hit the place between sentry duties and was confounded by three statues. Normally, you'd only find one."

He nodded in agreement.

"But I knew that the one facing the Holy Mountain would be the correct one, because of a stone tablet I'd unearthed earlier at the official tomb of the princess. The thing nearly fell on my head when I discovered it attached to the underside of her crypt. But it didn't, I'm here safe and sound as you can see, so don't get yourself all riled up."

"Okay." He took a deep breath. "And where exactly did the eyes point?"

She saw the exact second his interest flared to full throttle, pizza forgotten. She had him in the palm of her hand now.

"The statue's eyes stared at an old grated door that led down a stone staircase. I knew I'd have to be careful — this kind of thing is almost always booby trapped — just like the Oak Island Money Pit, so I crept carefully down the ancient stone steps. But as luck would have it, my foot pressed on a wrong spot and the damn staircase collapsed!"

"Holy shit! So what did you do?" Truman stared at her, unblinking.

"Held on for dear life to the edge, swung my legs back up and continued my journey of course."

"God, you're going to be the death of me. Remind me not to ask for too many of your exploits in explicit detail. But continue. I've gotta to know how it went."

"Well, a hidden side tunnel was revealed by the fallen

staircase and I headed right down it. At the bottom, I found the ancient stone altar that the princess had originally prayed to. Got down on my knees—" She stopped to give a wide smile as his eyes smoldered with renewed passion. "And the action of my weight on the stone triggered the mechanism, causing the priceless bowl to rise up from the bottom of the pool. I nabbed it, and the rest is history."

"No one tried to take it from you?"

"Well, they tried, but I slugged them with it—it's quite a sturdy relic—escaped, and took Will's plane back to Canada. Damned useful, having a good friend with a Lear jet."

"There is no way I can top that story." He leaned over and took her face between his hands. "You are physically beautiful, no denying that, but it's your beautiful mind that's behind it all. That's the most beautiful thing of all. I am one lucky man to be with you, darlin'."

Chapter Nineteen

"The best defense is a good offense." *Don Bain*

"Arms high, aim low — kick, block or twist. Run!" Sweat pouring down her face, Casey pushed her nearly exhausted body through the actions for the umpteenth time as the drill sergeant yelled out the moves. The Street Smarts advanced class was held in the basement of the local YMCA. Twenty other women were also lined up ready to part with their cash to keep up their street moves. Insurance that most likely meant she'd not need the moves anytime soon. But if she did, she wanted the actions to be second nature. And the workout beat any other she'd ever done, only rivaled by martial arts.

"Focus! Remember, in a street situation, the one who walks away unscathed is the winner. You got three seconds to make it happen." Evan Cleaver walked around behind the women, still screaming orders. "Widen your stance, Lisa. And for God's sake, duck! When you kick him in the nuts, he's going to fall forward, breaking your nose or giving you a concussion, disabling you for that vital few moments you need to escape."

Groans and grunts came, each woman pushing her limits.

"Okay, better. Let's call it a night. Any questions?"

Casey gave Evan a quick salute, turned on her heel and hurried away to hit the showers, letting the steady stream of hot water soothe her aching muscles. Ten minutes later, hair still half-wet, she tugged on her clothes. She was running late.

She exited the building, turning left toward the well-lit car park. A few early stars twinkled in the sky, the rest obscured by a maze of city lights. The odor of hot French fries from the fast-food joint across the street made her mouth water uncontrollably. *Oh, boy.* Her stomach clenched, agreeing that eating would be a terrific idea. She moved her canvas carryall to a more comfortable position on her shoulder, keys in hand, and walked over to her vehicle. Then made an about-face. A quick detour for fries. What could it hurt? She needed some sustenance if she was going to keep up with Truman's appetites. Awesome about described it. And last night had been just as awesome as the first time. Too bad tonight he'd flown to New York to see his ex-in-laws. But entirely necessary. She sighed aloud. He'd be back soon. *Suck it up, buttercup.*

She lined up with the other locals in the small porch-like partition that separated the cooks from the customers. It ran along the front of the joint, meant to protect the customers from the inclement weather. The French fries at VJ's were so legendary that everyone was used to shuffling along the narrow walkway to place their orders and wait for pickup. The business was set up in an ancient one-story building and had been situated across from the CN Union Train Station for what seemed like forever. Just down the street from the Fort Garry Hotel. Another legendary Winnipeg spot.

She gave her order, the sound of burgers sizzling on the grill sweet to her ears, and stepped back to wait. Nodded at the next person in line. There was no seating inside, but a few wooden picnic tables were lined up in the parking lot. She absently watched a seagull swoop down and nab a French fry from the ground through the glass.

"Large order of French fries for the pretty lady," the fry cook sang out. Casey looked over and grinned at the man. As always, his face was shiny with sweat from the heat of the fryer, but his smile was genuine.

She sprinkled salt on her order and vacated the hut. On a whim she sat at one of the tables, stepping over the wooden bench to sit down. A wasp was lazily waddling across the tabletop and she shooed it away. Fat sparrows rummaged the area for fries as well, easily sharing the bounty with the gulls.

Oh, God. So good. She began stuffing hot fries into her mouth like a mad woman, each delectable morsel better than the last. Soft and yielding inside, salty and crispy outside. *Perfect.*

She was half-finished when Lisa hurried up, her own large order of French fries spilling from their white sack with the usual cardboard tray placed underneath for easy handling.

"Hey, Casey. Mind if I join you?"

"No, of course not." Casey gestured at the table.

"Man, my muscles are screaming at me," Lisa said as she lowered her body onto the wooden seat of the old picnic table, carefully avoiding snagging her clothing. "I shouldn't have missed last week." Lisa was lithe, thin as a rake, really, with sharp facial features. Her long brown hair was pulled back in a tight ponytail, showing off her high cheekbones, while thick bangs framed her dark brown eyes.

"It's always worse when you lay off," Casey agreed.

"I sure admire your devotion. You must practice a lot to get as good as you are," Lisa said with admiration around a mouthful of food. "Any person who attacks you is going down for the count. And if it's a man—" She shook her head slowly to make her point. "Look out! He's going to be searching for his clackers on the ground!"

Casey laughed out loud, delighted by the image. Any man attacking a woman deserved whatever he got.

"Yeah, just one nut shot and it's all over. Sucks to be a man sometimes. I don't know how they walk around with those things, anyway," she joked.

A commotion sounded behind her. She swung her head around to check it out. A man was busy slapping his upper body with his right hand to knock away a wasp, but what he'd forgotten was that hand held a hamburger. The patty landed on his shoulder, ketchup and mayo dripping down his clothing, the bun on the ground, which an enterprising bird spotted and nabbed in a split second. Casey pressed her lips tightly together. Mirth threatened to explode. The man must be allergic to react so violently and she shouldn't laugh. Her stomach began hurting in the effort to hold it in. She didn't dare look at Lisa for fear of losing control.

She finished her fries, made her excuses to Lisa and threw the empty cardboard box in the garbage can. Now, she had the strength for anything.

This time, she got into the SUV, locking the doors immediately. Not the best part of town for a woman alone. Though if anyone tangled with her, he'd be picking his clackers up off the street according to Lisa. She grinned again and pulled her seat belt around her body, locking it in place. Her cell phone rang and she dug it out of the top pocket of her carryall.

"Hey, Miranda. What's up?" She envisioned her friend, cute pixie haircut, violet-blue eyes and enough energy to light up the Toronto CN Tower.

"You still planning to head to the island tomorrow?"

"Yeah, bright and early. Why?" *A few days away with Truman. Priceless.*

"I want to spend some time there. See if I can catch a glimpse of that Devil Dog ruse. Or better yet, get a photo. Set up surveillance as well and maybe catch who's doing all this."

"Sure, why not." Lacey, Lily and now Miranda. It was shaping up to be a quite a trip, long as there was no sniping at Truman. He'd earned a free pass for now, maybe forever. And all her friends had been informed of that fact.

"I can't come right away. Got something on tomorrow. You're going to be there for a few days, right?"

"Not sure exactly how long. A couple of days, for sure. I don't have a class until next Thursday. Depends on how long it takes to find what we're after." Casey was careful not to spell out all the facts over the phone.

"Good. See you soon."

"Bye." Casey shoved the phone back into its slot in her carryall and started the vehicle. She was about to back up the SUV when her Spidey sense clicked in. Big time. She scanned the area through the tinted windshield and side windows, checking for what was causing her sixth sense to go on such high alert, watching for any movement.

Then she spotted a dark figure lurking in a shadowed doorway about fifty feet away. It was too dark to make out any facial features but the person was wearing a black duster-like coat to their knees. Too tall and heavyset for a woman. The person standing so still and staring back at her made the fine hair on her neck bristle. She absently rubbed it. Was this connected to the break in or just another odd coincidence? Fuck. She didn't really believe in coincidences when it got right down to it. She reached inside her carryall again and nabbed the Taser supplied by the twins.

Enough of this shit!

Ignoring her instructor's voice screaming "No!" ringing in her ears, she opened the driver's door and bounded out of the vehicle, heading on a collision course with the interloper. Confronting was definitely not part of the three-second rule.

* * * *

Truman sighed. Time to get it over with. He knocked on the door of Hailey's parents' new townhouse. The pair had followed Hailey to New York in a recent move to be closer to their daughter and he had not yet visited them. Staying in a hotel alone without Casey sucked, but he planned a quick turnaround and they would be heading to Oak Island in the morning, anyway. He'd been surprised at the chancellor being rather reluctant to give him the necessary time to deal with this, then giving in. Casey knew her stuff, recognizing the man's shortcomings. Just the thought of her brought a smile to his face, his mind and body remembering their first amazing nights together. He closed his eyes and took a deep breath, thinking of what might have happened if the ruse had not been exposed in time. What he would have lost.

The red painted door opened. He centered himself, bracing his feet.

"Hello, Truman," Alec's voice rang harsh and clear. The man looked the same with his bristly gray hair and rough features from a lifetime spent working on projects all over the globe, his slate-blue eyes able to quell most men at twenty paces. His being on the road so much had been his daughter's loss. She'd just wanted her father home and would do anything to please him. Truman had gotten along well enough with his father-in-law, that was, until the divorce. Then all bets had been off. Suspicion sidled into his mind. *Is this the guy behind some of the shit going down? I wouldn't put it past him. The damn bastard has always been slippery as an eel, especially in business doings.*

Truman cleared his throat. He had a duty to let the family know what was going on with their daughter, to see that they knew to find her help. No matter what Alec was up to.

"Alec. I hope you and Mary are well."

"You can skip the pleasantries and just get to it. Why the visit?"

"I need to speak with you."

A short pause as the man's face turned even grimmer if that were possible, any veneer falling away. "Why? It's not a convenient time. Just say what you have to say and go." Alec's voice held deep suspicion under its steely edge. He stood as if guarding his own castle, his wide shoulders filling the doorway.

Truman tensed. This was more animosity than normal, making it even harder than he'd figured on. And now more awkward as well. Not something he wanted to get into on his ex-father-in-law's front steps. "Have you heard from Hailey lately?"

"Sure, she calls her mother every day like the great

daughter she is." The accusation that he was undeserving of such a devoted woman was clear. "Why?" Alec barked.

"Ah, well, she's been in Winnipeg, Manitoba these past few days. I've seen her a few times, as a matter of fact."

"Have you done something to my daughter? Is that why you're here? Because if you have, *so help me God*, I'll see you strung up!"

"No, no. Nothing like that. Um, maybe if I show you a couple of photos you'd be better able to understand the situation." Truman's mind rushed to make his case. He wanted no doubt left in the man's mind that his daughter needed help.

"Photos?" Alec sounded taken aback.

"Yeah. Give me a sec." Truman fiddled with his cell to find the file Casey had given him and loaded it, turning the phone around to face the older man.

"Okay, you just need to compare the two, taken about ten days apart." Truman kept his voice neutral, but his heart pounded loudly. This was going to hurt like hell. And why wouldn't the man let him inside? Make this a bit easier. It made the old guy looked guilty as hell.

Dead silence while Alec frowned, studying the two incriminating photographs. Truman waited while the seconds ticked by, hoping Alec wasn't having a heart attack. Maybe he would instead. His heart was still thudding too rapidly. He took a deep breath. Calm down.

"What the fuck is this? What are you trying to pull off?"

The words, more suited to some sort of mobster than an alleged businessman and delivered in a hard, suspicious bark, stunned Truman. "Hailey needs your help, Alec. She's under some kind of delusion that this will bring us back together again. I just couldn't stay quiet and not give you and Mary a heads-up. I beg you, please, please see she gets help. She needs professional assistance. And tell her she'll get most of the Templar treasure—if it's still there. Casey—my partner—and I have sworn to give it all to her, minus the government's fair share, of course."

The door was slammed in his face.

* * * *

Avoid — Counter — Escape. That was what she was supposed to bring away from the classes, not perform her own personal version of never back down.

But before she could reach the man and get a good look, he made an about-turn and raced back down the alley, his footfalls echoing on the pavement in the darkness, his long coat billowing out behind him like an unfurling flag. Taunting her to follow. She stopped at the entranceway, breathing hard. She had gone from sitting to running full tilt so quickly her impromptu meal was now in her throat, threatening to express itself. Chasing him down the shadowy alley seemed beyond foolhardy. She swallowed hard, wishing she'd skipped the fries.

The man had vanished like a fart in the wind. With so many doorways to hide inside, he could leap out from, she was left standing and peering into the blackness, wishing to confront him. Maybe she could have learned who was behind all the shit. She sighed.

Might as well go home.

A shot rang out. *What?* Pain seared her upper arm. She dropped to a crouch. Where had the bullet come from?

Move. Don't stay a target. Her training kicked in. Big-time. Zig-zagging back and forth, she made it to her vehicle, keeping her head down all the way. Focused on getting safely inside. *Damn, I wish I had a gun.* How she'd have loved to shoot back. Teach those fuckers a lesson. 'Course, it was crazy talk — the last thing her instructor would suggest was escalating the situation. But, oh, it would be so sweet.

Behind the wheel, she checked the area.

All quiet. Not that it would stay like that for long. Someone had probably heard the shot, might be calling nine-one-one at this very moment. Pulling down the shoulder of her black hoodie that hid the bloodstains, she surveyed the damage.

The bullet had nicked her upper arm, leaving a gash. Thank goodness it was her left. It needed attention, cleaning and possibly a stitch or two, but nothing she couldn't handle. She'd better get a move on before the police arrived or she'd be in for hours of questioning. Last thing she needed.

On the short drive home, she considered her options. The best one was to tend the wound first, before infection set in. She admitted to some shock. The biggest shock being that someone had shot at her on the quiet streets of Winnipeg and thought they could get away with it. Obviously, it had everything to do with the greed for gold. Either Soapy's or Oak Island's, with her instincts leaning towards the latter. But she and Truman had promised the ex a full share. Surely, she'd back off now? It just didn't make sense. Why shoot her when she'd given in on that score? Maybe it really was something to do with Dawson and the gold she'd found? Her mind kept going in nauseating circles.

She drove into the driveway, placed the SUV in park, turned off the motor. Thank God. No one home. She just needed to get inside unseen and get on with things.

Upstairs, behind the closed door of the bathroom off her bedroom, she pulled out her extensive medical kit from under the sink. It wasn't the first time she'd been attacked and it would not be the last. No way would she ever be deterred and give up the pure adrenaline rush of finding treasure.

She downplayed the incident in her head. Perhaps it had been a stray bullet. Crazier things had been known to happen. But deep down, she understood she was working at fooling herself. Making it easier.

Turning her mind to the business at hand, she cleaned and dressed the wound. The powerful disinfectant burned like hell, but she poured on more to be certain. She probed the site, looking for any tatters of fabric that could cause a future infection. Finding none, she pressed a sterile pad against the gash.

Probably the hardest part was going to be hiding it from

Truman. He might not take kindly to his woman getting shot at. She slapped a bandage on and swallowed painkillers. *Call it done.* Another battle scar. No doubt a doctor would have treated it differently. But it would have taken up a considerable chunk of energy, considering the average wait time in a hospital these days. Though maybe for gunshots, it might go faster. She just didn't have the patience to find out.

She walked back into her bedroom, the bed calling to her, her body heavy now with the adrenaline rush evaporating. *Just a few minutes. Truman won't be back till morning, anyway.* She lay down, pulling the afghan Aunt Milly had made for her up to her chin. Fast asleep in a second.

She woke with a start. Glancing at the clock on the bedside table, she read the red digital numbers: six a.m. She had slept clear through the night. Groggy, she sat up. Today they were heading back to the island and she needed to get her ass in gear. Checking her messages, she quickly texted Truman, assuring him she was all set to go and would meet him at the plane in an hour. No need to fill him in on small details that would just worry him unnecessarily, right? Her conscience squeaked, but she hushed her up. Who was in charge of this operation, anyway?

Chapter Twenty

The Times They Are A-changin'. *Bob Dylan*

Truman loaded the last bag onto the plane, hefting the tent beside all the other luggage piled up in the cargo hold of the Cessna. All the extra bodies had surprised them at the airport. Not exactly what he had planned. He shook his head. At least they'd have some privacy at night on the island, as they were the only ones camping full-time, the rest booked in a motel. Perfectly fine with him. Not to mention having a private plane at their disposal sure beat flying commercial all to hell. But from the array of bags, he'd guess they were going to Oak Island for a month, not the scheduled three days. And with enough food rations to keep an entire army's belly full on the march.

It wasn't an entirely new experience running with such a big team. He'd been on archeological digs, of course, and treasure hunts before, here and abroad, just never with a pair of divas like the twin tornadoes. *Now they even have me doing it, calling them that.* He shook his head. Life had changed. And definitely for the better.

He caught a glimpse of the woman responsible for his new-found happiness, then smiled at her antics. She was busy talking with the other Ringers. He'd lay even odds they were conspiring and hatching some wild plan as they stood close together on the tarmac. *Lord give me the patience.* This was going to be some trip. William James Thornton III, or Will to his friends, joined him.

"You up for this, Truman? Sorry you got set up like this. Hell, I did, too. I expect you would have preferred to head to the island alone with Casey," he said.

"Is any man really ready for this?" he joked. "But it might be good to have extra bodies around. There's been threats against our digging on the island. And that break-in at Casey's house."

Will grimaced. Truman liked him. He wasn't what he'd expected. Nicknamed 'the Wall' due to his massive size, he was a former university linebacker with a full dark beard — not the typical rich man's son. He'd even done a tour of duty in Afghanistan and in Iraq. The weight of war was obvious in his solid demeanor.

"Yeah, I heard about that. Best to have backup just in case. Anyone else know your plans for going there today? Other than this group?"

"No. We kept it quiet."

"Exactly right." Will grunted. "No point in broadcasting your intentions."

"Casey shared a bit of your history. Who were you with during your tours of duty?"

The man's eyes turned wary. "Just a regular army grunt — nothing special."

"Casey mentioned you're also rather handy around the house and help out the twins," Truman said, in an effort to lighten the mood. *What was Will not telling him?*

"Yeah, well, they've helped me a lot," Will said with a shrug. He smoothed down his beard with one hand, his eyes taking on a distant look. "Saw me through some tough times, especially Lacey. She's good at getting my mind off the things I've seen."

"Women can get your mind of a lot of things, even work, when they want to," Truman joked. He settled his gaze fondly on his new woman.

"You got yourself a good one there." Will nodded in Casey's direction.

"And don't I know it," he agreed.

"Time to get this show on the road, ladies. Plane's loaded and ready for takeoff," Will said, raising his voice. A few heads swiveled their way, but a couple of fingers went up in the air, a pantomime of just-a-minute, one less polite than the other.

"Told you." Will raised his eyebrows at being given the finger by Lacey. "See, it's starting already, the setting of the ground rules. 'We'll be with you when we're damned good and ready'. She's not happy unless she's breaking some poor guy's balls."

Truman snorted. *Damn, this is going to be entertaining if nothing else.*

A couple of hours later, Will set the plane down smoothly on a runway at the Halifax Airport. Convenient. Turned out he needed the extra hours to keep up his license. It left Truman alone to deal with the Ringers. He was beginning to enjoy the unexpected camaraderie. *Don't get too comfortable. Remember the warning about Oak Island.* He sobered immediately. He'd need to stay sharp.

Everyone pitched in to load the bags into the two rented vehicles for the hour-long trip down the 103 to Oak Island. He took the wheel of one of the SUVs before anyone else could volunteer, watching Lacey nab the driver's seat of the other right out from under Will's nose. He shook his head. *Figures.* But he'd bet his bottom dollar, if it was warranted, Will would stop her in her tracks. The man *had* been to war, after all.

Lacey led the way, peeling out of the parking lot with a gleeful expression firmly in place. She was driving too quickly in his opinion. He set his own pace, enjoying having a beautiful sane woman at his side and an adventure to look forward to. Who knew what could be revealed in perhaps a matter of days, if not hours?

Fog, the scourge of mariners, was moving in as they turned onto the causeway that led to their island. Add heavy currents, a granite ocean bottom scraped raw by Ice Age glaciers leaving behind a multitude of ledges and reefs hidden by the waves, and he could well understand the vast number of shipwrecks over the past three hundred years. Hell, Sable Island, farther out to sea to the west, was even called the Graveyard of the Atlantic, an apt name considering its brutal history of devouring ships.

He shivered. A ship breaking up, spilling its crew and passengers into the frigid waters of the Atlantic — he'd have to be a robot not to care. Casey laid her hand on his knee, dispelling the dismal image.

"You okay?" she asked, her eyes searching his.

"Just fine," he reassured her, wishing it was nighttime and they were in their tent. Alone. Thank goodness there were only a few hours of daylight left.

* * * *

Working together, the crew set up home base. Rebecca immediately got to fiddling with the VLF prototype ground imaging machine that had been offered by Ava's older brother, Cash. A high-tech wizard and talented inventor, he was as good as they got. The Ringers often teased him about being the Canadian Q.

With a large grin, her adorable friend announced to all and sundry, "I'd bet the ranch this sucker can find anything. Well, I'm off, ready for my maiden voyage. Wish me luck!"

"Good luck, Rebecca!" A chorus of goodwill followed her into the woods, lugging the space-age device and a portable shovel with all the excitement of Christmastime and the best present ever found under the tree. Her very own version of the official Daisy Red Ryder Range Model BB Gun with a compass in the stock from *A Christmas Story*. At least it was taking her friend's mind off the stolen manuscript.

Casey took a moment to enjoy the view of Truman's butt as he leaned over the cooler to grab a six-pack of beer. She still hadn't shared what had happened, the wound hidden under layers of clothing. But she was better prepared today. Just let those fuckers try something and she'd show them a move or two.

"Treasure hunting's thirsty work," he announced. "Any

takers for a frosty one?"

"Duh!" Lacey said, grabbing two for herself and Lily.

He handed Casey a beer and Will nabbed one as well.

"A toast to finding what we came for and finally solving the mystery of Oak Island," Truman said, holding up his beer for the toast, the metal tabs on the beverages bursting open and making a series of clicking sounds all around their impromptu circle.

"To Oak Island and the treasure," Casey said, taking a cool, refreshing gulp. It had been a long time coming.

"Guys! Come here! Quick! I've found something important," Rebecca called out from near the spot she'd vanished only a short time ago.

"Beginners' luck?" Lily asked.

"Well, there's only one way to find out," Casey said, heading after her friend.

"Casey! Look at this!" Rebecca glanced up at her approach. She'd shoveled a surprising amount of dirt. It was mounded all around the hole that measured about two and a half feet across and more than two feet deep. She was breathing deeply, and no wonder. She must have worked like a madwoman to have moved so much soil so quickly.

"You've been working out," Casey teased her, standing near the edge and watching her friend brush away the clay soil from around a hard object projecting out of the ground. It looked like an old wooden chest. "Here, let me help."

Casey leaned down and grasped the edge of the object with both hands while Rebecca used the shovel to brace underneath, levering it out, ignoring the pain in her arm and hoping she didn't bust a stitch or two. Maybe she should have glued the wound together instead. Grunting from the strain, they determinedly shoved the object up and onto the side of the hole. About eighteen inches across by twelve inches and nearly a foot deep with some kind of engraving in the flat wooden top, it was locked with rusty iron padlock.

"Wow, it's old. Maybe it's a pirate chest!" Rebecca said,

the glow in her eyes making Casey smile.

"Talk about beginners' luck." Casey gave her a quick hug.

"I hope it contains something interesting. Heavy enough," Rebecca said, squatting and running her hands over it, checking it out. The hinges were rusty and decaying, though the wood was intact, preserved by cold winters. Lucky also that the chest had not been subjected to wet conditions, like if it'd been buried in the Oak Island swamp nearby.

"Let's wait to open it. Then everyone can share in the excitement," Rebecca said, picking it up with both hands and holding it tightly against her body. She gingerly made her way around the large hole, the chest weighing her down. Casey picked up the shovel and began throwing the dirt back in. The last thing they needed was someone breaking a leg in the middle of the night. Tromping down the soil with the back of the shovel, she found Cash's discarded imaging device, shouldered the items and hauled ass back to camp.

When she got there, everyone was huddled around the picnic table, the newly found artifact proudly displayed in the center, already the subject of much awe and speculation.

"Maybe it's from Captain Kidd's crew?" Lily asked her voice tinged with reverence.

Casey laid the items aside and joined them.

"What took you so long? We thought you'd never get back," Lacey grumbled good-naturedly.

"Thought I'd save you breaking an ankle or two. I refilled the spot. Okay, I'm here. Whatcha waiting for? Let's open it!"

Rebecca leaned forward, dragging the chest closer to her body. She chewed on her bottom lip as she struggled with the rusted lock. Everyone's attention remained focused on each miniscule action of her fingers, the women and men silent witnesses to history in the making.

Finally, Rebecca resorted to using a screwdriver to force the lock, conveniently handed to her by the ever-thoughtful Lacey.

"Oh, God, I hope I don't damage it too much," she

exclaimed, grimacing as she worked, trying to pry it free.

Then, with a squeak of protest, the lock gave way.

Bated breath.

Eyes on the prize.

The lid opened all the way to an upright position, exposing the chest's contents for the first time in what could have been centuries. Musty air escaped. Rebecca sneezed, turning her head away to avoid contamination. Casey fancied she heard the chest give a sigh of relief in giving up its contents. What glory could there be in staying hidden away?

Only those in front of the chest could see, so everyone moved around to the one good viewing spot, crowded in like sardines in a tin can. Truman was pressed against her back, his hard, lean body tantalizing hers. *Sweet.*

"I feel like I should be wearing white gloves," Rebecca said, her voice wavering with emotion, her fingers trembling.

"No time. I gotta know, Becca. Now!" Lacey wailed in desperation, feigning hanging herself. Regular diva stuff.

Casey focused on the contents. The first items they saw just below the lid looked to be old documents, letters perhaps, aged yellow and sprinkled with darker spots, the edges curved and warped.

Rebecca reached in and removed the thick sheath of paper, a dry rustling noise the only sound. More dust and mold spores sprung into the air, disturbed by the breeze blowing off the ocean. Casey sneezed this time, wiping her nose on her sleeve. No time to find a tissue.

Rebecca read the lines aloud, stumbling where words faded, "'My dearest Penelope, with my last few breaths and fading strength, I put pen to paper with the hopes that someday these words shall reach you. How I long for your sweet smile and the…laughter of our children one more time before I am called from this Earth.'"

She stopped reading suddenly, swallowing hard, before resuming her recital, "'I trust you will speak with my brother whom I gave monies to be set aside for you and the children, to keep you in your…accustomed style. The thought of you without the necessities and small daily pleasures of this life would cause me great suffering. I miss you all terribly and think of you with each passing hour.'"

Casey could see Rebecca's hands shaking even as her own vision blurred from the tears that were welling up, tightening her throat. With admirable courage, her friend pressed on, "'We were beset by pyrates and in attempting to outrun them were run aground by a most terrible storm to this God Forsaken Island. It is only the memory of you in your best Sunday bonnet and the children frolicking on the grass when we would picnic on those glorious summer days on the banks of the River Thames which sustains me. Golden days must surely await us yet in heaven. Until we meet on the other side, your loving husband, Randolph Thomas Scott. Esquire. In the year of our Lord, August fifth, seventeen hundred and twenty.'"

Silence. A few sniffles.

"Oh, that poor man." Lacey began weeping openly. Will gathered her into his arms, pressing his face against her hair.

Casey glanced up at Truman, caught a glimpse of moisture pooling in his eyes. Her heart swelled with a rush of feeling so wide and deep she was overcome, her legs gone wobbly. *Life can be stripped away so quickly.*

Truman reached out to steady her as she swayed.

"Hey, you okay?" he asked, his blue eyes darkening with concern.

"Not sure," she whispered, swallowing hard. "That was pretty intense."

"I think we just found the real treasure," Lily said, drawing everyone's attention once more. "Somehow we have to get this letter to the rightful owner. I don't care what it takes. We have to do this, right? Say we can do this?"

"Of course, we have to. Count me in," Lacey said, dabbing at her eyes with a tissue.

"All for one and one for all," Rebecca said.

They looked over at Casey with questions plain on their

eager faces.

"Well, of course," she said, pressing her lips together as more emotion threatened to well up.

"I want in. Could I be an honorary Ringer just this one time?" Truman asked. "I think that's about all I could take, though."

"Me, too," Will added.

"I vote yes. They were both here for this, they should both have the pleasure of seeing it through to the end," Rebecca said.

"All in favor?"

A chorus of yeas.

* * * *

"Yeah, they're back and they've brought reinforcements. Six of them. Four women and two men. They've set up camp again and are snooping around. What should I do?" Byrne brightened with the vision of all that fancy pussy inhabiting his island. Maybe he could scare those twins enough to come running to him? Any port in a storm.

"I had hoped it would not come to this," the man said his voice cold, the underlying threat clear. "Well, it's their choice. Not like they haven't been warned off."

Byrne shivered, as though a ghost had just walked over his grave. He shook his head to dispel the notion.

"What do you want me to do?" he asked, licking his lips.

"Nothing. It's time to take matters into my own hands."

Byrne frowned, biting his tongue. This was a first. He'd hoped for more direct intervention on his part. Earn a little more cash. Not that he was greedy, mind, but living these days was expensive. It was well past time that a quick shot over the bow would do much convincing. Time to send these suckers a real fuckin' message. And he was just the man to do it. Might even take mercy on that fancy pussy if they'd see their way to giving him a little.

"Okay, if that's what you really want. But I think it's

a mistake. I'm here right now and can create some big problems for them before the day is through. Just say the word." Byrne let his disappointment and warning hang out there before the guy hung up on him. *Shit heel.*

* * * *

"Look at this!" Lacey said. Rebecca was busy reading the Penelope Papers, as they were now referring to them, looking for more answers, while Lacey scrounged through the coins she'd laid out on a tea towel. They'd also found artifacts under the papers. A snuff box made of horn with a little dusty tobacco still nestled inside, the initials *R.T.S.* carved into the bottom, a comb made out of wood, some faded hair ribbons and a small drinking vessel also carved from horn. Tucked under the cache of coins was a King James Bible produced by the King's Printers somewhere between 1614 and 1649. Produced on one hundred percent rag cotton linen, it had held up amazingly well over the centuries. All the stark remnants of a man's life cut tragically short.

"There's a willow tree on one side," Lacey said flipping the small coin over with her fingers. "What do you think it is, Casey?"

"That's a Massachusetts shilling—a New England coin, minted between 1652 and 1660, one of the most sought-after early coins minted in North America. The last willow tree coin I heard about sold at auction for a whopping hundred thousand dollars." Casey filled in the information. The course on numismatics was proving valuable.

"Too perfect!" Lacey broke out into a gleeful smile. "Money to fund our operation."

"Most of the coins in the series go for a few thousand dollars, depending on condition. But these are in mint condition. Prime. There are also coins with pine trees and oak trees engraved in them," Casey said, finishing her history lesson before adding, "And you know if we find an heir, we have to turn these over to them, right?"

Lacey pouted, nodding reluctantly.

"I love being with a beautiful, smart woman," Truman said, complimenting Casey.

"And I love being with a handsome, supportive man," she quipped back. He hugged her closer to his side, kissing her lightly on the lips. She wanted more. *So. Much. More.* The past few days had awakened a deep sense of how precious life was. But making love would expose her condition. She needed to keep a lid on things until they left the island with the treasure. 'Better to offer an apology after the fact than ask permission beforehand' pretty much summed up how she lived her life. She wasn't going to let her involvement with Truman change that.

"Get a room, you two!" Rebecca teased, glancing up from reading, her lips twitching. Along with the letter, there were other papers, maps and a ship's journal she was busy studying.

Perhaps it was the Penelope Papers, but having him back in her life was almost too good to be true. Where it would all lead? Not today's problem.

"I need to take a walk, sort this through in my mind," Rebecca said, getting to her feet and carefully laying the papers back in the box.

Casey sobered. A family had lost a husband and father. What did it matter if it had happened three hundred years ago? For the Ringers, and especially for her sensitive writer friend, it was happening today.

"I'll come with you," she volunteered.

"No, but thanks. I need to be alone." Rebecca softened the shake of her head with a smile. Then turned and slipped into the woods that led to the shoreline.

Truman came up from behind her and embraced her. "Everyone's a bit torn up by events, darlin'. Don't take it to heart."

She stood still for all of two seconds. "I'm starved. Let's

have a barbecue."

"How about we go to town and eat?"

"Are you kidding? After all the food Rebecca made us bring along?" Plus, staying on the island made guarding the treasure easier.

"Okay, works for me," he agreed. "What do you want me to do?"

"Light the briquettes. Kind of old-fashioned, but it's the absolutely best way to barbecue a fine steak, I promise."

"You got it. Hey, Will, want to help?" he called out to the silent man sitting at the picnic table, observing the twins catalog the coins for prosperity.

"Sure."

The two men bent to the task. With a quick spring in her step, Casey made the hike to the spot she was positive held the key to Oak Island. *Thank goodness. Undisturbed.* She sank onto her heels beside the spot they'd marked with a few stones, wishing they could dig now. *What's stopping me?* She got to her feel and hurried back to camp, grabbing a shovel and flashlight from beside the tent. The others were turned away, busy. Only Lacey glanced up from the picnic table, giving her a questioning look. Casey waved her off.

She'd just take a quick perusal. What harm could it do?

A few minutes later, certain she was well out of earshot, she forced the sharp blade into the hard-packed soil, wincing at the pain in her arm. Maybe this hadn't been the best idea. Nah, when had it ever stopped her before? She'd had more than her fair share of battle wounds. Using her foot for leverage, she removed the first shovelful. The clay was an ornery competitor and soon she was sweating heavily. Stopping to swipe at her brow, she took a deep breath.

The odor of fresh-turned earth permeated the air, making her nose twitch uncontrollably. On the next thrust into the soil, the shovel jammed back into her shoulder as she struck something hard. Wincing, she ignored the pain. *Great. Only three feet down.* Her job just got a whole lot easier. The parallels to the original Money Pit did not escape her as she dug. She just hoped to be luckier than those guys. Two hundred plus feet down was a little out of her range with a shovel. And a sore arm.

Working furiously, she soon exposed a huge stone slab. *Hmm. Perfect.* The island was legendary for its stone clues that may or may not lead somewhere. The stone was flat, showing evidence of likely being man-made. She ran her hand across the smooth surface, scraping the remaining dirt away with her fingernails, stunned to see a pictograph and words carved into its surface. The St. Clair family coat of arms. A shield with the holy engraved cross of the Sinclair clan, three boars' heads in a separate rectangular section and the letters *I.M.S.* and *I.C.* displayed separately—an exact replica of the one displayed in the sacristy in Rosslyn Chapel beside the east window—and, best of all, a name and date.

She whispered while tracing the ancient lettering with her forefinger, "'Dated thes 1398. Prince Hendire Saint-Clair, laird ay Orkney, Baron ay Rosslyn.'"

Translated to, Dated this 1398. Prince Henry St. Clair, Laird of Orkney and Baron of Rosslyn.

Clear as a bell.

She sunk back on her heels. Flabbergasted.

Proof positive of the Zeno Narrative, the recorded history and map of Prince Henry visiting the New World nearly a hundred years before Columbus. Staring her right in the face. She swallowed hard. *Awesome.* She'd just helped rewrite world history.

She leaned forward to read the writing beneath.

"'Push ben fear tae be rewarded fur aw eternity.'"

Push through fear to be rewarded for all eternity.

What the hell does that mean?

Her heart now hammering uncontrollably, she took in the significance of the historical find. Something important was hidden here, something important enough to warrant being placed under the memory stone for posterity. Important enough for Prince Henry to have left his ancestral home.

Was this it? She'd bet her bottom dollar on it. Truman was going to be so stoked. Well, if he forgave her for getting here first. And not telling him about being shot at.

She quickly took a photo before levering the heavy stone to the side with the shovel. The last thing she wanted was to have anything happen to the priceless artifact. Headed to a Maritime museum, if she had any say.

As the stone jerked away from the force she exerted, teeth gritted, the other end of a stone slab began to rise out of the ground, confusing her. And the more she tried to lift the stone away, the more it rose, as if on a teeter-totter. What the hell was it? Damn, a second stone slab under the first, not the layer of oak logs she expected.

Crap. Where were the logs? What did this mean?

It took all her effort, but she pried the rock free and the slab of rock rose perpendicularly to the ground, exposing what was underneath. *Oh, God, it looks like a coffin.* It *was* a coffin, its lid partially rotten away. She didn't want to look closer and she sank down by the hole, spirits low, thoroughly creeped out. How could she disturb someone's burial place? Maybe it was a treasure guardian, like the pirates were legendary for? Some honor. Dying to protect treasure.

Gathering all her courage, she took a deep breath, peering into the bottom of the coffin using the flashlight to check around. *No body in sight. Whew.* Of course, she couldn't really expect one, after so many years. As she stared down at the box, thinking about the strangeness of it all, she found she could see right through the bottom in one spot. She shone the flashlight. The ground was open underneath.

Maybe the well or something of equal importance was still here. She had to know. Now. Her stomach rumbled again, like distant thunder.

Heartened, she stood, more determined than ever. Nearly out of time. Dusk was descending, the fog thickening. Chilly fingers of damp air made her shiver. Pea soup. And not the good kind.

She just needed to break open the bottom of the casket. She laid the flashlight aside and made the sign of the cross, praying for forgiveness for what she was about to do. Using the shovel like an ax, she hammered away at the broken spot, enlarging it.

After a series of loud bangs, expecting everyone to show up from the confounded noise, she could see what lay beneath. The flashlight illuminated a large chest, likely made of oak. Stereotypical pirate fare with a fancy curved top and rusted hinges. No damn well. Rebecca would be disappointed. But they would not go away empty-handed. And, just maybe, there was a clue in the chest. Thoughts of another treasure hunt made her swallow hard. She licked lips gone dry.

She should just go get the others. But the song of adventure thrummed through her bloodstream, firing her imagination. More history lurked at her fingertips. Her body flushed hot despite the chill in the air. She had to know. She *lived* to know.

Chapter Twenty-One

"An object, lost and hidden, waits and whispers."
Anonymous

Truman placed the perfectly cooked steaks on a large platter, his mouth watering.

"Time to eat. Where's Casey?"

Lacey gave a guilty start. "She took a shovel and went that-a-way." She pointed in the direction of Nolan's cross.

"What? She's digging out there alone?! Damn it all to hell! So help me God, if she's hurt herself again—" Truman raced toward the cross, ranting all the way.

He looked around frantically. *Where?*

The hole loomed suddenly in front of him, making him stop short, almost tumbling into the opening as he planted his feet, swaying back and forth in an effort to regain his precarious balance. *What was Casey thinking?*

He peered over the edge. And there she was, standing in the bottom of the hole, leaning over at the waist and rummaging around in an opened chest.

"Look, a map and coins!" she said as she caught sight of him, her voice excited beyond all measure.

"What the hell are you doing down there?" he demanded. "You might have been hurt?" Then he took in the full picture of what he was seeing. "And is that a coffin?"

"Ah, yeah, I had to break through to get at this chest. Don't worry—no body. Jump down. It's only a few feet. See what I've found. A map well-preserved with mercury that shows the other spots where Templar treasure is buried. *Unbelievable!*"

Truman shoved his hands through his hair and tugged at the roots. He wanted to scream, but her face was so animated, like a kid in a candy shop, that he just stood there. Dumbfounded pretty much summed it up.

"That's something, all right," he managed weakly. Lame as hell.

"Something!" She sounded outraged at his use of the word. "It's the find of the century! Well, this and the stone with the 1398 date on it."

"Stone?"

"Yeah, didn't you see it? I left it up near the edge for safe-keeping."

"I was a little busy worrying about you."

"Oh, sorry, didn't mean to worry you. But isn't this amazing!"

"Yeah, it certainly is." He shook his head. Casey was even more amazing. And once he'd calmed down, he'd tell her so. "Move over. I'm coming down."

He jumped into the hole to assist her in retrieving the chest from the ground, landing on the balls of his feet.

"Get that end and we'll haul it up," he instructed. Casey nodded and picked up her end as he hefted his. They pushed it up through the open coffin lid, the chest proving awkward and heavy to deal with. It took a bit of work, but finally they had it sitting on the edge of the hole. He gave her a hand up, joining her there.

"I would like to be in on this kind of thing from now on," Truman said, earning a contrite look from Casey as they took a breather, standing beside their haul. Now that he could see she was all right, his stress evaporated. "You know, we got us some fine tuning to do, darlin'. It's that or you're going to be the death of me."

"I'm truly sorry I worried you," she volunteered.

"Yeah, well, treasure hunting alone is a dangerous operation. I would prefer you give me notice in the future so that I can be there. Would that be even a remote possibility?" This was not a woman for ultimatums. At least, he was too smart to fall into that trap.

"Since you asked so nicely, I'll take it under advisement," she said with a smirk that held a promise to try.

"Good place to start as any."

"I had hoped our theory about a well was true, but it's not looking good," she grimaced.

"By the way, thanks for sharing all your facts with me," he snarked, bringing on another smirk.

"Well, I'm not used to having a partner outside the Ringers. Going to take some getting used to."

"Yeah, me, too. Never had to work with such a headstrong woman before."

She swatted his arm. He wanted a hug. Hell, he *needed* a hug.

He pulled her into his arms, breathing in the precious scent of her hair, savoring the warmth of her body tight against his. A rustling slight sound alerted him to company. He looked up to see two men standing above them, one holding a gun pointed right at him. *Damn it! I should have been more alert.*

"My, my, what a pretty picture. Your father-in-law or should I say *ex*-father-in-law would be so proud to see how well you've gotten on with things, Truman. Seducing another woman and forgetting all about his precious daughter. Hailey was smart to divorce your ass."

Truman held on to Casey, trying to direct her off to the side.

"It's that creepy duster guy!" Casey shouted, trying to launch herself at the man. Truman held on tighter.

"Relax, I'll take care of it."

She narrowed her eyes, a mulish look on her pretty face.

"Malcolm," he said, recognizing one of the two thugs. A seedy guy who'd long been on the fringes of Alec Sinclair's 'business' dealings. The tall man was dressed all in black today and wearing a long trench coat, a black fedora obscuring his face. Beside him was a younger, shorter man also dressed all in black. Malcolm held the gun. His tight expression and steely gray eyes suggested he'd have no problem using the weapon.

"And, yes, I know what you must be thinking — you're quite right, I will use it if I have to," Malcolm assured him. "Okay, back away," he ordered.

"You know this guy?" Casey said, giving him an assessing glance.

"He's Alec Sinclair's man. Alec, my ex-father-in-law. Known for his rather shady business dealings."

"So that's who's behind it?" Casey asked.

"Is Hailey working with her father? Is that why she showed up here pretending to be pregnant? So, they'd get a share of the treasure no matter what?"

Malcolm's eyes narrowed. "Are you fucking with me? No, don't know nothing about that. I work for Alec. Don't know nothing about a fake pregnancy. Besides, why take a share when you can have the whole thing? Alec would never settle for anything less."

"So you guys were behind all the warnings and the break-in?" Truman pressed.

"Yeah." Malcom gave a cold chuckle. "That worked like a charm. You treasure hunters are all alike. So fucking predictable. Make it a bit harder for you and you're guaranteed to head off to find it. Makes it so much easier for the rest of us, so I'm not complaining."

"Now what?" Truman asked, eying the thieves.

"You know how this works, Truman. We take the box and the stone. Then we leave and you say nothing of this if you know what's good for you," the man said. "Keep in mind we'll know if you do — we're always watching."

"You don't get to take my treasure! Bad enough you stalked me and shot me —" Casey demanded, giving the taller man a belligerent glare, hands on her hips.

Truman stared at her. "Someone was following you and you didn't think to mention it to me? And fucking *shot* at you!" he said, his temper flaring, shock slamming into him.

"Yeah, well," Casey said, shrugging it off. "The guy ran

off before I could get a good look, but he was tall, just like you," she accused the man, her gaze flashing with anger. "And if you broke into my house and took my friend's manuscript, *so help me God*, I'll not let this rest until—"

"You're either very foolish or very brave," Malcolm interrupted. "Enough talk."

He waved his gun to punctuate his remarks.

Truman took a deep breath, recovering from the shock. He'd deal with that later. Right now he needed his A-game more than any other time in his life. He racked his brain for an idea, any idea. But with Casey and the other women there, he would prefer the men just take the treasure and go. The thought of anyone harming one hair on his precious Casey's head made him shake with anger. More anger even than what she had kept from him. He'd tear these men limb from limb before he'd let anything happen to her on his watch. Anything else, that is. Liam Neeson in *Taken* would have nothing on him.

"Move away," Malcolm ordered. "And one more thing. I want your phones."

"No!" Casey began to protest, her expression turning to one of disbelief. Of course, she'd taken photos. Smart to strip them of their phones.

Malcolm grinned evilly.

Truman's hackles rose on the back of his neck. His feet planted on the hard-packed earth, he waited. Maybe they'd slip up. The thought of them just walking away with the legacy that Casey had worked so hard to find disgusted him to the core. It overrode everything else in that moment.

"Think I don't know how this goes?" the man scoffed, moving forward to grab at Casey's phone which she'd just dragged reluctantly from her pocket. He jerked it roughly from her stiffened fingers. Truman clenched his teeth so hard they began aching in violent protest.

Casey caught his eye. He read her intentions clear as a bell.

He made a split-second decision.

Then the man turned with a smug expression to toss it triumphantly at his assistant.

A moment's distraction.

Just enough.

Truman rushed forward, tackling the man's legs and throwing him onto the ground. A whoosh of air left the derailed thief, the gun flying from his hands into deeper grass.

Casey went for the other man who moved forward to aid his partner, kicking him lightning fast and so hard in the groin he slumped to the ground, dead weight. Rolled away in acute agony, she damn well hoped.

Out of the corner of his eye, Truman saw Casey race for the gun, grabbing it when she reached it. Perfect.

Then he got too busy rolling on the ground with the outraged man. Fighting him tooth and nail.

Time to end it.

He slugged the man in the jaw, thinking of him shooting at Casey, drilled his head into the earth. A hard clip from the right, then the left. Boxing moves always came in damned handy. Once. Twice. The man's arms came up in protest, trying to push him off.

Truman held on.

"Ready to give up?" he growled, taking an elbow in the ribs for his trouble.

One more solid slug to the man's jaw, adrenaline masking the pain in his hand.

The fight went out of the man. He nodded once, his expression one of resignation.

Truman helped him to his feet.

"Maybe you're not such a stuffed suit after all," Casey smirked, a smug look brightening her expression as she joined him. She kept the gun pointed at the men.

"So that's what you thought?" he said, arching one eyebrow in derision.

"Well, at first. Not now, of course. You got game."

"Let's get these guys back to camp," Truman said with a

grunt, pleased at her assessment. He took the gun from her hand and turned it on the pair. "Okay, move it."

Malcolm mumbled something they couldn't hear, his mouth already swelling from the slugs to his jaw. The other guy finally found his nuts and got to his feet. The pair trudged down the path, Truman keeping the gun pointed at them all the way. Fuckers had shot at his woman. They were lucky to be still alive.

"What the hell!" Will said, untangling his long legs from under the picnic table and scrambling to join them when they reached camp.

"What happened?" Everyone sprang to their feet. Gathered around.

"This pair of fucking dirtbags pulled a gun on us. Insisted they were taking all the treasure. Even after we offered the Sinclairs a full half-share. The old man is behind all this. Hailey's father," Truman said, motioning to the men to get down on the ground. He wondered if Hailey was also more involved than just setting him up with the fake pregnancy, as if that weren't enough, though he doubted it. He'd already offered her a share. She'd be crazy not to just take that. Then he realized what he had just thought. Hailey was half-crazy. Maybe it had been a kind of failsafe plan. Get them one way or the other.

"So, why warn you guys off? It only makes you more determined—*oh, yeah*, that's why," Rebecca said, the light dawning.

"Alec knows of my legendary stubbornness. And I see we share it in spades, darlin'." He gave Casey a conspirator grin.

He turned his mind back to the matters at hand. "Grab some rope, Will. We'll tie them up. Oh, and something to shove in their mouths to shut them up with while we think what to do with their sorry asses. We'll park them in the tent for now."

Casey joined her friends, watching the action on the

sidelines, giving them a wide grin of triumph as the men took care of the would-be robbers. The treasure and stone were collected and stowed away as well. "What these clowns didn't realize is their plan wouldn't have worked, anyway. I've already sent the photos to a secure email account as a back-up plan. A precaution I always take when in the field just in case I damage my phone. We've got photos of the treasure map, inscribed stone and chest just waiting for us when I log in. And one of these for good measure!" She reached down and dug a coin out of her pocket. And not just any old coin, but a coin of two men on horseback. A Knights Templar gold coin. Priceless.

"Way to go!" Lacey said. They fist-bumped to seal the deal.

She handed the coin to Truman as he joined them. He held it in the palm of his hand.

"If you think this makes it all right that you didn't tell me about being shot at, you're sadly mistaken," he said, a definite edge to his tone. She sensed the others backing away, giving them space. "Let's go for a walk. We need to sort this — now."

Oh, boy. She swallowed hard. He wasn't planning on making this easy to tap-dance over.

He stopped at Joudrey's Cove, the spot she'd run to when he'd been in the wrong. Damn, now the shoe was on the other foot. She looked over at the stump where they had made up the first time.

Casey pursed her lips, trying to figure how to explain it. "I am sorry about what I did. I knew you'd just worry and I thought if we hurried and got the treasure, we might be gone before anyone knew we were here. Your ex-father-in-law must be working with that Bryce guy to know about this so soon," she speculated.

"Maybe. But I'm not letting this go that easily," he said. "Let me see it," he demanded,

"What?"

"Where you were shot. I need to see it."

She bit her lips and pulled down the edge of her top, exposing the thick bandage. "It's just a scratch. They only winged me. Remember, they just wanted to keep me interested, not kill off the golden goose."

"God damn it all to hell, Casey!" he said, his eyes darkening into thunderclouds. She was grateful he didn't look under the covering, exposing the raw wound inside.

"Did you at least go to the hospital?"

She shook her head. "They'd have to involve the police, and I didn't want that. I'm fine. Okay? I said I'm sorry. What else do you want from me?" Her heart began beating too rapidly. Had she destroyed the incredible sense of unity and togetherness they had just begun? Was it going to be all over before it had truly started?

"I want you safe and you're making that impossible. I don't know if I could stand it if anything happened to you. If we go any deeper into this bond that's growing between us—I can't lose you, that's the thing. And I need to trust that you will at least try to stay safe and let me know when things like this occur. I'm not saying I ever want you to stop being who you are—you're a free spirit and I admire that—just take a moment to recognize others want what's best for you, too. When I think what might have happened—" He raised a shaky hand to his head, running it roughly through his hair. His expression bleak, he looked away from her. "I don't know that I can go on with—what's developing between us—without your promise. I'm falling in love with you, Casey, and it scares me to death."

She bit down harder on her lips, drawing blood. This was bad. She reached out a hand to touch his arm. "I am so sorry. I wasn't thinking right. I see that now. Please, I don't think I could take it if you don't forgive me. Please, look at me, Truman, say you'll give me another chance. I can learn to do this better. I promise."

"No false promises between us. It has to come from your heart," he said, swallowing hard, his eyes locking with hers.

"It does. My heart says I can do this. I promise you from

this day forward to not hide what is going on from you — ever again. Please, say it's going to be okay between us. I've fallen for you, too. I'm in love with you, Truman."

He nodded and opened his arms. She stepped into them. They hugged for a long time while she listened to his heart through his sweatshirt, the space between beats slowing as his breathing returned to normal. A sound heart. One that could take them the distance.

She settled back to earth as he pulled away a bit.

"Thank you," he said, hugging her again, experiencing a feeling unlike anything he had ever had before. His whole being lightened.

"No, thank you. It's really going to be okay now. Let's make a pact, here and now. To only believe the best of the other. Until they prove differently."

"I like that idea." He kissed her tenderly on the lips. How had he gotten so lucky?

"No more secrets, eh."

"No more secrets."

"We should get back. We got a situation to deal with and the others will need our help," Truman kissed her forehead, clearing his throat. "We'll talk more later," he said. The look in his eyes promised more than just talking. She let out a sigh of relief. It really was going to be okay. Truman loved her. The thought fully registered. And she loved him. They could work out anything.

"What are we going to do about them?" Lily asked as they made camp, pointing at the tent.

"Let them go later after they've cooled their heels for a while. Catch and Release, just like Parks Canada advises with small fish," Truman said with a half-grin, giving Casey's hand a warm squeeze.

Casey nodded. "Works for me. Any chance of a beer?" she asked, her mouth gone dry.

"I don't know about you, Truman, but I brought along

239

a bottle of the finest quality Scotch a man should buy. And proper glasses. None of this red plastic shit. Care to partake?" Will asked.

"Thanks," he said. "I could use a bracer."

With everyone settled back down at the picnic table, Truman raised his heavy-bottomed crystal glass, turned golden from the generous amount of expensive Scotch splashed in by Will.

"To the truth of the Sinclair Clan's claims of visiting the New World before Columbus."

"You are aware that in 1965 the Vikings were proved to be the original discovers of North America? Remember the Vinland map authenticated by Paul Mellon, a Yale University alumnus," Rebecca said, pursing her lips.

"Yeah, but it's dated 1440. This new map pre-dates it. Right?" He looked to Casey for assurance. She nodded, verifying the claim.

"Then there's Helge Marcus Ingstad and his wife, Anne Stine Ingstad, the famous archeologist, who in 1960 discovered the remains of houses at L'Anse aux Meadows, at the northern tip of Labrador. They found tools radio-carbon dated to c.1000, the same year the sagas attributed to Leif Erikson's voyage to Vinland. Even the Smithsonian Institute in Washington was notified of the conclusive proof of a Norse settlement," Rebecca added.

"I don't care who was first. All I care about is seeing Truman's heritage never gets into the hands of any thieving bastards connected to this pair." Casey gave a curt nod toward the tent, shutting down any extraneous discussion.

"*Our* heritage, darlin'," he said with a smile.

The thought brought her up short with wonder. She liked the sound of that.

"Don't forget we've got a new mission to get the Penelope Papers to their rightful owner, not to mention next year's treasure sea hunt to prepare for and some side trips planned with Miranda and Elin," Rebecca warned, ticking them off on her fingers before reciting a few favorite lines from *A Song of Drake's Men* by Alfred Noyes, "'The moon is up, the stars are out, The wind is fresh and free. We're out to search for gold tonight, Across a silvery sea.' It's the Spanish Main treasure we've deep sea diving for, right?" she asked, confirming her poem was the right one.

"We're the Ringers, for Heaven's sake! Goes with the territory to take on the world. You know, I've always had a hankering to go after Queen Antoinette's jewels, the missing Crown jewels of London and Ireland, Scepter of Dagobert, Elin's Lost Imperial Fabergé Egg. And Confederate Gold, not to mention the Treasure of Lima and—" Lacey ran down the list with breezy assurance, as if it all was just a day's work away.

"Enough! You darn well know that's an impossible wish list for managing all in one year, Lacey Cameron. That's going to take the best part of the next decade or two," her twin interrupted, rolling her eyes.

Truman chuckled. "Going to be quite the year. I hope my visa can be renewed when the time comes. I wouldn't miss any of this for the world."

Casey sat upright, stunned.

She'd forgotten he was on a work visa. The thought of him having to go back to the United States at some point was a hell of a wake-up call. She wouldn't stand for that. Whatever it took, he was in her life now and she'd fight tooth and nail to keep it that way. No matter the baggage or what other surprises lurked in the woodwork. She was not letting go of a partner she respected, enjoyed every second with, intelligent as all get out to bounce ideas off, and not unimportantly, lusted after. And who loved treasure hunting as much as her. The complete package. And now they had declared their love. Perfect.

"You're not going anywhere, Professor Truman," Casey said aloud, while adding silently, *even if I have to marry you to keep you in Canada.* "We've got too much living to share. Not to mention, you made a pact with the Ringers to help return the Penelope Papers. Break that promise at your own risk. Just sayin'!"

Truman leaned over and kissed her, the taste of the fragrant Scotch warm on his tongue.

"I most certainly am not going anywhere without you. Someone's got to keep an eye out for you," he whispered against her lips, making her heart sing, his actions waking up the lust monster lurking inside. She moved in closer to him, enjoying the thrill of pleasure coursing under her skin, her body sensitive to his every movement, breathing in the fragrance that did such amazing, crazy things to her libido. She nuzzled against the side of his neck, kissing the warm skin just below his ear…

"Get a room, for heaven's sake!" The twins spoke in unison this time, making everyone laugh. How had she gotten so lucky? Humbled and grateful, tears came to her eyes and she blinked them away before anyone could see.

"What the hell's going on here?" Byrne demanded, striding into camp, his face even more florid than normal. The man looked around the area as if he expected to glimpse something more than he was seeing, staring at the zippered shut front door of the tent as if someone was going to jump out at any moment.

"Something we can do for you, Mr. Byrne?" Truman asked with a sigh, keeping his voice calm with difficulty. The man was tied into this somehow, he was more than certain. But backing up his intuition with real facts — difficult to prove.

"I know what's going on!" Byrne blustered. He would have a heart attack if he wasn't careful.

"And what is that?" Will demanded, his expression gone cold, the warrior housed in his massive body exposed.

"And who the fuck are you?" Byrne turned on him, though when he caught a glimpse of the size of Will he looked less certain for a split second.

"William James Thornton the third. And who might you be?"

The man's eyes narrowed. "Mr. Thomas Byrne. Say, aren't

you the heir to the Thornton fortune? The idiot who went to war when he didn't have to?"

Will went deadly still. "Yes, I served my country. And proud of it."

"You still haven't answered my question, Mr. Byrne. What are you doing here?" Truman asked.

"I'm getting to that. I've got it right here. A cease and desist order on the property that says you have to stop digging—immediately." The man held out a piece of paper, a look of smug triumph failing to mask the anger.

Truman got up and took the item from the man's hand. Gave it a quick perusal. He kept a smile from his appearing on his face with great difficulty. A little late.

"No problem. We'll be packing up directly."

"What?" The man looked almost dismayed, as though he was itching for a fight. His frustration was clear, as if he were certain something or someone was hiding just out of sight, but couldn't do much about it. "Well, see that you do," he blustered. Lame as hell. *One almost had to feel sorry for the guy. No. Not really.*

Silence descended while Bryce turned on his heel.

"So, what say we pack up and haul ass home?" Truman queried as the man finally disappeared from view. *Adios.*

"Perfect," Casey said, a grin widening on her face as she whispered in his ear, "I love it when you don't sound like a department head."

"Too late, 'cause I'm going to be all over your ass getting you to write the definitive report on the final reveal of the Oak Island mystery. That reminds me—there's one more thing we have to do before we leave the island."

She followed him, a nice change for Truman, her eyes filling with wonder as he set up the event. Nice.

They were high above the prairie skyline when it began getting hits, and by the time they landed, it had gone viral. The whole world was now in on the Oak Island mystery being solved and the remarkable woman who had done it. A YouTube video that re-created the excitement of the actual find, minus the robbery, of course. Though that might have made it all the more potent.

* * * *

"I hear congratulations are in order, Miss Madison," Chancellor Adams' voice echoed in Truman's office, coming over the speaker phone. Couldn't even manage a personal visit though their whole Archeology Department was in attendance, celebrating, including her new teaching assistant. She rolled her eyes. Truman gave her a look that said *behave yourself*.

"This is quite the coup for our university in more ways than was realized at first. Apparently, this kind of thing goes over well with students and brings in extra revenue sources. Selling ad space on YouTube, TED talks, and even offers for you to lecture in international universities and the like. Your video will be added, of course, to our long distance V-pod education resources for students of archeology to access. It was thought your use of a drone to show an overview of Oak Island was particularly effective and should be used in all future on-site demonstrations." His tone sounded pompous with a side order of baffled, but she knew he was trying to tell her she'd done her school proud.

Truman nodded at her as Adams cleared his phlegmy throat, pausing his spiel.

"Thank you, Chancellor. I'm just pleased that I could help in some small way."

"Well, keep up the good work, Miss Madison." The call ended.

"Now was that so hard?" Truman asked.

"You have no idea."

Chapter Twenty-Two

"A merry life and a short one shall be my motto."
Bartholomew 'Black Bart' Roberts

Six weeks later

"Okay, Ringers, and oh yes, honorary Ringers," Casey corrected herself as Truman gave her a glance. "This is it." Her words came out a bit breathless.

She looked over at Rebecca, the treasure chest of Randolph Thomas Scott, esquire, hugged tightly against her body. She was giving it up today to the rightful heir and she looked off-kilter, half-saddened at giving it over and yet happy to give it to the right person. An emotional mix Casey understood all too well.

"Well, knock already!" Lacey said, her eyes rolling with impatience. "They know we're coming, right?"

"Yes, of course," Casey said. They stood together on the screen porch of the home belonging to the closest living descendant of the man. A young woman named Helen Sinclair Brown. The family's cottage, located on the shoreline near the city of Halifax, faced the British Isles far across the sea, a poignant reminder of the man who'd died on Oak Island. Shocking as hell to have discovered the woman resided in Nova Scotia, after a merry chase across England. But before Casey could raise her hand, the door flew open.

"You're finally here!" the young woman said, her brown eyes lit up with an inner fire. Her smooth brown hair framed a sweet face, a few small smile wrinkles just developing around her eyes, testimony to a happy nature.

A man stood behind her, with two small children peering out at them from behind his knees, both wide-eyed and cute as buttons.

"Come on in," the man said, gently easing his wife and children out of the way.

"Yes, of course! I've forgotten my manners in all the excitement," the woman exclaimed.

"You must be Helen," Casey said, holding out her hand before making introductions. "I'm Casey Madison and this is Rebecca Fairfax, Lacey and Lily Cameron, Truman Harrison and Will Thornton. Everyone who was there when the chest was found."

"So nice to meet you all. This is my husband, Brian," Helen said.

More handshakes before trooping into the living room. It was a nice, middle-class home, with a well-lived in look. A few children's toys were scattered about the rug and Helen bent to move a bright red toy fire engine out of the way.

"Please excuse the mess. Soon as I pick everything up, they're right back at it again."

"No worries," Casey said.

Casey took a deep satisfying breath and squeezed Truman's hand. The family's financial future was also going to be assured by the coins found in the treasure chest. Treasure hunting—one of its best moments. And now that she had finally gotten tenure, one of her finest hours and thanks to Truman's help, she was gaining a new-found respect for following some rules. And she knew she was helping Truman learn the value of breaking some—only the right ones, of course. For a second she felt such happiness she was not certain her body could contain it.

She waited patiently while everyone settled down, the offer of refreshments declined, and asked, "Do you have any questions before we hand the chest over?"

"Do you think there's more treasure still on the island?

You know, in the actual Money Pit? I mean, who goes to all the trouble for nothing, right?" Brian asked, leaning forward on the sofa as he waited for their answer.

"Personally, I think what may have happened is that it fell deeper into a cavern, likely natural to the island, back when they exploded all that dynamite. They were trying to block the man-made tunnels to keep it from flooding the original Money Pit, but it didn't work," Casey said.

"Very possible," Truman said, nodding his head. "Good theory," he added, earning a smile for his compliment.

"Hmm, I was wondering—I know you said it was Captain Black Bart Roberts who most likely attacked Randolph Thomas Scott's merchant ship, leaving him on that godforsaken island to die, but did you find out if anyone else made their way to the island? Was he all alone there all that time? Did he die alone?" Helen asked, her eyes darkened by emotion.

Casey cleared her throat. "Looks like it. He never mentions anyone else in the journal."

A moment of silence. Broken by the little boy pushing his fireman engine across the rug, pretend siren going a million miles a second. He had a black plastic hat perched on his head, the badge claiming him to be Fire Chief of the department. Beyond cute. And completely oblivious to who his distant ancestors had been and the important role they'd played in the history of Nova Scotia.

"I really appreciate your going to all this trouble to get the treasure to us," Helen said, picking her daughter up and cuddling her close. The toddler lay her head against her mother's breast, her eyes closed, her thumb instinctively seeking her mouth. A tug on Casey's heartstrings gave her pause.

"It was our pleasure, ma'am," Truman said.

"How did you come across the treasure, if you don't mind me asking?" Brian's brows knitted over eyes filled with curiosity. Casey tore her glance away from the mother and daughter. Nodded at Rebecca.

"I was using my new VLF prototype ground imaging machine to test it out. Complete accident—beginners' luck really," Rebecca said.

"Well, it turned into a lot of luck for our family," Helen said. "And we're also fortunate a son of Penelope and Randolph Scott emigrated to Canada after his father never made it back home, looking to find word of him, or we'd not be living here today and I'd not have married our Brian here." She looked up at her husband, love obvious in her tender expression. "And had these two wee ones. Funny how things turn on a dime."

"Yeah, funny that," Truman said, giving Casey a look. Remembering how they'd met, Truman's chagrin at being dumped into a sinkhole made her smile, before he added, "But I also believe that what is meant to be will be. I, too, gained a lot from the experience of what we discovered on Oak Island. And found this incredible, amazing, wonderful woman at my side. Life doesn't get any better than that."

"No, it does not. I'm happy for you. Maybe you'll be having one of these soon?" Helen patted her daughter's round little tummy, making her giggle. "You'll be staying for supper? Our small way of saying thanks."

Casey spoke up quickly. Too much of this would ruin her. "Wish we could, but we have another appointment tonight. Maybe another time?"

"Sure! You're always welcome here."

A short while later, the crew exited the cottage and made their way back to the rented vehicle.

"That was really nice," Lily said, buckling her seat belt. The pair had taken over the front bucket seats, leaving everyone else to pile in behind.

Her twin snorted. "God, could you just imagine living like that and being tied down with kids and diapers. Ugh. So not for me!"

"Lacey! You're incorrigible. That was such a sweet family. I'd give a lot to have that."

"And give up the life you have now?"

"Wait! You two haven't figured out that you can have it all yet?" Will scoffed. "Lots of women have married, had children and gone on to make their mark in the world. What about Jane Goodall? Or Amelia Earhart—oh, yeah, she married but had no kids. But then there's that female pirate—Anne Bonny, she had a passel of them with her husband."

"She escaped to the high seas. Sure they were all her husband's?" Lacey joked, turning around to give Will a look.

"Lacey! The woman's dead and buried. Don't slander her name," Lily warned, wagging her finger at her.

Casey took Truman's hand, giving him a playful eye roll.

"You want children, darlin'?" Truman asked lightly, massaging her hand, sending tingles up and down her body.

"Maybe. Some day. But that decision's a long way off."

"Not as far as you think," Rebecca warned. Apparently unabashedly eavesdropping. She was a writer after all—it was almost a prerequisite.

"Medicine's making advances all the time in that direction. Women have babies in their forties and fifties. Even in their sixties," Casey said.

"Enough talk about children already!" Lacey complained. "Everyone up for tonight? Got enough bear spray in case one of our competitors shows up?"

"Lacey! You can't mace everyone you don't like. It's public land. And we're the ones with the original map," Lily said, ever the voice of reason.

"Well, I sure hope no one else got there first," Casey said to no one in particular, praying the map they'd found on Oak Island was the only one in existence. And to think it was only one island over from their first dig. She shook her head. A few of the other islands held secrets too, and soon all would be revealed.

"We find what we find, darlin'. There's lots more treasure hidden on this planet than we can ever recover. If those men get there first or someone else for that matter — so be it," Truman said, calming her fears.

"What did I do to deserve you?" Casey said, warmed by his continuing hand massage now sending delicious pleasure to other more sensitive body parts, giving her ideas.

"Oh, God, here we go again!" Rebecca joked.

"You guys are so not invited on our honeymoon. In fact, I'm not sharing the destination, even if you try to torture it out of me," she said, setting the ground rules before Truman added his piece.

"Hmm. Rescuing me from a sinkhole tops my list at the moment. Though I enjoyed rescuing you back even more, and you can blame that on my DNA. I'm hot-wired to want to take care of you. Let's see what tonight brings. I got lots of ideas of how you can thank me later." Truman brought her hand up and kissed the back of it, sending more thrills chasing through her. "You've taught me so much, darlin'."

"Yes, I have. But tonight, yes, I think I can arrange a demonstration just for you," Casey said. "Thank you," she whispered in his ear. "For being you. You're the best."

He gave her such a warm smile she almost stopped breathing. She filled her nostrils with his scent, becoming such an integral part of her DNA. Of course, her Ringers would always be important to her. But now a new part of her heart and life had opened up and was taking priority. A love bigger than anything she could have imagined or hoped for. Life changed and, sometimes, for the better. A whole lot better.

"All in a day's work, darlin'. And a Sinclair never forgets their oath of loyalty. I've pledged to be yours. That I can promise you."

Her heart expanded and just the right words came to her. "And I promise you the same, Truman, to be true to you and no other." The timeless words might have been spoken from others long past, but in the moment, they resonated and said it all.

More books from Totally Bound Publishing

Book one in the Marilyn Club

The Munsters had their niece, Marilyn. Buzzard's Breath has Emily Redfeather. Being the only 'normal' one in the bunch ain't for the faint of heart.

Book two in the Sassy With Sir series

Black Ops with benefits, spy cop secrets and criminal attraction. An agent finds his kink match on a sizzling Santorini stakeout.

Monique Mackenzie has everything a modern woman could dream of – a fabulous career, great clothes, a lovely home and wonderful friends. She could have anyone she wants. But one man doesn't seem to notice her at all – her boss.

Book one in the Corporate Heat series

Taylor's suddenly thrown into the dangers of the corporate world and her only protector is her hot, anonymous one-night stand.

About the Author

January Bain

January Bain has wished on every falling star, every blown-out birthday candle and every coin thrown in a fountain to be a storyteller. To share the tales of high adventure, mysteries, and full-blown thrillers she has dreamed of all her life. The story you now have in your hands is the compilation of a lot of things manifesting itself for this special series. Hundreds of hours spent researching the unusual and the mundane have come together to create a series that features strong women who don't take life too seriously, wild adventures full of twists and unforeseen turns, and hot complicated men who aren't afraid to take risks. She can only hope the stories of her beloved Brass Ringers will capture your imagination as much as they did hers when she wrote them.

If you are looking for January Bain, you can find her hard at work every morning without fail in her office with two furry babies trying to prove who does a better job of guarding the doorway. And, of course, she's married to the most romantic man! Who once famously replied to her inquiry about buying fresh flowers for their home every week, "Give me one good reason why not?" Leaving her speechless and knocking her head against the proverbial wall for being so darn foolish. She loves flowers.

January Bain loves to hear from readers. You can find contact information, website details and an author profile page at https://www.totallybound.com/

Home of Erotic Romance